CONFESSIONALS

MIKE ROBERTSON

authorHOUSE·

AuthorHouse™
1663 Liberty Drive
Bloomington, IN 47403
www.authorhouse.com
Phone: 833-262-8899

Published by AuthorHouse   05/08/2023

ISBN: 979-8-8230-0774-0 (sc)
ISBN: 979-8-8230-0773-3 (e)

Library of Congress Control Number: 2023908359

Print information available on the last page.

This book is printed on acid-free paper.

THE VESTMENT

His family was religious, seriously religious. The fact was that religion had dominated a good part of his childhood. The family believed in the divine authority of the Almighty or, more accurately perhaps, they were afraid not to believe. They were Roman Catholics, Catholics who were comfortable in the knowledge that they belonged and were, therefore, pursuing the one true faith. They were convinced, somehow, that billions of people who were enlightened by some other spiritual belief, would be consigned to the perpetual damnation of hell once their time was up. When he was younger, he was familiar, maybe too familiar with all the trappings of that one true faith. There were the sacred signs watching over him, watching over everything he did. The symbols of the Supreme Being and the faith in that Being were everywhere it seemed. He thought about them all the time, the curious ceremonies of the Church, the mysterious Latin words muttered during Mass, the reliefs representing the Stations of the Cross on the walls of the church, the spectres lingering in the confessional, the strange theatre of the benedictions, the solemnity of communions, novenas, even vespers, whatever they were supposed to be, all intended he thought to ensure that he stayed on the right path to heaven. They all belonged to him at one time or another, all of them.

Then there were the priests, the caretakers of the doctrine. They were mysterious men, odd individuals who were cast out of the most mystifying of circumstances, curious characters who Richard thought were out of place almost everywhere but in a church. The parish in which he attended church was fortunate enough to be blessed with three priests, all different in character but all similar in function. There was Father Purchell, the senior partner and principal navigator of the theological fortunes of his congregation. Then there was Father Quinn, a perplexing man who had a well meaning manner as well as a well known drinking problem. And finally, there was the younger but much admired Father Griffin who, at least in comparison to his two colleagues, appeared to be a recruit barely out of the seminary. The two older clerics were fat, clumsy men, Friar Tuck types, who had presumably lost much of their hair and almost all of their theological zeal. On the other hand, Father Griffin, while he was given to a penchant for serious prayer compared to the tepid passion exhibited by his older colleagues, at least was thin and was often celebrated for his full head of head. Richard's mother, in a moment of weakness no doubt, thought he was sexy although she didn't use the word. Richard's father objected although without much conviction. But one could tell that his mother's remark, however inappropriate it may have been, still must have bothered him.

All of them, himself, his brothers Jack and Stephen and his best friend Peter had frequent opportunities to observe liturgical procedure first hand, all being pupils in an elementary school which, being across the street from the church, conducted much business with the Almighty. By the time he had graduated to high school, Richard had experience with all manner of prayer and worship. Aside from significant events like Christmas, Easter and Lent, there was first Fridays, second Tuesdays, rosary weeks, holy weeks, and special liturgical spectaculars like Ash Wednesday and Corpus Christie. There were also regular benedictions, occasional retreats, novenas, devotions, high mass on Sundays, and the occasional marriage and funeral. All of them, all four of them were being employed as altar boys at one time or another, slowly had grown weary of such gatherings. They had grown bored with the gospel, particularly it seemed with the continual tedium of having to kneel, sit and stand as they participated throughout the services.

They had grown frustrated, in so far as any twelve year old could become frustrated, with the tyranny of certain elements of religious ritual. They had become tired with having to file up for communion, God help anyone who failed to make their way to the rail, their sins absolved, their parents there to witness. They were also apathetic with the lassitude of still another round of religious homilies by that spellbinder of a speaker, Father Purchell, whose sermons often sounded like presentations at an insurance seminar. They would squirm, restless in the pews like prisoners in a cell, waiting for the festivities to be over. The boys would whisper urgently to each

3

other until caught, whisper again, and then wait with the sweeping of an invisible ecclesiastical clock, for the conclusion. Church please be out.

Still, despite his growing reluctance to continue to pursue their spiritual beliefs, Richard and Peter both received documents entitled a "Certificate For Religious Instruction" signed by Father John D. Purchell himself. It was a verification of their profession of faith and renewed their promises of the Christian life. The certification was witnessed by the Inspector of Schools, whose signed name could not be distinguished. It was provided to the both of them a month before they received their grade seven report cards. Both Jack and Stephen presumed they would receive certificates when they graduated from grade seven the next year.

Despite their reservations with their fading faith, the group still held in high regard in those days when they were the altar boys, a group to which they thought they were obliged at one time to join, much to their parents' relief, in order to escape, even for one moment out of many, the boredom of sitting in the pews with their prayer books in their laps. Still, the entire experience was adventurous enough Richard had recalled, the black or red cassocks, the stiffly starched soutanes, and the prospects of an appearance before a packed house on Sunday the main pleasures. To continue with their piety, or whatever spiritual ambitions they still maintained, they soon continued to accept their careers as acolytes. They found themselves sacrificing early morning sleep and some weekday evenings in order to fulfill their obligations to religious service. So it came as no revelation that barely into the second year of their tenure, Richard being almost out of elementary school, almost thirteen years old by then, all three of them, Peter's brother Stephen having been excluded as a conscientious objector for reasons he never did disclose, were still celebrants. He did, however, remember that the three of the remaining altar boys had embarked on the hazardous course of laughing at the hand that blessed them.

At first, it seemed little more than harmless fun, a way of passing the time before and after the occasional tedium of their sacred duties. It was there on the altar, the sword battles, mock fights, and imagined attacks on each other, all of which employed, in one way or another, some religious article as a prop. The church, of course, provided the enterprising acolytes, much in the way of utensils for their entertainment: candles snuffers with long ornate handles, innumerable crucifixes, chalices, cruets, silver containers of unknown purpose, and many other curios of the religious theatre. It was like being backstage on Broadway. They eventually expanded their taste for such improprieties, extending their unacceptable behaviour to include the looting of the lost and found cabinet, the unauthorized ringing of the church bells, and their continued standby of on altar pugilism, a relatively obscure art in which Richard and his brother attempted to hit each other with whatever was handy during the consecration of the mass. Still, they only tussled during the early morning services on the weekdays, hoping that there were few or no parishioners to witness their nonsense. After all, such behaviour would normally be considered disturbing enough to prompt even the most casual of the faithful to demand they be suspended from service and banished to the basement. In fact, one such critic of their heretical performance, having collared them at a boy scout meeting, condemned them to the eternal fires, a power which the two of them did not previously know he possessed, The critic was called the "man with the smelly feet", so named because he was cursed with unfortunate feet odour that, despite his obvious respectability, his assumed wealth, and a big black Cadillac sitting in the parking lot. He could not take off his shoes during services without offending most of the congregation.

The boys never, from that moment on, exhibited their talents for disruption, unless assured absolutely of the discretion of their audience. They were still clever enough to avoid any lapses in bad judgment. If there were more than a dozen celebrants present for a mass or if anyone in the church at the time looked to be younger than seventy years old, they would control themselves until they were clear of the altar. Still, there were times when they were caught, once when Richard's brother Jack was in the process of belabouring him with a particularly vicious pillow which, when it was not being pressed into service as a weapon, was used by the priest in kneeling. They were, or so they came to suspect, dangerously close to excommunication for actions which were described by Father Purchell as the "work of godless hooligans", whoever they were. But they were saved by the great Christian virtue of forgiveness. The good Father did, however, elicit a promise from the brothers to reform their behaviour. Unable to continue their squabbles publicly, as their rehabilitation was being monitored by all three parish priests, the two of them resorted to covert insubordination, a policy which, while it limited the range of their infractions, did allow them some minor godless hooliganism like using the serving dish at the communion rail to look down the blouses of the grade seven girls.

One day, before serving mass, they were reposing in the sacristy, which was, at least to a mind untutored by liturgical tradition, a kind of halfway house between the residence of the priest and his place of business. Richard and Jack were scheduled to serve mass while Richard's friend Peter was there to join the brothers on the way to school. Waiting for whoever was to say mass, they came upon a closet containing a collection of priestly vestments. They were first curious but soon lapsed into customary thoughts of trickery. Selecting an Easter ensemble complete with gold illustrations on a virgin white chasuble, they immediately set out to satisfy whatever mischievous possibilities the discovery suggested. Peter, who was generally the boldest of the bunch, immediately slipped the garment on over his head in an elaborate burlesque of the priests he had seen do the same thing. Although the chasuble was presumed to be well suited to their original purpose, it looked quite ridiculous on Peter, as if specifically designed for parody, when worn with basic dungaree and sneaker. It looked like he was wearing a weird rain slicker. Suddenly and surprisingly, they had been expecting no one for at least fifteen minutes or so, Father Purchell appeared in the corridor leading from the altar back to the sacristy. Predictably, the boys immediately froze, nervously regarded Purcell's advancing shadow and then actively panicked. They couldn't think of a single explanation, a plausible excuse eluding them. After appraising their situation for a good ten seconds, they made their getaway through their rear door, down the backstairs, and out into the church parking lot where Pete found the presence of mind to put his jacket on over the chasuble which had initially precipitated much merriment in them. All three of them were developing a bad case of nerves peculating in their tummies, thinking about returning into the church for relief provided by the washroom in the basement.

Instead of the washroom, they continued to scramble and withdraw from the church. By the time they had reached the field beyond the church parking lot, it could have been Golgotha that day, they were nervously alternately between laughing at their larceny and wondering what they should do next. After catching their breaths, briefly regaining their equilibrium, the three of them stooped over looking like drunks with the heaves. Peter, the main perpetrator, finally spoke. The field was eerily silent, his voice sounding like it could be heard blocks away. "Now what guys? Shall I go back with this under my arm and tell Purcell that I just picked it up for him at the laundry?" All three of the thieves stood staring at each other. Peter continued his frivolous humorous proposal. "Wait, wait, I know. I could say that my mother knitted it for him. No, better than that, that the old man picked it up wholesale on one of his buying trips to New York. Sure, why not? Anyway, any better ideas?"

Despite their perilous circumstances, they all found the fortitude to snicker when Peter got out of the vestment and folded it, with uncharacteristic care, into a neat bundle. Richard suggested that maybe Peter should have disrobed in a telephone booth. "Like Clark Kent.", he quipped. Peter retorted by noting that the closest telephone booth was in the basement of the church. Jack then made an obvious suggestion. "We can't go back to the church now. Maybe we should wait." The three of them just looked at each other and shrugged. Jack looked like he was clearing what may have been tears out of the corner of an eye. Peter was still holding the neat bundle. He then spoke up. "How about if we just toss the garment? Just throw it in the first garbage can we can find. Or maybe we could leave it somewhere in the field, bury it under a tree or something. And to hell with worrying about it. Okay?" The other two offered a couple more shrugs. The fact that Peter used the word hell startled Jack, who was still fiddling with his eyes. Richard observed and used the word again. "And we could end up in hell if somebody finds the bundle." After a few moments of reflection, during which time the three of them were shuffling their feet, Peter came up with a conclusion, a final conclusion. "Hey, I don't think we can come up with a better idea. And when you think about it, it's not a bad plan really. And since we have to settle this as fast as we can, I don't think we have any other choice." Richard and Jack waited for the suggestion. They were disappointed but in someway not surprised. Peter explained. "We'll bury the cloak." Another pause. "Look, we have ten minutes before mass starts, so we'll have to start digging, okay?"

The three of them had actually started to scrape the

ground when Jack, coming out of one of his dazes, started mumbling in a low, frightened voice. "We just can't do it, just can't. I mean, let's face it. It's desecration, sacrilege, just like we learned in religion class. I mean, He knows you know." Jack was looking skyward. Richard and Peter glanced at each other, almost rolling their eyes. "We can't just bury holy vestments. It's just not right." As it turned out, it did not take them long to capitulate to Jack's spiritual objections to their plan to bury the vestment. In fact, all three of them, not just Jack, were disturbed by the thought of divine retribution, even the cynical Peter admitted that he had read, where he couldn't say, of deaths brought on by presumably deranged people biting into the Eucharist or humming derogatory hymns. And this, not to place too fine an edge on the matter, seemed to them a similar transgression. The three of them were worried that they would be potentially in hot water with the Almighty. For a moment, they stood under that flat November sky as if they were attending their own funerals. It was as if they were waiting for lightening to strike. But instead of lightening, there was no heavenly event descending on them save the ominous threat of snow flurries. And, as Peter was to remark, they could have consulted a weatherman before they decided on their next move. On the other hand, they didn't have much time.

After church, where they nervously served mass like they were about to face charges, they went home. For reasons none of the three of them could quite fathom, Richard was left in possession of the purloined garment, hidden inconspicuously in the bottom drawer of his desk at home, resting beneath the latest copy of a magazine that he thought was dirty, and his six hundred page baseball encyclopedia. He hoped that his mother would not look through his desk before they decided what to do. He felt that the three of them could more easily discuss the matter of the vestment's disposal a couple of days later at school. Still, it was difficult to consider an appropriate plan since the three of them began to think that they were possessed with some sort of mysterious curse. In fact, Peter the most dubious of the three when it came to the idea of a hex even the thought of blaming the supernatural when he lost his wallet the Sunday after they lifted the chasuble. Meanwhile, Jack did little to allay his fears, not to be confused with the previously unflappable Peter. From the beginning of the entire incident regarding the stolen vestment, Jack once stated that if the Almighty was out to punish you somehow, there just wasn't much you could do about it. He constantly bothered Richard and Peter with tales of divine intervention into his school work, precipitating bad weather and prompting all sort of bad luck, or so he claimed. In fact, it went so far that Jack began to imagine that Father Purchell had noticed the missing vestment and had consulted the police.

Despite their frequent deliberations concerning the appropriated garment, the three of them could not come up with anything approaching a sensible plan for ameliorating the situation. In the next few weeks, they considered and rejected a series of schemes, which ranged from sneaking the garment back into the sacristy cabinet to possibly destroying it. Jack proved to be the least effective conspirator, unwilling it seemed to accept any idea without any sort of precedent, a task that proved fruitless since their knowledge of religious history did not include any familiarity with the robbery of holy vestments. There were also theological matters to be considered and although the three of them were tempted to pass the entire question onto a higher authority, they were able to restrain the urge through actual fear.

Within a couple of weeks, they had at least settled on a plan, no matter how begrudgingly accepted by the cautious brother Richard. They were to set out on a train trip downtown, canvas the available pawnshops, a new experience for the three of them in any event, sell the garment, a possibility that caused Jack more consternation than he had been already dealing with. On the other hand, in a surprising suggestion, Richard, who was still alarmed by the theft of the garment in the first place, also wanted to engage the services of a confessor at one of city's churches. In other words, he wanted to go to confession, normally a duty that the boys dreaded, sort of like a visit to the principal's office. He was successful, however, in convincing the other two to seek absolution. At first, Jack and Peter looked at Richard as if he had suggested that all three of them turn themselves in either to the police, the diocese, their church or Father Purchell himself. But the two of them came to realize that they would have to agree with Richard. All three of them would have to seek penance. Finally, they also agreed that if the pawn shop option was to fail, their visit to confession was to also include abandoning the garment in the church, trusting that no one else would be possessed of sufficient villainy to steal holy vestments rather simply turn them in. It was settled. They would first visit the pawn shop, selecting a shop called Henry's on Ste- Catherine's, and then, further to Richard's demand, seek penance in a nearby cathedral/ church, Notre-Dame de Lourdes.

They had selected the next Saturday for their visit to the pawn shop and then to the church. Both Jack and Richard admitted to being nervous the night before, both joining their parents in reciting the rosary which was broadcast on the radio every evening at seven o'clock. To further assist in their devotions, both boys, who usually participated in the radio rosaries reluctantly, followed the broadcast with a certain level of sincerity, even using their mother's spare rosary beads, the ones with luminous beads. The next morning, Jack remained unwilling to join the other conspirators, necessitating his brother to try to convince him otherwise. Richard managed to change his mind by offering Jack fifty hockey cards. It was, all things considered, an auspicious beginning to the day.

It was Saturday, a rain shrouded Saturday, grey shaded enough to somehow reflect their predicament. The boys' mother made a mild attempt to stall their expedition, making the boys' worry a little more acute, while their father had fortunately already gone to work unaware as he usually was of any problems with the boys. In addition, Peter was sufficiently tardy, forcing them to scurry through puddles for a train they barely boarded before it swept out of the station to Montreal, all with that accursed garment tucked under Richard's arm in a plain paper bag. As they were not accustomed with train travel, what with their entire universe usually within walking distance, they were quite apprehensive about the prospect of confronting the big city with little or no knowledge of what they would encounter. Jack, when he not mumbling mea culpas about what they were about to do, complained about the fare. Richard and Peter, obviously less interested in the cost of a train ticket, invested their travelling time in a discussion of approaching a pawnbroker and the ancillary proposal of seeking absolution in a confessional.

No one knew why but Peter took the lead in outlining their approach to the pawnbroker. "Just don't say much. In fact, don't talk at all if you can help it. You remember Ted McCarthy, don't you? Well, he told me after he pawned the radio he lifted out of Mr. York's car that unless you know what you're doing, don't say a thing. And well, you've got to admit, we don't know what we're doing." Richard then added an unexpected comment. "Okay, so let's not do it." Peter looked at him as if he was kidding and then responded somewhat sarcastically. "What are you talking about, moron? Boy, you really know how to ruin a train ride." He then smiled. "Yeah, that's one thing you seem to know how to do." Richard didn't want to let the comment slide. He continued the conversation. "Come on guys, there's still time to quit. Let's just forget the whole thing. Okay?" Peter responded again. "You have to be crazy, Richard. You know that we don't have any other idea. Besides, you want to waste the fare?" Jack was looking out the window and then whispered, "I also wanted to go downtown on a train too."

Within fifteen minutes of disembarking at Windsor

Station, they had arrived in front of Henry's on Ste. Catherine's Street. As expected and perhaps feared, the shop's window was dank and disagreeably cluttered. It was entirely predictable, at least to the three of them. They had previously imagined it. As they looked through the front window, they saw hanging from the ceiling an array of articles, mostly musical instruments it seemed, the entire arrangement sending a faint and disquieting shadow across a dark stained hardwood floor. Jack and perhaps the others could feel that a ghost might reside in such a room. They glimpsed the owner through the window. It seemed natural to assume that anyone found behind the counter in such an establishment was the proprietor. And there he was, a chalk faced man who could be in his seventies, his skin corrupted by years, if not decades of skulking through those ominous shadows, only his eyes seeming to indicate consciousness. He was also smoking filter less cigarettes, the smoke drifting about the store like ominous clouds. The three visitors stood staring through the door for quite an interlude, more afraid than appreciative of the curious atmosphere, Jack particularly panicky, having taken a couple steps backward.

After a few minutes, the pawnbroker finally took notice of them through the window and hobbled, if not lurched toward the door and opened it. "Well, young gentlemen, buying or selling this morning?" All three boys remained and stood silent. Jack took another step back, as if Henry the proprietor, assuming his name was Henry, was about to attack him. He wasn't. "Come on now, boys, let's speak up. A guitar maybe learn to play, be a big star. Speak up, come on. I don't got any time for a sales pitch. And if you three are thinking about a little larceny, you should know that I'm used to dealing with that sort of thing." Peter, who had convinced himself and his two buddies that he was the most sophisticated of the group and therefore their spokesman, replied on their behalf. He somehow took on the tone of phony street bravado although it was a trifle rehearsed. "We're selling, pal, selling." The pawnbroker leaned back. "What's with this pal stuff? The name's Stein, that's Mister Stein to you, and as you can see, I'm not anybody's pal." Richard pointed to the name Henry emblazoned on the front window of the shop. Mr. Stein saw Richard pointing to the front window. "Henry was my father's name. Mine's Samuel." The three boys nodded. Samuel Stein then continued the conversation. "So anyway, what are you boys selling?"

Richard, who was still holding the paper bag, gently handed it over, as if he was handing Mr. Stein a gift. Stein removed the vestment out of the bag and slowly affected a puzzled look on his face. Peter explained. "Well, it is kind of hard to describe really. We were told that it is very valuable though." Stein took the vestment as it was passed to him from the bag and then offered an opinion about it. "Maybe it is evening attire, for what kind of evening I don't know. Where did you find this anyway? I mean, look at it. What kind of weirdo wears this kind of of thing? Who? I mean, look at this cape. Christ?" Peter, the wit, followed with a comment. "I think you're getting warmer." The boys realized that a further explanation would be required. Meanwhile, Mr. Stein continued to inspect the garment.

Richard elbowed Peter and took over the explanation of clarifying the identity and purpose of the garment. After all, he realized that he had no choice but to turn to the truth. He then told Stein that the vestment was called a chasuble and was worn by Catholic priests during religious services. Mr. Stein endured the explanation without comment. After Richard had finished his treatise on the garment, he and the other two boys were politely asked to leave the shop when Mr. Stein politely declined to purchase the chasuble. He informed the three of them that despite many customers with peculiar tastes, no respectable pawnbroker would consider handling such an item.

He then offered the boys a surprising admission. Stein said that even though he seldom went to church, or synagogue Richard later thought was more likely, he was devout, religiously observant in a quiet way. He believed in the Divine he said even though he hardly even attended services, no matter what organization they represented, a comment that could not be understood by neither Richard nor Peter nor Jack, all three of them looking somewhat confounded. Mr. Stein then removed the vestment completely from the wet paper bag, placed the garment in another paper bag which he had lifted from the counter beside the cash register and handed the package back to Peter. Although Peter was evolving the temerity to perhaps say something flippant to Mr. Stein as they started to make their exit, he and his two friends stayed silent. They were relieved to escape Stein's establishment without disturbing his spiritual beliefs. They were out the door with the vestment. They still had it. Ironically enough, it was time to visit the Notre-Dame de Lourdes to seek penance, first for stealing the vestment and also for possibly offending Mr. Stein's spiritual beliefs.

INTRODUCTION
TO CONFESSION

Even since he was first told to attend confession, when he was six or seven, Richard was seriously troubled by the obligation. The parish priests, the teachers, his parents, they all instructed him that it was necessary in order to prepare for communion, receipt of the Eucharist being the highest step in his ascent toward heaven. To Richard, and likely most of his classmates in Saint John Fisher elementary, the idea of locking yourself into a confessional, which was akin to some sort of medieval dungeon, and admitting your supposed sins to God through a priest was so terrifying as to evoke bladder and bowel problems before, during and after the ordeal. Back then, when kids were lost in a major childhood fear, the conclusion of confession and the requisite recitation of prayers for penance, even those that would eventually grow up to be criminals, could be said to be in a state of grace. Mortal or venal sin, it didn't seem to matter much. When one was that age, sin was just something that priests, teachers and parents could punish you for. When he thought about it every time he went to confession, most, if not all of the transgressions that he testified as sins were little more than childhood errors, misdeeds against acceptable behaviour, the recollections of which could be repeated to the confessor and hope that he would accept them as forgivable violations of whatever spiritual principle you were supposed to accept.

Still, the process itself was enough to frighten anybody that age. Here they were, six or seven years old, scared enough by the formalities of just being in a church, compelled to line up for confession, thinking that the confession was actually talking to God through a priest. They were worried that the Divine could be summoned if any of the kids said the wrong thing. When it was their turn, something that they instinctively dreaded, they would enter a dark room no larger than a clothing closet, kneel down in supplication, their trembling hands together in forced prayer, and wait for a priest to slide a latticed panel no wider than a pane of glass across a grate that separated the confessor from the penitent. The priest would then provide a solemn greeting of some sort and ask for disclosure, all in a voice that sounded like it was coming from some region of heaven or hell for that matter. Young penitents would then tremble through their testimony, after which the priest would order an act of contrition, a prayer that was assumed by congregants to satisfy the Divine, and then receive their penance, a decade or two of the rosary beads the usual sentence, after which they would be granted their freedom, the recitation of prayers the sole cost of immunity from any guilt or punishment or both.

Compared to the punishment that they could expect from their parents, their teachers, or any other adult who they could possibly offend, the prospects of reciting prayers did not seem so bad on reflection, particularly when compared to a half of dozen wacks of the strap on each hand, eventually called the biffs by the time they got to high school. One would mumble the prayers as quickly as one could, hurriedly genuflect and depart from the church before the confessor was finished with the next few customers. Most of the kids thought that it was important that they exit the church before their confessor had the opportunity to leave the confessional. Most boys had the inexplicable belief that if the priest who had heard their confessions saw them outside the confessional while they were reciting their penitence, their prayers would somehow be rendered invalid, as if God would not have heard them. It was the sort of theological quandry that would baffle young minds until they were old enough to forget about their dilemma.

And forget about it they did. Over time, maybe several years, the anxiety had worn off, not entirely, but enough to reconsider their approach to confession. For example, by the time Richard proposed the confession in connection to the vestment they had lifted from the church and were attempting to pawn, any anxiety about confession he might had eventually faded, not completely but enough to prompt him to reconsider his approach to confession. It was now no longer the frightening prelude to an unfortunate religious judgment but one of the many disturbing obligations that were forgotten the older they got. He began to understand that the act of going to confession itself, like other religious activities, was more symbolic than actual, more theatrical than real. But Richard still felt that he had no choice but to continue to confess, if for no other reason than his parents would be profoundly unhappy if he wasn't attending confession on a regular basis.

So, despite the absence of any serious sin, most Catholic kids like Richard remained regular patrons of the confessional, prepared to admit and ask forgiveness for misdeeds at least once a week, a pattern that Richard and others followed until they were in the grade seven or so, by which time they had concluded that their sins, such as they may have been, did not merit the constant remorse that their frequent admissions inside the confessional suggested. At that age, Richard and presumably others his age believed that the only other group that seemed to go to confession as often as they did were elderly women who, for some reason no one could fathom, must have been as sinful as hell, so great was the need to unburden themselves in the confessional. The pursuit of penance became so routine that the young and the elderly people must have wondered why their confessors did not take note of it. Richard, among others, could not figure why the priests to whom they confessed, Fathers Quinn and Griffin particularly, had not asked them to express their spiritual regret less frequently, so bored must they must have been with their constant recitation of the same sins for which they sought forgiveness. They could have been asleep for all they knew.

Disobedience of teachers and parents, minor tiffs with brothers and sisters, and what little profanity they were capable of using could be said to be the favourite misdeeds, the most reported in the confessional, at least until such time as they managed to discover and pursue more heinous behaviour. As mundane as their sins seemed, most of what was said in the confessional was basically forgotten anyway, their actual sins too infrequent to actually require more a genuine confession. As a result, most penitents, including Richard, Peter and even Jack, discussed the possibility of inventing violations of some commandments to which they could confess, just to determine what kind of response they could provoke from the bored priests to whom they usually confessed. But aside from manufacturing crimes which they could not possibly commit, like stealing a teacher's car, they could not come up with any transgressions noteworthy enough to hold the interest of their inquisitors. So Richard and pretty well most of his friends went about the banality of routine confessions, mindlessly going through rote recitations of wrongdoings for which they could but not always did claim responsibility, if not guilt.

That all changed when they discovered sex or more accurately sex discovered them. They were twelve years old, some of them thirteen when they inexplicably, if not accidentally developed a frantic interest in all matters sexual, masturbation and dirty pictures being the most frequent pursuits. At least until the boys stopped going to confession altogether, impure thoughts and actions were their usual refrain there. By the time Richard came across his proposal to confess to the theft of the vestment, he had not been to confession for at least six months, the most previous occasion just before going to midnight mass on Christmas, a family tradition.

As Richard was to admit to his two pals in crime, attending confession remained a painful duty, even for those mainly unblemished souls who had nothing worthwhile to confess. He repeated to Jack and Peter that the idea of slipping into the stale darkness of a booth barely larger than a standing clothing cabinet to squint at a bored stranger, dressed in a black cassock, redolent of cigarettes and incense, seemingly whispering to himself remained a fright. He would be expected to confide his private activities to a total stranger nothing other than a fright. Recently, despite his doubts, as he had become old enough to understand the gravity of confession, medieval images of sinister, even hideous faces floating about like black clouds, smoke rising heavily out of huge steaming cauldrons, and the pitiful cries of accused heretics giving testimony on the rack always seemed to fill his head during such moments. Richard recalled a teacher in grade five, informing his students, with a strange reverent glee, that hell burned without flame, meaning that that one could suffer the torments of fire without end. Richard always seemed to remember that anytime he was prepared to enter the confessional. World without end was a concept that was right up there with sex in the complete and utter mystery department.

But after the ordeal of confession began, as he entered the holy cubicle, these nightmarish thoughts became suddenly foreign, almost as if they had forgotten all about his fears. But here he was, standing in the Notre-Dame de Lourdes church, a church that looked like a Gothic mausoleum, waiting with the prospects of a large crime on his conscience, hoping to receive absolution for his sin of ecclesial theft. Asked by Peter and to some extent by Jack to explain his reason for proposing that they seek forgiveness for the theft of the vestment, Richard told them about advice he had received from a fellow student named Doug Jackson. While Richard could not remember the circumstances of Doug's transgression, he did recall that he had had the presence of mind to suggest that admitting their sins to a complete stranger in a strange church, specifically an unknown confessor, was recommended. So the young Jackson advised him to attend an unknown church, particularly one as distant and busy as Notre-Dame de Lourdes for example. After all, did this downtown church not deal with large volume forgiveness? Yes. It seemed like an easy way out.

By the time the three of them entered the selected church, they were relieved to discover that there were at least three priests on confessional duty. In fact, four confessionals were open to dispense forgiveness to hopeful penitents. They were relieved that they were able to risk the possibility of boring three different confessors with three identical stories. Richard drew a Father Lawrence or so it announced on a little card, much like a business card, pinned to a curtain that hung on the door to his confessional booth. Richard had never seen calling cards for priests before and was momentarily confused as to the procedure. There was a certain levity to the situation. Should he introduce myself? Present his own card? Shake his hand? He did not have the time, however, to reflect about such matters. His time in fact passed quickly enough when an old woman made a surprisingly hasty exit from visiting Father Lawrence. He hoped to be as fortunate. It was automatic.

He provided a short introduction to his sin. It was as heartfelt as possible. "I confess to Almighty God and you, Father, that my friends and I stole a holy vestment belonging to my parish priest." "A what?" asked Father Lawrence. "I think it's called a chasuble, a white chasuble." Richard answered. He sounded nervous. Father Lawrence then asked, "You stole only that one vestment?" Richard immediately replied, his voice still low. "Yes, Father, only that one." The father then coughed and continued his inquiry. "Tell me, son, why did you steal the vestment? And don't be afraid, God wishes you to make a clean breast of things. He is prepared to forgive but He must know the details." Richard continued his explanation. "I guess we just took it, my two friends and I. I don't know why. We were just fooling around in the sacristy before serving mass, trying on the vestments in the cabinet and everything. And then we thought we saw Father Purchell coming and we ran from the church. There wasn't time for my friend Peter to take the chasuble off. We were worried about being caught." Father Lawrence asked through the screen. "But why, son, why?" Richard again explained. "I don't know. It just seemed like fun at the time."

Then confessor Lawrence asked another question. "Where is the vestment now?" Richard's face moved closer to the grate. "We brought the garment here and we had hoped to maybe leave it here, if that's okay I guess." Father Lawrence offered guidance. "Well, as you probably know, the theft of a priest's vestment is serious business. I will take the vestment but I think you should return it to Father Purchell. But I guess you're too scared. God understands your fear. For your penance, I want you to say several decades of the rosary. And now don't forget your Act of Contrition."

Richard agreed and started to mumble the prayer. He was then surprised by Father Lawrence. "Tell me, son, do you think that you or either of your two friends have vocations?" Interrupting his prayer of remorse for a moment, Richard asked, "A vocation to the priesthood, Father? No, I don't think so." Father Lawrence tried to persuade Richard that he may have had a vocation. "I wouldn't be too quick to deny a vocation. Judging by the desire of you boys to wear the vestments in the first place, followed by your unwillingness to just throw the garment away, well, this seems like powerful evidence to me of a vocation. Haven't you ever thought about it?" "Yes, Father. Everybody does, I mean, we go to a Catholic school, we go to church a lot, we've been altar boys for years." Richard said. Father Lawrence commented, "But no more church I suppose, not even when you were stealing the vestment. Not even then. But I would think about it if I were you. Maybe a few decades of the rosary will straighten you out. And son, remember to leave the vestment in one of pews outside the confessional. Now finish your Act of Contrition."

━━━

Richard met the other two outside, they had waited for him under the dark brow of the church sculptured portico. They did not speak until they were a good five blocks away, at which point the three of them had grown weary of their grim silence. Soon, they were laughing with all the delirium of a prisoner just granted a stay of execution. In fact, when they had relaxed enough, even Jack complied, to reveal their penance to one another. There was Richard's month of rosaries, Peter got three decades of the beads, and Jack, who was probably the most guilt-ridden and therefore likely the most contrite earned himself a mere two decades of the beads. But it was left to Peter, the original perpetrator, who provided the group with the appropriate epitaph to a saga of such consequence, to explain his penance. Fact was that the boys hadn't been on the train home for five minutes when Pete admitted that he didn't even own a rosary, a remark that caused convulsions of laughter in the three boys that the conductor had to warn them about horseplay. Richard still remembered that they seemed to snicker for the duration of the journey.

For a time after the confession, Richard couldn't encounter a priest, even on a crowded street, without recalling the question he had received about a vocation to the priesthood. For months, he contemplated the question, even though no one ever asked him again about a vocation to the priesthood. He couldn't avoid the question. After all, his life, at least until he was in high school, was to some extent circumscribed by religion. It was a pervasive part of his life, and the lives of friends like Peter, Peter's brother Stephen or his brother Jack. At home, at school, before hockey games — they were still regularly imploring the Divine until they were almost fourteen. Faith eventually became a tiresome duty, from which there was no escape. It was saying grace at dinner.

That was to change.

AFTER THE CONFESSION

It took a little less than a day before the three boys who had failed in their effort to pawn a priestly vestment, only to end up having a confessor named Father Lawrence to agree to take possession of the garment, to leave the episode behind. They entertained themselves with replays of both their visit to Mr. Stein at Henry's pawnbroker and then the confession at Notre-Dame de Lourdes. All three of them, particularly Jack, the youngest of the trio, admitted being initially frightened by Stein the pawnbroker, only to gradually be appeased by Stein's apparent old world charm. They also had to acknowledge, at least to each other, that they were nevertheless spellbound by the shop itself. They were surrounded by shadows, the reflections off the dim lights on the ceiling, the abundance of merchandise hanging off the walls and under the glass counters, The three of them were also beguiled by the musty aromas, combined with Mr.

Stein's continual smoking, and assorted vapors drifting about the store.

Peter, who was initially the least intimated by Stein and his shop, thought that Stein reminded him of the main character of a movie about a pawnbroker who was a Nazi prison guard hiding in a poor section of New York twenty years after the end of World War II. He had forgotten the name of the movie, a gloomy black and white feature that both he and his father had watched on television a couple of months previously. Peter's father obviously admired the movie, suggesting that the lead character may have won an Academy Award for his performance. Richard didn't know much about movies, either at a local theatre, a drive-in, or on television. He preferred regular television shows, *Twilight Zone*, *Perry Mason* and *Bonanza* being among his favourites. Peter liked the *Untouchables* and the *Dick Van Dyke Show*. Being a little younger and a little less sophisticated than his two friends, Jack was a fan of *Lassie*, *Captain Kangaroo*, and *Leave It To Beaver*, all three of which were often broadcast as repeats. Peter, Richard and Jack all watched the *Ed Sullivan Show*, which was watched by most families.

In any event, despite their initial fascination with Mr. Stein and his pawnshop, they eventually forget about that trip, concluding that none of the three could not anticipate any situation in which they would call on Mr. Stein in the future. After all they thought, they did not own anything nor could they foresee owning anything that might lead any of them to try to visit Mr. Stein's store or another store owned by somebody like Mr. Stein. In addition, and perhaps more importantly, despite the show of bravery by both Peter and Richard in dealing with Mr. Stein, their experience did not diminish their apprehension regarding pawnbrokers in general. Fact was that anyone who knew anything about pawnbrokers, including kids like Peter, Richard and Jack, were aware or at least suspected that many of the items on sale in any pawnbroker shop were probably stolen. Anybody who watched movies, television shows, read detective stories, or happened to pass by any pawnshop anywhere in the city were likely suspicious of such entrepreneurs. To them, the prospect of rummaging through the merchandise on sale in any such shops seemed dangerous somehow, like taking a chance of running into an unsavoury individual, if not a criminal. Peter claimed that the older brother of one of their classmates at Saint John Fisher elementary often contributed to the inventory of a pawnshop in Lachine.

Aside from their experience with Henry's pawnshop, which was eventually forgotten by the boys with the priestly vestment to sell, there was the memory of their adventure going to confession in the Notre-Dame de Lourdes church. Peter and Jack had pretty well forgotten most of the details of the confessions that they had made, including the names of the priests who had heard their admissions of sin. They had remembered their penance, Peter to recite the three decades of the beads, who said that he only recited one decade of the beads. Jack said that he faithfully recited his complete sentence of two decades. Richard, who had been given a month of the rosary, completed his penance. Jack did, however, admit to Richard that unlike his other two friends, he was still committed to confession. While at one time he usually went to confession every two weeks or so, a schedule authorized for years by his parents, he continued to seek absolution in accordance with the once every two weeks timetable after confessing to a Notre-Dame de Lourdes cleric. As he was to later admit to Richard, deciding not to share his reaction with Peter who would have laughed, Jack confided that his five minutes in the confession was not enough to disrupt his faith in confession in general. Although he couldn't provide an explanation for his continued belief in confession, it was still little more than an obligation that his parents, his teachers, and the parish priests still imposed on him, a paint-by-numbers requirement as Peter was to call it.

As for Richard, although he didn't mention it to Jack and certainly not to Peter, he suspected that there may have some sort of spiritual reason for the survival of his attitude toward confession. Simply, Richard thought the Divine may have been behind his search for absolution. While he didn't relate his inspiration to Jack, Richard was convinced that he had been somehow enlightened by the Divine, perhaps a spiritual hallucination, like a remembered prayer. Still, all of this wasn't much of surprise since Richard was still reciting several decades of the rosary several evenings a week, a custom that his parents had pursued for years further to a religious show that had been on the radio for decades. So it was understandable that even several years later, Richard was pursuing absolution from not only one of the three priests who were still serving the spiritual needs of the congregants of the Saint John Fisher church as well as Saint Ignatius high school where confession was much promoted, the fact that more than half the faculty was populated by Jesuit priests easily explaining it. So he continued to rely on the capacity of confession to alleviate any guilt he may have incurred due to the sins he would regularly confess.

On the other hand, the further he aged into his teens, Richard began to believe that his dependence on confession, if dependence was what it was, would diminish. He begin to think that the religious faith of kids around his age had ultimately faded, not like his parents' generation who persisted in their attendance at church and went to confession regardless of how old they were. Fact was that Richard's father was a church warden, a parishioner appointed to assist Father Purchell in the administration of the Saint John Fisher parish. In addition, his mother was about as devout as could be, daily rosary, weekly confessions, framed portraits of religious figures hanging on walls throughout the house, every attribute of a religious belief. There was no doubt that his parent's faith had a serious effect on Richard's attitude toward religion and attendance at church. But that too had withered.

While Richard's brother Jack continued to regularly attend church, Richard eventually did not, notwithstanding his parents' unabated faith. In that regard, Richard would pretend to attend church at a later time than his parents who would normally patronize Sunday morning mass at an earlier time. As a substitute, Richard would spend his church time sitting in the bleachers of the local baseball park. Interesting enough, he often joined other recalcitrant teens who were also skipping services. Richard eventually became friendly with them, often discussing their parents' continuing requirements that they attend church. Still, despite his disinclination to the religious dictates of his parents, Richard often had to attend mass at times during his week at school. It was compulsory for all students. After all, this was a school administered by Jesuit priests. In those circumstances though, many if not most students attending mass at school did so with some reluctance although they generally tried to appear pious, trusting that it would fool their teachers. Whether the priests or the teachers were deceived, it did not seem to matter, the boys going to church usually once a week satisfied the devotional requirements of most of the Jesuit clerics who taught at Saint Ignatius.

By the time Richard graduated from Saint Ignatius High School, he was almost bereft of religious conviction of any kind despite its continual promotion by most of the faculty who were ordained Jesuits. In fact, when he graduated in 1966, almost half of the thirty teachers on staff were priests. Some of them, precisely four of them, actually taught courses on religion, which all students had to study in at least one of their four years of high school. By the time of his graduation, after four years in Saint Ignatius, he could not remember any of the particulars of the course in religion which was taught in his first year by Father John Murphy. Years later, Richard had developed a theory that religion was usually taught in the first year of high school because thirteen and fourteen year olds were less likely to question any of the doctrines of the Catholic religion than say sixteen or seventeen year olds. Although former students with whom Richard shared his opinion disagreed with him, they had to concede that the older they got, the more likely they were to question religious beliefs, a conclusion that was easily reached he thought. So it was no surprise that by the time he was handed by a diploma by the principal of Saint Ignatius, he was virtually an agnostic.

As for the matter of his plans for his future after his high school graduation, Richard was bewildered. His parents told him to pray for guidance although Richard didn't take the advice too seriously, despite his mother's formidable counsel. On that point, after several months, Richard would finally go on to admit to his mother that while he did try praying for guidance, he was never provided with any career inspiration. While the admission disappointed his mother, she did propose that he consider seeking the advice of an employment agency, a guidance counselor or, at the most drastic, a psychologist or even a psychiatrist. Instead, after discussing his future with a couple of former classmates who had no doubts regarding their own futures, that was to attend post secondary educations, his old friend Peter was scheduled to go to Queen's University, while Nelson, whose father was a draftsman, was planning to go to a local trade school. They both were able, unintentionally since they never attempted to advise Richard, to convince him to consider continuing his career plans in Saint Ignatius College, a decision that he ended up concluding that post secondary education was better than working, particularly since his only future work possibilities involved working in some sort of factory. Richard's mother was overjoyed with his proposal, convincing her he assumed that her prayers on his behalf had been successful. As for Richard, he had successfully deceived his mother, never taking his mother's advice regarding prayers but pleased to discover when she expressed her happiness with the way things worked out. Richard's mother was now pleased that her son had a future.

In addition to thinking that she had successfully encouraged Richard into praying for guidance about his future, she also managed to secure a tip from one of the parishioners at Saint John Fisher regarding an application for a summer position with a local factory manufacturing plastic bottle caps. Richard, who had started applying for summer jobs a month before graduating, was relieved when his mother provided him with the recommendation that she had received from a friend who attended the same church. Predictably, Richard met with a Mr. Gallagher of the Foley Plastics Company within days of receiving the advice of his mother. A week after the interview, Mr. Gallagher telephoned Richard to offer him a job as a labourer, specifically maintaining a plastic injection machine in Foley Plastics. As soon as his mother was informed, she immediately proposed that they both attend mass the next chance they had. Although Richard normally avoided mass, Christmas and Easter the exceptions, he agreed to accompany his mother, no reason to decline the offer coming to his mind.

Morning masses were held three days a week at seven o'clock, on Monday, Wednesday and Friday. Richard and his mother attended on a Monday. There were less than a dozen parishioners in attendance, all but Richard and his mother likely to be over seventy years old. Based on his years as an altar boy, that was predictable, there not being too many times that he ever observed anybody in attendance on weekday mass that wasn't a senior citizen. The mass was conducted by a Father Grady, who had replaced Father Griffin who had left the Saint John Fisher parish a couple of years before. In addition, there was only one altar boy serving the mass. Like Richard and his mother, all but one of the congregation sat in the first two rows of pews. The only individual who didn't sit in the first two pews was an elderly lady who spent most of her time knitting. She sat throughout the service, Richard noting that it was apparent that she couldn't kneel. There were maybe half a dozen other old ladies in attendance who never knelt. The other attendees knelt, leaning forward on the rail of the pew in front of them.

A few moments before the mass actually began, Father Quinn appeared from the hallway to the right of the altar and slowly shuffled toward the confessional, opened the door and disappeared inside. It was apparent that Father Quinn, who was hard of hearing, was prepared to hear confessions, which seemed a little peculiar since most of the potential penitents were elderly ladies at the early mass were also hard of hearing. Richard's mother noticed his surprised expression and whispered that Father Quinn was probably preparing for confessions from students from Saint John Fisher elementary. The next mass was scheduled for eight o'clock that morning. It was usually reserved for students, again for three days a week. Richard recalled that he had confessed to Father Quinn occasionally when he was still in elementary school, remembering that the good Father would often hear confession while he was well on his way to slumber or was struggling with a hangover. After any morning confession to Father Quinn, Richard would reflect on the possibility that any absolution granted by Father Quinn was probably worthless, that is as long as he still believed that seeking penance from Father Quinn would allow him to partake in the Eucharist, which at one time was supposed to be important to him.

That morning, Richard's mother also suggested that in addition to attending the service, Richard consider going to communion, a proposal that would require him to seek absolution from the slumbering Father Quinn. His mother asked if he was in the "state of grace", a question that prompted Richard to nod affirmatively, even though it wasn't true, having decided that he would again appease his mother, considering her efforts on his behalf. So he accompanied his mother to kneel at the altar rail to receive the Eucharist and was guiltless about taking communion without receiving absolution. His mother was happy.

A CHANGE OF HEART

Her name was Catherine Morris and Richard met her in a course in Theology in his third year at Saint Ignatius College. He had failed his first year at Saint Ignatius College, spending almost that entire year either drunk or stoned and therefore declining to attend classes. The second year, he did a little better academically, actually passing while in his sophomore academic semester, he decided to take a Bachelor's degree in the Arts with a major in English Literature. For some presumably traditional reason, a course in Theology was a curious subject for Richard to take in pursuit of his Arts degree. Catherine Morris was in her freshman year of Saint Ignatius College. She was also taking Theology in pursuit of a Bachelor of Arts degree. She sat in front of him in that class, which was taught by an older priest named Father Breslin, and he watched her furiously taking notes as Father Breslin, at least in the first class the two of them took together, elucidated about why theology mattered, a question that he said was asked by everybody who ever took the course. He really didn't know why he took the theology course in the first place, thinking that maybe the fact that the line for the introductory theology course was much shorter than the lines for the other courses. Richard had been in the lineup for a second year philosophy course but changed his mind when he also noticed that aside from the length of the line, there was an attractive girl in the line for the theology course. She happened to be Catherine Morris who later turned up sitting in front of him in that first theology class.

The curriculum required the purchase of a text book entitled "Theology: The Basics". A new copy of the book was available at the campus bookstore for $9.99 while a secondhand copy could be purchased for $4.99. According to the one of the sales clerks at the bookstore, there were only a few used copies of "Theology: The Basics" available, suggesting that perhaps not many students had taken a theology course in the first place. In this regard, one of his classmates in the theology course said that there was only two other theology courses offered by Saint Ignatius College and only a very few students were studying theology. At any level. Only Richard, Catherine and seven other students were now taking introductory theology. In other words, theology was not very popular with students taking any courses in the Arts faculty. Fact was that theology was up there competing with the classics as the least popular courses. One of Richard's professors at Saint Ignatius observed that there could soon be more professors teaching theology than students being educated about theology by them.

His friends from school, almost all of whom were now sophomores, not having failed their freshman years, asked Richard about having registered for the theology course, an unusual choice for almost any student in the Arts program or any other for that matter. He couldn't tell his friends that he decided to take theology because he had instantly developed an attraction to one of the female students in a nearby registration line. At first, he would shrug his shoulders and tried to avoid the question by changing the subject, mainly by asking his colleagues why they selected their courses. It was evident that Richard's strategy, however feeble, wasn't working. Again, he avoided telling anyone the real reason for registering for Theology 130, claiming that he understood that theology was not a demanding course. In fact, Richard said that a neighbourhood guy had told him that his older sister had taken the theology course several years ago and told him that Father Breslin was one of the few professors in the college who based their grades entirely on home assignments rather than written examinations. In other words, Father Breslin's theology course was a comparatively easy course. He was not convinced, however, that anyone believed his explanation, thinking that maybe his friends thought that his judgment had somehow gone awry, an explanation that could have fit anybody choosing theology over any other subject in the curriculum. On the the other hand, his mother was predictably pleased. She didn't need an explanation.

During the first three classes of Theology 130, Father Breslin spoke endlessly about the origins of theology to a collection of eight students, one registered student having already dropped the class. There were six females, including Catherine Morris and two males, Richard and a guy named Lee MacKay, the latter having contemplated enrolling in Saint Sulpice Seminary in downtown Montreal. That explained the reason that MacKay kept on questioning Father Breslin when he was outlining theology as an academic discipline. Like most of the classes that Father Breslin conducted, most of the eight of the students, that is of course when all eight actually showed up for class, had difficulty staying awake. Father Breslin didn't seem to mind that most of the students weren't paying attention to his lectures. Unlike most professors and instructors, Father Breslin did not follow the textbook, preferring to expound on the genesis of religious theory in his own way, often confusing the students who were actually listening to him. While Richard, along with most of the class, was fighting to stay awake during the Father Breslin's lectures, Catherine Morris was taking notes, one of the three students who were actually listening. Aside from occasionally gazing at Catherine, a habit that he tried to hide, he noticed that she was recording Father Breslin's remarks with a fountain pen, an unusual choice of writing utensil for a college student. He thought that it gave him the opportunity to engage her in conversation. Fortunately, he was sitting behind her.

He whispered although he quickly realized that given Father Breslin's blather, he probably would not have to. He tried to sound simply inquisitive. "That's a nice pen. You don't see many students using a fountain pen." Catherine turned around toward Richard, looked at him with a slightly coquettish smile and then returned to keeping notes on Father Breslin's discourse. Her face had been less than a foot away from him. He had less than thirty seconds to examine her face. To him, she was fetching, could had been a model he thought. She had a short hairstyle, surprisingly stylish for a college student although she wasn't wearing a lot of makeup. Richard thought she didn't need any. His interest in her in the registration lineup was now more than understandable. After a few moments, she responded to his observation with her own comment. "I guess you don't need a pen of any kind to take notes since you don't seem to be taking any." Richard offered his own smile and offered what he thought was a witticism. "I don't need to take notes, I have a pretty good memory." She then turned back to looking toward the front of the class. Their conversation, as brief as it was, disturbed a girl sitting beside Catherine Morris. She might have been one of the students who had been napping. She gave him a slightly dirty look and returned to her nap.

Richard managed to stay awake through the remainder of the class. He had intended to resume some sort of chat with Catherine Morris but a classmate, an obvious friend, interrupted her short conversation with Richard. The two girls left the class in discussion. Four of the class in attendance had to be roused when Father Breslin concluded the session, informing the students that the next class would cover the origin of theology in Christianity as defined by a historical figure named Thomas Aquinas. Only the aspiring priest Lee MacKayseemed to recognize the name although Richard suspected that Catherine may have heard of him as well. Father Breslin was kind enough to inform them as to the precise section of "Theology: The Basics" in which Thomas Aquinas was discussed.

Richard attempted, in so far as he could, to sit close to Catherine Morris for that class. That required him to wait until Catherine arrived for the Breslin's class, which was scheduled for ten o'clock every Tuesday morning, the purpose to determine where she intended to sit in the eighteen seat room on the third floor of the main college building. He had assumed, correctly as it turned out, that Catherine was punctual when it came to attending every class. Usually, she was already seated when he entered the room. Richard would sit behind Catherine although not always directly behind her. In that event, he would sit behind her as close as he could. She would allow him a slight smile every time he followed her into the room although he wondered whether she might have suspected that he was interested in her. He hoped that that wasn't the case. She looked reserved, the type of person who would be upset if she thought Richard was somehow preoccupied with her. On the next Tuesday morning, when they were scheduled to be educated on the views of Thomas Aquinas on theology, as almost always Richard sat in the row behind Catherine, not specifically right behind her but one seat to the left.

As soon as all the students were seated, only seven showed up on this particular Tuesday, Father Breslin started his presentation on Thomas Aquinas and his opinions on theology. Father Breslin began his lecture by pointing out that Thomas Aquinas was a Dominican friar who was born in Sicily and eventually become a Catholic saint. He spent a good part of his discourse talking about

45

the admiration that Aquinas had for Aristotle, a reference that prompted one of the students, a female student named Warren to ask about Aristotle, an inquiry that seemed to not only surprise Father Breslin but everyone else in the room. Richard noticed that a broad smile emerged on the face of Catherine Morris. She was not alone in seeing the possible humour in Miss Warren's question. Even Father Breslin saw the humour as well, first replying to her inquiry by identifying Aristotle as a Greek sculptor. He then lightly chuckled and after leaning over to inform Miss Warren that he was a Greek philosopher, returned to a discussion of Thomas Aquinas. He introduced his academic sermon lectured by explaining that Saint Aquinas defined theology as being constituted by three aspects: what is taught by God, what is believed in God, and what ultimately leads to God. But he also cautioned them by saying that scholars initially pursued theology as an academic discipline without a formal affiliation to any particular church.

Lee MacKay, who was likely the most knowledgeable of the eight students, nodded and informed Father Breslin and the class that he understood that several colleges and universities were established primarily to train students headed to the clergy. Father Breslin agreed with MacKay's assertion, noting that Saint Ignatius College was founded about a hundred years ago by the Society of Jesus, an easily understood claim in view of the dozens of Jesuits who taught in both the college and associated high school. Father Breslin agreed however that theology was originally pursued as an academic discipline without any formal affiliation to any particular church and without any focus on ministerial training. To support this contention, Father Breslin said the theology courses in Saint Ignatius College could be more easily defined as religious studies than theology, a more formal term. Father Breslin then pointed out that Theology 130 would cover a variety of issues such as the anthropology of religion, comparative religions, the history of religions, the philosophy, psychology, and sociology of religion.

Richard had tried concentrating on Father Breslin's explanation regarding the origin and purpose of theology although he was often distracted by the attention he was paying to Catherine Morris. On the other hand, she was not distracted, seemingly transcribing pretty well everything Father Breslin was saying. He noticed that she was using a different fountain pen than she had used during the previous week's class. By the time the class ended, two students detained Father Breslin as he was leaving the classroom. Apparently, the two of them still had questions for Father Breslin about either theology or Thomas Aquinas or both. Breslin tried to avoid the two students but was delayed long enough to speak to one of them. Richard thought her name was Mary while her friend's name was Lorraine. Father Breslin looked annoyed and was trying to escape their attentions. He heard Lee MacKay comment as he passed the Father and the two girls. "He's probably late for vespers." and then snickered. Richard, who had planned to catch Catherine Morris for a moment's conversation, watched her pass him in the corridor as he had turned to possibly hear the Breslin's exchange with Mary and then MacKay's remark.

He had intended to follow her and maybe speak to her but decided against it, as she had disappeared into the crowd of students in the hallway. He stood against the wall of the corridor and observed Father Breslin deal with his predicament. He was still trapped just outside the classroom by Mary and her friend Lorraine. He had looked exasperated as the two students had moved closer to Father Breslin, their faces less than a foot from his face. He tried to escape the students' attention but every time he moved, the girls moved with him, essentially preventing him from leaving. Richard must have stood across the hall watching Father Breslin fending off the two students for five minutes before escaping from the theological inquiries of two students in Theology 130. By the time Richard left the scene, Catherine Morris had disappeared. He would have to wait until next week's class for any opportunity to speak to her. Richard then watched Father Breslin go down the corridor.

Richard then headed for the library and its basement where he could drink coffee, smoke cigarettes, and maybe find someone to talk to. He often met up with a recently inducted friend named Bill Wade who was majoring in history.

Aside from watching most of the people in the basement socializing, he and another student Bill Wade had struck up a conversation regarding their courses, none of which they shared. The courses taken by Bill Wade were studies in Russian history, his preferred academic pursuit. He was almost frantically interested in Russia and its history, having even attended a couple of lectures about Russian history by the local Communist Party. So it was natural that Wade would choose to major in history once he entered Saint Ignatius College. On the other hand, although he had chosen a major in literature, Richard received the occasional inquiry about his registering for one of the three theology courses offered by Saint Ignatius College. Almost everyone who knew about Richard's choice of theology thought it strange, if not bizarre.

Although he did admit to more than one fellow student that he was a student in Theology 130 because he thought the course was relatively easy, particularly because the professor, Father Breslin, did not require written examinations. Wade did not believe him, asking Richard for another justification. He could not tell him or anyone else for that matter that he had registered for the course because he found one of his future classmates attractive. But he came to realize over the past several weeks during which he had listened to Father Breslin and read the "Theology: The Basics" that he was beginning to rediscover the religious belief that he was thought had vanished a number of years ago. Not that he was ready to rediscover the inclination to return to the church, not having seriously attended services of any kind since he was compelled to by the Jesuits in Saint Ignatius High School several years ago. He could not decide, sitting in the basement of the college library, whether to admit to a renewed religious sentiment even to himself. He would sometimes ponder the possibility when he wasn't daydreaming about Catherine Morris or actually listening to Father Breslin going on about the history of the academic discipline of theology. Regarding the latter, Richard had to admit to myself that he found the origins of the study of theology almost fascinating, prompted by Breslin telling the class that a number of universities, including Harvard, Yale, Princeton and Saint Ignatius College itself were founded primarily to provide theological training of clergy. Richard was not surprised therefore that Father Breslin, who was one of the three dozen Jesuits teaching at the college, did point out that Saint Ignatius was one of the list of universities and colleges that had been established in order to solely instruct clergy on theology.

Their regular conversations in the basement of the library continued although not entirely on their studies, the two of them sometimes discussed sports, university politics, and the occasional commentary on the crowd of girls who also frequented the basement. Bill often spoke of his plans to pursue a postgraduate degree in history, maintaining that Queen's University in Kingston supposedly had an excellent masters program. During one of their subsequent dialogues on their respective university schooling, the issue of Richard's study of theology came up again. Anytime there was an empty interval in their conversation, Bill would bring up his apparent interest in theology, in which he continued to have a certain curiosity since, as he pointed out to Richard on at least two or three occasions, he understood, having been told by the chairman of the college's history department, that there were professors in the Arts faculty who believed that there would soon be more individuals in Saint Ignatius College teaching theology than actually studying theology. There used to be three professors in the Theology Department to cover their classes, the fourth professor the chairman of the department, Father Noll. All four of them had been Jesuits priests. Now, maybe ten years later, only Father Breslin was left. Bill then said that the same situation probably would someday apply to the Classics Department as well.

Richard had another opportunity to initiate a conversation with Catherine Morris when the class which preceded Theology 130 in room 308 of the main building, specifically freshman Political Science, lasted a little longer than scheduled. The six theology students who intended to attend the class were lingering outside the room. Father Breslin, looking a little displeased, was standing across the corridor. He was ignoring the six students waiting with him. Catherine Morris was casually speaking with the girl who had entertained the class by asking Father Breslin that dumb question about Aristotle. Richard managed to take up a position leaning on the wall beside Catherine Morris and at the first opportunity, asked for her opinion of the course.

"How are you finding the course? I know you're paying attention because of the notes you continue to take. I mean, I see you're still using a fountain pen." observed Richard, offering Catherine a hopefully engaging smile. Catherine Morris turned away from Mary, who was no longer speaking, to face Richard and answer him. "Sure, I find the course fairly interesting though the subject matter is a little, say we say a little dry, though as you probably know, Father Breslin could be a little more entertaining." Catherine then asked Richard for his opinion of the course.

He was somewhat surprised by Catherine's question although he should not have been. He stood mute for a few moments and then gave Catherine a barely comprehensible response. "I don't really know. I can't really say. I admit that I don't always pay attention — no, change that, I admit I often have trouble paying attention but when I do listen to Father Breslin, I find what he has to say is worth hearing. I don't know if you know it but I used to be a practising Catholic so some of which Father Breslin has to say about theology or religion makes me suspect that I may still have some faith left. Anyway, the course made me think about any faith I may still have."

Catherine looked like she was preparing to reply to Richard when the poli-sci class was finally dismissed, its students started to leave room 308, a large crowd was suddenly congregating in the corridor and the noise level rose substantially. Father Breslin and his theology students waited for a couple of moments as the room emptied and then started to file into the room. Before he and Catherine Morris entered the class room, she turned and suggested that they maybe could meet for a cup of coffee on Friday. Richard was understandably pleased. Catherine smiled and took her seat in the front row as Father Breslin shuffled to the front of the class. As usual, Richard sat behind her. Before she took out her fountain pen and her notebook, she asked him to pick a location where they could meet that day, saying that her last class ended at four o'clock. Richard suggested that they meet at the small cafe off the cloister between the the main building of the college and the high school. At that time of day, there were likely few patrons. Catherine Morris agreed. Richard was nervous. It felt like a first date that wasn't.

Catherine Morris was already sitting down in the cafe off the cloister on Friday afternoon when Richard arrived for their rendezvous at a little after four o'clock. She was reading and nursing a cup of tea. She looked up with the same beguiling smile that she gave him when the two of them met during the opening class. They exchanged greetings and Richard sat down at the table. After the salutations, Richard caught the eye of the cafe waiter who was wearing a cassock under a white apron. Catherine leaned over and whispered, "His name is Brother Allan, he told me that he is nineteen and is studying to be a Jesuit priest. He and two other brothers serve coffee, tea, simple sandwiches and plain pastries." Richard ordered coffee and a strawberry tea cake. Brother Allan brought the coffee and the desert cake over almost immediately. Richard thanked him and wondered about what he would be teaching in ten years.

After Richard poured some cream in his coffee, a spoonful of sugar and tried a fork full of strawberry cake, Catherine smiled again and then asked him about his course load. It was fairly standard curriculum. Aside from Theology, Richard listed four other courses: English Literature, History, Political Science and Sociology. He told Catherine that he had failed his first year in Saint Ignatius College although he did not provide any reason. Richard then asked Catherine about her coarse load and was understandably surprised when she enumerated eight courses, two more than normally carried by most students. She was taking courses in Classics, French, History, something called Pastoral Care, which Catherine described as the study of emotional, social and spiritual support for religious and non-religious purposes, Philosophy, Psychology, Religion and finally Theology. It struck Richard that Catherine Morris probably had unusual academic ambitions for a freshman. He also had a faint, fleeting thought that Catherine Morris may have had more a spiritual rather than academic motivation for her choices of study. Richard also thought that Catherine may have had a scholarship.

Richard felt compelled to comment. "Catherine, that's seems like an a fair amount of education for a freshman. Most students take five or six courses and that's hard enough." Catherine smiled again. "Yes, I often have to work a little harder than I did in high school." With that remark, she pointed to the books in the shoulder bag lying at her feet. Richard said, "I can also see why you taking theology, that and religion and pastoral care. They kind of go together." Catherine quietly giggled and then explained her choices. "Well, my uncle was a priest at Saint Monica's in NDG and now is a pastor at the Douglas Mental Health Hospital. And I went to Sacred Heart before coming here to Saint Ignatius. So I guess you can say that I was influenced." Richard slowly nodded and looked at Catherine with a sympathetic look on his face. He then made an obvious observation. "So I guess you were brought up seriously religious."

Again, Catherine allowed Richard a small smile and quietly answered. "My mother was devout, very devout. Her aunt was a nun and I think my mother might have thought of joining her in a monastery but my father came along and I guess she decided that she would rather live with my father in NDG than with the Sisters of Charity convent on Guy Street. So she never become a nun but I know she hoped that I would think about it." Richard leaned back and exhaled. "And I thought my upbringing was pious?" commented Richard and leisurely rolled his eyes. Catherine noticed and smiled again.

———

As usual, he didn't see Catherine until the following Tuesday, the possibility of the two of them running into each other during the school day or another day unlikely, Theology 130 being their only common course. More like an impulse than an explanation, Richard visited the cafe off the cloister on the following Thursday, two days after their last theology class together. He intended to study the cafe clientele, looking for Catherine who he hoped had stopped by the cafe for a tea after her last class that day, having studied class schedules to determine when her classes were. He ordered a cup of coffee from brother Matthew and pretended to read from a history book about the Russian revolution for about twenty minutes before he gave up surveying the cafe and left. On the train ride home, Richard spent most of his time looking out the window and wondering why he had just invested maybe half an hour looking for Catherine Morris in the cafe off the cloister even though she wouldn't probably be coming. It was now clear to Richard that his simple attraction to Catherine Morris was now more than that. It was a serious infatuation.

On the following Tuesday morning, prior to the start of theology class, Richard resisted the urge to take up a seat beside Catherine. But he still took up his customary position behind Catherine. Catherine provided him with her familiar smile. Father Breslin was preparing to enlighten his students with the life of Saint Ignatius of Loyola, the founder of the Society of Jesus, when Lee MacKay asked whether atheists studied theology, a casual observation that Father Breslin had made during the immediately previous class. It was obvious that Father Breslin was uncomfortable with the question, suggesting that academic as opposed to ecclesiastical interest in the subject was declining, academic interest in theology slowly disappearing in Canadian universities and colleges, many courses often necessitating scholarships to attract students. Father Breslin went on to bemoan the fact, pointing out that when he was training to be a priest, there were many more theology courses then than there are now. Somehow, he managed to avoid answering the question about atheists. Mr. MacKay responded with a nod and a frown. Richard wondered how anyone would know. He also wondered why atheists would want to know anything about God anyway.

RICHARD RETURNS TO CHURCH

Over the course of their continued engagements over tea and desert, Catherine and Richard persisted in discussing, among other things, their religious experiences. That was their primary ambition but they were not limited to the subject. Regarding religion, Richard confided once again that he had slowly lost his faith in his adolescence but he admitted that he had recently begun to reconsider it, basically because of, amazingly enough, his continued attendance at the theology class. While they would predominately discuss the issues that emerged from Father Breslin's classes, whether they were theological, philosophical or sociological, they would also appraise other matters as well, including the ambitions for their futures, their social lives, which in Catherine's case seemed negligible, if not non-existent, their classmates, not only in Theology 130 but the other courses as well, and general campus events, particularly in the Arts Faculty although both of them were not that interested. There was also a flicker of romance, at least as far as Richard was concerned, their dalliance consisting of Richard occasionally brushing against one of Catherine's hands while they were exchanging cream and sugar during their Friday cafe dates. Rather than infatuation, he was developing a deep affection for her.

After several assignations at the cafe, Catherine asked Richard directly if he would consider accompanying her to a mass which was regularly held every Wednesday morning at eight o'clock in the Saint Ignatius Chapel on campus. He should not have been and was not surprised when Catherine made the proposal. It seemed entirely predictable. At first, he told her that he would think about it. "I can understand that. After all, from what you've told me, you may not have voluntarily attended church." Richard quickly realized that Catherine was right in her observation. While Richard was religious, at least until he was out of the elementary school, his devotion to church during those years was compelled not only by his parents but by his church, his school, and by practically every one he knew. But now, as he was leaning about an academic discipline that could help him understand religion and was being encouraged by a girl with whom he was smitten, he was facing the choice of belief unbound by convention. Or so he thought. During the next theology class, Richard said he would join Catherine for morning mass the next day.

The Saint Ignatius Chapel was the second building constructed on the plot of land first acquired by the Society of Jesus in the late nineteenth century. It was a relatively small church which originally provided spiritual services to around two hundred Roman Catholics who lived in the west end of Sherbrooke Street of Montreal. Richard entered the church through its two front doors and stood in the vestibule of the place inhaling the musky aroma of stained wooden pews, the fainted mist of incense, and old mold. He looked up at the altar and the sanctuary, a plain oak pulpit, a statue of Saint Ignatius of Loyola to the left of the lectern, confessional booths on both sides of the chapel and finally on the wall behind the altar was a replica of some famous Michelangelo painting, the title of which Richard did not know. On both sides of the church were four stained glass windows respectively and sculptured reliefs of the fourteen Signs of the Cross, seven on each side of the room. The ceiling of the chapel was made of dark wooden slats and the floor of smooth stone.

That first morning, there were maybe thirty parishioners seated in the first three pews from the communion rail, aside from several students, whose motivations Richard could only guess, dozens of regular churchgoers, and in the fourth pew on the eastern side of the chapel, Catherine Morris. Richard walked round the baptismal font to the right and headed toward Catherine Morris. He went by the empty confessional and reached Catherine's pew. She turned, saw Richard, greeted him with her usual sedate smile and moved to her left. He sat down and returned her smile. She handed him a prayer book, the Daily Missal, with one hand and briefly grasped his hand with her other. He had just opened the prayer book when a priest appeared from behind the crucifix on the tabernacle trailed by two altar boys. Neither Catherine nor Richard recognized the celebrant although it was evident that a number of the attending students recognized not only the priest but both of the altar boys as well. If Richard was still in high school, he might have recognized them as well.

The congregation knelt as the mass started with an opening prayer that practically most of the elder parishioners, a good number of the students and Catherine herself recited along with the priest. The prayer was in Latin. Not surprisingly, Richard could recall the prayer from his experience as an altar boy and tried to mutter along with the rest of the assembly. Once the prayer was finished, Catherine looked at him and smiled again. Richard looked up from his Daily Missal and returned her smile. He was kneeling about a foot from Catherine, close enough to think about kissing her. It was a brief interlude, during which he felt guilty and then returned to follow the mass. The gospel was scheduled next and the congregation stood up in unison. After an address narrating several paragraphs of a gospel, the presiding father provided an inspirational sermon for teachers and students, not to mention the rest of the congregation. After the gospel oration, the mass turned to the Eucharist Prayer, after which everyone was invited to take the sacrament of communion. The priest and one of the altar boys approached the communion rail as people began to line up to accept the wafer. As the priest placed a host on the tongues of those taking communion, the altar boy held a tray under the chins of those accepting it. As Catherine arose to join the line for communion, she looked down on Richard who was sitting and waiting for the communion to be concluded. "I guess you're not taking communion." said Catherine. Richard looked up at her and replied, "I remember that you have to be in a state of grace and I haven't been in a state of grace since I was in the seventh grade." Catherine nodded, looked past Richard toward the confessional over his shoulder, and commented. "I think you can solve that." Richard looked confused. He didn't really know what she meant.

Catherine and Richard met at the cloister cafe two days later, the usual Friday afternoon. He was waiting for her, sipping his coffee and taking the occasional bite out of a piece of chocolate cake. The waiter was Brother Nelson, the last of the three brothers serving patrons of the cafe. She arrived maybe ten minutes later, carrying her book bag, her last class being Psychology 101. She greeted Richard, sat down and asked Brother Nelson for a cup of tea. She asked Richard about his activities between his last class on Friday, Sociology 201, Introduction to Research Methods, which he said was more interesting than it sounded, and their meeting at four o'clock. Richard told her that he spent two hours in the library taking a nap at one of the desks in the back of the second floor, pointing out that he played hockey on Thursday evening and was normally fairly tired after his two Friday classes. Richard then suggested that maybe she too must have been fairly weary by the time the two of them met at the cafe on Friday afternoon. She commented, "But I don't play hockey on Thursday evenings." And then both smiled.

After enjoying their refreshments for several moments, Catherine brought up their attendance at church two days before. "So, Richard, how did you find church the other day? I want to tell you that you should be complimented for accompanying me on Wednesday. I was just wondering how you felt about it. Maybe you'll come with me next week. As I think I told you, I go to the chapel every Wednesday." Richard gazed off into the corner of the cafe for a moment, pondering his answer. There was another couple in that corner in an intimate conversation. He had thought about his attendance at the chapel for the last two days but was still not certain about his feelings about going to church for the first time in years. "I can't really say. I have to admit that while I was glad I went with you, I can't really tell you why. I can tell you though that I can't remember the last time I was happy to go to church, if ever."

Catherine accepted Richard's explanation and then followed her first question with a second after talking about the congregants at the Wednesday morning mass. Catherine said that aside from students who sometimes attended, the majority of the church goers on Wednesday mornings were elderly. Richard slowly nodded and remarked that when he was an altar boy serving early morning masses, most of the those in attendance were older people. "I always thought that any parishioner with a job or had to get kids off to school weren't going to early morning masses on weekdays. In addition, my mother used to say that older people were usually more devout than most people." The two of them agreed about the increased reverence of older people. Catherine then returned to her suggestion about his possible attendance at the next Wednesday.

"I can tell that you've thought about it and may be still thinking about it." said Catherine. Richard nodded again and leaned forward, giving Catherine an intense gaze. "Yes, like I said, I was glad I went to church with you. And I've thought about it, thought about it a lot." Catherine took his right hand in hers and responded. "And …" Richard stared in Catherine's eyes, his anxiety continuing to build and finally gave her the answer he assumed she wanted to hear. "I'll go to church with you next Wednesday. I want to. I may even take communion." Catherine leaned even further forward, kissed Richard on the cheek and told him that he would have to go to confession and receive absolution before taking communion. She then said that he could take confession during either the weekday morning masses, benediction services on Thursday evenings, vespers on Saturday afternoons, or during the Sunday masses, at 8:00, 9:00, and 10:00, the latter the high mass. Richard slowly shrugged and said that he had not been to confession for years, probably before his last appearance at mass in grade school. He also added that he doubted that his confession at that time was a honest accounting of his reputed transgressions, uncertain as to what constituted a sin worthy of reporting to a confessor, at least back then.

He decided, his guilt overwhelming him into deception, not to tell Catherine about his last confession, perhaps his only legitimate confession, the accounting he provided to an unknown confessor at a Notre-Dame de Lourdes church about the theft of the priestly vestment. Instead, he gave an abbreviated history of his experience with confession. "Most of the time, I just told the priest what I thought what he wanted to hear." Catherine looked a trifle surprised and asked for an explanation. "What did you think priests wanted to hear?" Catherine inquired. Richard answered quietly, obviously embarrassed about having just admitted something that seemed, once he voiced it aloud, almost preposterous. "I really don't know. When I was younger, like when I was in elementary school, I just confessed to the normal mischief, things like minor theft, swearing, and talking back to his parents. And then later, when I was in my early teens, I added impure thoughts and actions to my repertoire, which was true for the most part." Catherine tittered while Richard moved awkwardly in his chair. He was having difficulty sitting still. After an uncomfortable silence, he added an interesting comment that had been made by one of his confessors when Richard confessed to activity that every teenage boy pursued with almost constant enthusiasm. "He asked me if my sins were performed alone or with others." This time, Catherine's reaction almost turned more than surprise, almost astounded that a priest would ask such a strange question. Richard thought he saw three other diners taking notice of their conversation. He also suspected that Brother Nelson was following their discussion as well.

Their seminar regarding confession now over, Richard and Catherine collected their things and left the cafe.

Richard attended the morning mass on the next Wednesday in the Saint Ignatius Chapel in order to take confession. He arrived maybe fifteen minutes before the mass began, enough time to arrange a visit to the confessional. Catherine was already present, seated in the fourth pew on the eastern side of the church. Richard's turn for confession came after two old ladies were able to confess to whatever presumably venial sins of which they thought they were guilty. Richard entered one of the vacant confessionals as soon as it become available. Being an older church, it having been built almost a hundred years ago, the confessionals in Saint Ignatius were dark and disagreeable, the fragrance of oak panelling, the velvet curtains between the penitent and the priest, and the aromas of old lady eau de toilette dominating the enclosure. The scent of this booth reminded of Richard of the confessionals he entered when he was in elementary school, his olfactory sense obviously functional. The chapel was almost completely silent, the only sound being the noise of the several old women routing through their purses and murmuring to each other.

As Richard knelt in front of the curtain between he and the confessor, he happened to faintly hear the old lady who had preceded Richard into the other booth. The old lady sounded like she was weeping and occasionally exclaiming, in a whisper but in an increasing volume, that she was sorry about something or other. He was surprised. As he knelt waiting for his turn with the confessor, he tried to recollect past situations in which he actually heard either the other penitent or the confessor say anything. He sometimes heard or thought he heard priests ask the same question in identical words. He concluded that overhearing the old lady's weeping and whispering in a confessional was nothing other than an accident, a fluke. It was also a mystery that for some unknown reason continued to occupy Richard's thought after he had received sympathy or absolution or both and joined Catherine in the fourth pew. The mass had not started as yet. He sat down beside her. Catherine turned and patted him on the knee. A couple of minutes later, the priest followed by a single altar boy appeared. Neither looked happy.

Almost as soon as the mass started, Richard found himself surreptitiously inspecting the members of the congregation, specifically the elderly women who made up most of them anyway. He was looking for the woman who he might have overheard in the confessional adjoining his own. There must have dozens of elderly worshipers in attendance, almost all of whom were women. To Richard, all the ladies looked similar, all in elegant states of decay, cosmetics for elderly women applied haphazardly across their faces. To Richard, a lot of them looked like they were rehearsing for some sort of theatrical show. Either that, or they were related to both his grandmothers. In the meantime, Catherine had noticed that Richard was occasionally distracted as the mass progressed. So she was patting him on the knee and then whispering for him to pay attention, her tone growing uncharacteristically insistent. Richard took notice of Catherine's growing discomfort and by the time the service progressed to the serving of communion, he was paying rapt attention. He followed Catherine in the line for communion, having concluded that his surveillance of the old ladies was unable to identify the old woman who he had overheard in the confession.

He and Catherine returned to their pew after receiving the Eucharist after which the two of them were kneeling and then sitting beside each other. Catherine was holding Richard's hand, looking at Richard with a beatific smile. To Richard, it was almost as if Catherine had a halo surrounding her head, a sacred nimbus that was almost paralyzing him. Ten minutes later, after the blessing, the priest dismissed the congregation with the benediction "Go in Peace" in Latin. Catherine and Richard left the chapel, Catherine to French class at nine o'clock and Richard to the cafeteria beside the hockey rink for breakfast. After that, Richard didn't have a class until history at eleven o'clock. Before they separated, Catherine gave Richard another earnest look and left him with a memorable comment, "I must say that I'm proud of you. You must be rediscovering your faith." Richard wanted to answer but he didn't. He wasn't sure that he ever had any faith to rediscover in the first place.

On their next date at the cafe, Catherine had arrived early as usual. She arose from her seat and hugged Richard. It seemed obvious to Catherine that the possible restoration of his faith might have prompted him to accompany her to the Wednesday mass but his participation in communion during the last mass they shared confirmed it. So it was expected by Richard that Catherine would further explain her pride that she had expressed at the conclusion of Wednesday's mass. Catherine did not disappoint. She told him she had hoped that he would continue to maintain the religious faith he had recently resurrected following the epiphany she claimed had been revealed to him during theology classes and then early morning church services.

Richard did not entirely accept Catherine's observation, saying he could not assign his recent religious conversation to inspiration provided by the classes and her persuading him to attend mass. He said, with some hesitation, that while the classes and going to mass contributed to his newly realized belief, there was something inexplicable involved. Catherine looked at him with a look of excited sincerity and then made a surprising assertion. "I prayed for you on several occasions. I had hoped that my prayers would have some effect on your faith." It looked like there were tears in her eyes. Richard slowly nodded and added another conclusion. "I just don't know why." Catherine looked up and agreed. "Maybe I don't know either."

As the academic year headed toward the spring and its conclusion, Catherine and Richard resumed their reflections about his renewed religious conviction. As for their relationship, it had drifted from a caste romance to the status of good friends, an association that he had not maintained with anyone since he was in high school. Things had fundamentally changed after one of their Friday afternoon meetings at the cafe when Richard mistakenly tried to kiss Catherine. It wasn't a casual kiss, not a peck on the cheek, not a greeting, not a farewell. It was an attempt at a romantic kiss, in what would have been their first. Catherine slowly drew back, surprise an accurate definition Richard thought, and started to stand up as to leave the cafe. To Brother Allen and the three other customers in the cafe, there seemed little doubt that an astounded expression had appeared on her face and she looked like she was about to leave. Richard sat in silence for a moment before she picked up her bag and left the room. Neither of them said a thing.

It was several days later that Catherine's older sister, Patricia, joined Richard at a table on the first floor of the library. Richard had met Patricia Morris once, Catherine introduced them after theology class one Tuesday a month ago or so. Richard recognized her immediately but she still introduced herself. She said that while she was happy that he and her sister were good friends, in view of her lack of experience in matters of romance, she didn't want him to pursue her along along those lines. It was obvious that Catherine had told her sister about his attempted kiss. "I think you're too experienced for her. She needs someone who is as innocent as she is. I'm here to ask you to please not pursue her in any romance." Richard was stunned. Patricia then simply got up from the table at which they had been sitting and left, seemingly as quickly as she had arrived.

The kiss that Richard had unsuccessfully sought was intended to initiate their possible romance, if it was the direction in which he thought their relationship was headed. The fact was, however, their association was going in the opposite direction. In the next couple of months, not only did he and Catherine avoid any hint of future romance but had drifted away from any serious conversations, discussion of matters of faith no longer prevalent between the two of them. Richard started to concentrate on the course itself. In fact, he began to participate in class discussions, something he had never previously pursued, asking questions, making comments. For reasons he could not fathom, he had taken an interest in Father Breslin's elucidation regarding the seven sacraments of the Catholic Church, reconciliation or penance being of particular attention. He wondered about it constantly. The confessing of one's sins, formally called the Sacrament of Reconciliation according to Father Breslin, attracted most of his curiosity. Even since he started to go to confession again as a consequence of his attendance at the early Wednesday morning masses in the Saint Ignatius Chapel, he had developed a fascination with the procedure, the testifying of his sins to the priest. It had become an obsession.

So he began to spend a significant amount of time contemplating the meaning of mortal or venal sins, the kind of acts that qualified for admission in confession in the first place. He recalled the relatively simple process he undertook when he was going to confession before he abandoned it entirely in his teens. He would disclose any transgression that would or could prompt disapproval from anyone in authority, his parents, his teachers, the priests, even the Divine if He or She were available. Still, despite his frequent ruminations about sin, he would confess almost anything he thought might be considered not just sinful but inappropriate as well, rudeness, talking back, little white lies, and minor thefts, even sneaking the occasional sip from a bottle in the parents' liquor cabinet.

But during the theology class, particularly during its last two months, his consideration of the subject of confession had changed completely. While he had been educated on the characteristics of sin before he reached Saint Ignatius College, for example the Catechism of the

Catholic Church having been a constant companion in every class he attended in Saint John Fisher Elementary School, religious instruction become understandably more complex as his schooling went on. So it was no surprise then that the class began to review his thinking about sin. In this context, Father Breslin led the class on a discussion of the Ten Commandments during which the class had eventually concluded that maybe only five of the ten edicts could actually be considered immoral or unethical actions. In that regard, after some discussion, most of the class had agreed that the first four of the principles supposedly handed down to Moses on Mount Sinai had little to do with human conduct but were almost entirely relevant to the worship of God while the fifth commandment only concerned honouring your parents, a situation that most children acknowledged as normal, at least until they entered adolescence. As Richard could have expected, Catherine contributed little to the class discussion, although she did express a serious reservation about the suggestion that believers should simply ignore five of the ten commandments. In addition, it was apparent that Catherine may have spent much of the exchanges fighting back tears, dabbing at her eyes with a pale blue hanky while her friend Mary comforted her with the occasional embrace. Richard didn't know why.

It was during the next class that, in the continuation of its consideration of what constituted sin, that Richard himself raised the possibility of allowing the "Seven Deadly Sins" to guide their definition of evil, at least in terms of dealing with the complications of confession. He put forward for the consideration of Father Breslin and the class that every one of the "Seven Deadly Sins" was a transgression that should be included in any admission by anyone making their confession. When someone was uneducated enough to ask, Richard enumerated them: gluttony, lust, greed, wrath, sloth, envy, and pride. In some ways, as pointed out by class cynic MacKay, several, if not a majority of the sins were practices that were normally, if not enthusiastically pursued by many believers, no matter how ardent. That prompted several of the students to nominate those so-called sins in which they took a fair amount of delight. The two males in the class, Richard and Lee MacKay immediately voted for lust while the five women in the group selected envy and pride as misdeeds that could bedevil them. Finally, at first Catherine resisted naming any of the deadly sins as captivating but after considerable discussion among Father Breslin and the rest of theology class, she acknowledged that pride was her vice, an unfortunate addiction that grew out of the certainty of her faith.

As usual, it was Lee McKay who pointed out that it would be difficult, if close to impossible to name pride as a sin in the confession, his point that being proud was a continual misdeed and not like a normal sin, which she suggested was a singular act. Father Breslin looked mildly interested in response to MacKay's observation and then shrugged his shoulders, asking if anyone else had an opinion, asking specifically if Catherine cared to debate MacKay on the issue. After a short interval, during which Catherine assumedly pondered her view, she said that she disputed MacKay's view that pride was not a deadly sin. To support her opinion that pride was in fact a deadly sin, Catherine said that she felt like she had committed a sin anytime she exhibited pride and had felt guilty about it. Catherine provided the group with several examples of sinful pride about which she felt guilty. She said that censuring people that did not believe with the same religious conviction as she did or making uncomplimentary comments about other religions was obvious she said. Father Breslin was impressed with Catherine's justification for defining pride as a deadly sin, particularly about the relationship between sin and guilt, a perspective that the good Father thought was an admirable clarification. Even the continually skeptical MacKay was willing to consider her explanation.

The class discussion of the overall definition of sin then ended as the class itself concluded. Before discharging the class, Father Breslin said that that discussion was not over.

A Chaste
Romance Ends

Any kind of intimate relationship between Catherine and Richard had been fading over six weeks or so, his rather awkward attempt at a kiss quite possibly the obvious basis for the pivotal development, at least as far as Richard was concerned. Their deliberations regarding belief, however, continued, if not increased in intensity. Richard still maintained the hope that he could possibly revive any kind of romance with Catherine, if it actually prevailed in the first place, more a hope than a reality. In any event, Richard continued to discuss with Catherine any issues that were appraised by the theology class. In addition, and more importantly, he continued to accompany her to Wednesday morning mass and receive communion, necessitating Richard to occasionally visit confession, to ensure that he was in a "state of grace", a requirement for anybody receiving communion. During the month after Richard first took communion further to Catherine's constant persuasion,

Richard felt it appropriate to visit the confessional in Saint Ignatius Chapel twice, which was more than he went in the previous ten years. He was relatively charitable when it came to determining which misdeeds he was eventually to confess. He thought that applying a more expansive definition as to what constituted a sin was a wise way to impress Catherine, even if she didn't realize it. His ambition was to win her back, which was basically a fantasy since he had never won her in the first place.

Further, while he was pondering a course of action to renew Catherine's interest in romance, regardless of whether they were ever involved in any relationship that could be considered a romance in the first place, he continued to attend Theology 130 class. In addition, he increased his participation in the class discussions on various subjects that have had something to do with church history. In the last few classes, Father Breslin said that he was hoping to introduce a couple of interesting issues from church history. Since the class had been debating the history and current status of confession, a topic that had fascinated Richard ever since the matter was first raised not only during the class but also during his conversations with Catherine, when one of the students, it might have been Lee MacKay or someone else who brought up the subject of "plenary indulgences" although he didn't know their meaning.

It was evident that nobody else in the class but Father Breslin knew what "plenary indulgences" were. It was up to Father Breslin to explain to the class what "plenary indulgences" actually were. He smiled and mentioned that he had not heard the term for years, if not decades.

After several minutes, Richard came to a faint recollection that he had heard the term before, perhaps in elementary school classes during which "plenary indulgences" were discussed, likely in passing by teachers who might have been asked by a student who might have heard the term somewhere. So when Father Breslin began his report on the history of the term, Richard's memory grew stronger. It was during a recollection of his fifth grade teacher, Mr. Clark, explaining hell to his students when the term came up as an aside. Richard recalled that Mr. Clark took a certain delight in describing hell, actually telling his pupils that hell was a fire that burns eternally.

The students began to listen carefully to Father Breslin delineate the history of "plenary indulgences". He introduced his exposition by briefly talking about the conditions regarding the route to hell, particularly the consequences of confessed and forgiven sins to be paid on earth or in purgatory. When one of the students, a woman named Judy who seldom if ever spoke in class, continued to ask about purgatory, claiming to have never heard of the term, Father Breslin chuckled a bit and said that it was a state of suffering inhabited by souls making amends for their sins. Although the rest of the class seemed to have barely heard of purgatory, some of them actually rolling their eyes, Father Breslin admitted it was a relatively outdated concept but was still a notion that had a place in the church's belief mythology. "An indulgence freed the sinners from having to make amends for their sins. Usually indulgences were granted based on a sincere repentance, the intention to live a holy life, and reception of the sacraments of penance and communion."

Lee MacKay then asked if anyone ever paid for "plenary indulgences", mentioning that he had heard that it was a principal element of church corruption. Father Breslin nodded and said, "I'm sure it happened but it probably doesn't anymore. It has always been a sin but, as you say, the Church has sometimes been hypocritical. So I guess it happened, particularly if the sinner had money."

Some of the class continued to seem interested in Father Breslin's narrative about "plenary indulgence". Several students, Richard among them, admitted to each other their curiosity about the matter. Class specialist MacKay remarked that the Catholic Church must have been a helluva interesting organization at some point in the past, presumably in the Middle Ages in particular. That initiated an observation by Richard that he wished the class would consider the Inquisition in a subsequent class. The other two students agreed.

Richard initially thought that he would somehow slip Catherine a note about the changing nature of their relationship in view of her sister's recent counsel to him about the two of them. He had acknowledged to himself that Catherine was unlikely to have any experience with the kind of romance he had envisaged. He thought, in fact he was convinced, that Catherine was not only a virgin but may have never engaged in any sort of romance, regardless of its nature. But he could not come to any course of action to straighten out their friendship without ruining it. After dismissing the possibility of providing Catherine with a written message that he wasn't actively seeking her romantically, he decided that he would inform her at their next Friday afternoon date at the cafe, a plan about which he had been nervous but had grown a littler more agreeable after he spoke to her sister Patricia. He would then invest a couple of days rehearsing to himself how he would inform her of any change in their relationship, that is if it was necessary.

Friday afternoon came quickly enough for Richard to avoid the kind of anxiety he might have otherwise anticipated. He practised what he would say to Catherine all three nights just before falling asleep until Friday arrived. He arrived at the cafe before Catherine did, an unusual development. He had Brother Nelson bring him a hot chocolate and a raspberry scone and waited for Catherine who came into the room no more than five minutes later. She sat down, ordered tea and toast and gave Richard her customary smile. Richard immediately went into his practised script, interrupting Catherine's report on her class on pastoral care. He reached across the table and patted Catherine's forearm.

"Catherine, I've been thinking a lot about our friendship. I have come to the conclusion that we are friends. You remember that I tried to kiss you a while ago. At the time, you looked uncomfortable, maybe even a little frightened. So I didn't try to kiss you again. I hope you're okay with that."

An endearing smile spread across Catherine's face. She returned Richard's gesture and patted him on his forearm. She then tittered a bit. "Sure, I'm okay with your restraint. I was a bit surprised that you wanted to kiss me. It was a nice thought I guess but I wasn't interested. I'm still not." Catherine gently looked at him and patted his arm again.

"Still friends, okay?" It may have been a question more than a reassurance.

Richard softly smiled, shook his head and then started to change the subject. "Did you find the discussion the other day on plenary indulgences educational?" Catherine nodded and answered his question. "I was wondering when you were going to bring that up." She delayed for a moment and then answered directly. "I guess I should admit that I already knew a bit about indulgences. Father Breslin pretty well covered the subject but he could gone a little further." Richard predictably commented. "Further! What do you mean, further?" Catherine moved closer to Richard at the table and continued the conversation in a whisper. "Well, I've read that the provision of "plenary indulgences", the purchase of the forgiveness of sin was fairly common in the the church in the Middle Ages and led in some way to the Reformation. Martin Luther thought that the Church was corrupt and the granting of indulgences was one element of that corruption. That corruption resulted in the emergence of the Protestant Reformation. That was back in the 1500's."

Understandably, Richard was not conversant with the history of the Protestant Reformation and basically looked at Catherine with a blank look on his face. He then said that maybe he should take another theology course. Either theology or a history course. "On the other hand, maybe it would also do me some good. As you know, I've become interested in religion since I started taking Theology 130 and started going to church with you." He then laughed a bit. Catherine then concluded their contemplation of plenary indulgences by expressing a hope that Father Breslin would continue his exposition but expressed some doubt. "We only have a couple more classes left." Richard shared that doubt. "That's too bad. Corruption is always interesting, no matter where or when it happens. Maybe you should ask Father Breslin about that." Catherine looked a little embarrassed but agreed. "I'll ask him, privately."

It was getting close to five o'clock, cafe closing time, and both of them had to leave to catch their buses anyway. They would see each other the next Tuesday in class. For a moment, Richard thought about checking the Protestant Reformation in the library. He would visit the library and research the Protestant Reformation, Martin Luther and corruption in the Catholic Church in the Middle Ages. In addition, it would be another way he thought to forget about Catherine romantically and return to seducing her intellectually, if that's what was occupying his mind. After all, Catherine seemed to almost have almost forgotten the incident, confessing that she wasn't interested in his apparent intention anyway.

He went to the library on Monday to investigate the origins of the Reformation and the influence of Martin Luther, the so-called "Little Monk", on its evolution. As tiresome as his research had seemed the first hour of that morning, Richard finally came across a section in the Encyclopedia Britannica regarding the prevalence of corruption in the church during the Middle Ages. One of the principal issues covered by the Encyclopedia included a section on the granting of indulgences in the Middle Ages by the church, an activity that bothered Martin Luther to such an extent that it become a crucial part of his "95 Theses", the subliminal document that he wrote in 1517 to establish the origins of the Reformation. Since Father Breslin had explained "plenary indulgences" to the theology class only five days ago, Richard's interest was obvious. The Encyclopedia described indulgences as blessings that the church could use to absolve sins in exchange for money, the difference between "an indulgence" and "a plenary indulgence" being that the former applies to only part of the punishment while the latter applies to all punishment, including sins committed by the dead, a possibility that enraged Martin Luther even more. Richard also noted that the Encyclopedia included a paragraph on the most famous peddler of indulgences, a salesman named Johann Tetzel who managed to separate many peasants from their limited financial means in order to help free themselves or a loved one, living or dead, from years of torment. It was said that Tetzel would travel from town to town, presumably German towns, claiming that a little money would save sinners from the suffering of hell.

Reflecting on the article, Richard wondered if indulgences were still accepted by the Catholic Church as a legitimate response to sin. He assumed that instead of confession, an indulgence could be purchased and whatever punishment that was due could be absolved. On the other hand, it was standard that sinners could simply visit a confessional, confess their sins and seek repentance, accept penance, recite an Act of Contrition, receive absolution, and then perform their penance, almost always prayers. All without having to purchase an indulgence. Accordingly, as far as Richard understood, the only advantage that indulgences would have if they were still a legitimate part of Catholic Church doctrine was to provide forgiveness to sins committed after the sinner's death. But indulgences were banned by Pope Pius V in 1567. In any event, he thought he would demonstrate his research efforts to Catherine the next day in theology class, his intention to continue to share theological interests with Catherine. It was unfortunate that he never got the chance.

Father Breslin opened his class the next day by informing his charges that he intended to continue class consideration of corruption in the Roman Catholic church in the Middle Ages following last week's discussion of the widespread use of indulgences during that period. "I had the impression that most of you were fairly interested in last week's dialogue about indulgences in the Middle Ages. In addition, I thought that maybe some of you were also wondering about corruption in general, of which indulgences were a major part. So instead of discussing the sacraments or the miracle of faith for example, which are issues that we could be covering over the last two classes we will have together this year, we will continue to examine corruption in the church in those years." There were enthusiastic whispers heard from the eight students who were listening to Father Breslin. It was conspicuous that the class would rather listen to a lecture from Father Breslin about past corruption in the church as opposed to any other issue that could have been explored by the class in its last few weeks of the academic year. Father Breslin acknowledged their academic preference with that creepy little smile of his, an expression that sometimes frightened his charges even though that was not his intention. The usually inquisitive students, Lee MacKay and Grant Beattie joined Richard and two other students in moving to the edge of their seats, obviously preparing to listen to Father Breslin's presentation about the history of church corruption. Catherine and Mary seemed to be the only students who were not happy with the change in curriculum.

That class started with Father Breslin telling his students that Martin Luther defined corruption as deviating from the word of God. Surprisingly, he did not blame Church leadership but the Church itself. Fact was he said that the perception of corruption changed when the congregation started to notice clergies' wealth and how it was exhibited. He noted that the wealth was gained through the selling of indulgences, which the class already knew, and other items. The church bought and sold its properties, its jobs, its forgiveness of sin through indulgences, its nepotism, and its involvement in education and politics. Regarding the latter, Lee MacKay interrupted Father Breslin by asking about whether the relationship between former Quebec Premier Duplessis and the Catholic Church in Quebec was indicative of corruption. Father Breslin smirked and said, "Maybe, a lot of people continue to think that that was true."

The rest of the class was devoted to discussing examples of church corruption that several students could recall from their experiences. At least two of the students, including Lorraine Laflamme, another student who seldom, if ever spoke in class, shared stories about priests whose alcoholism was so well known that parish deacons supposedly seriously considering asking the diocese to remove the priests from their posts. The two students also said that they remembered that altar boys were sometimes asked to ensure that fruit juice was substituted for wine in the chalices used in church services. Father Breslin replied to those stories by identifying alcoholism as disagreeable, anti-social behaviour but not corrupt. Another student, the predictable Grant Beattie reported that an old pastor from his parish ended up driving a different automobile annually, suggesting that maybe he was dipping into church donations to purchase a new car every year. Father Breslin shrugged, stating that it would be too obvious, unlikely to escape detection by church hierarchy, the parishioners, or maybe even the press and therefore was not really corruption.

That portion of the class ended without any further suggestions being offered by either Father Breslin or any of the students. Before dismissing the class, Father Breslin announced that they were to provide him with a short essay on any aspect of the course that improved their understanding of history, religion, or the Roman Catholic church. The essay would then form the basis for their final and only grades for the course. As the class began to leave, Richard hurried out of the room to catch up to Catherine. He reminded her that both of them would still be attending mass the next morning in the Saint Ignatuis Chapel. Catherine, who hardly participated in the class discussion on church corruption, nodded and hurried down the corridor.

As Richard watched the ladies disappear down the hall, he thought about whether he still had a reason to accompany Catherine to mass on Wednesday morning. He frequently wondered whether he ever had a rationale to keep Catherine company in church, his original motivation, his romantic interest in her, having slowly faded, leaving his growing belief in the Catholic faith the likely basis for going to church with her. In any event, Richard had plans to not only meet Catherine at mass the next day but to also visit the confessional. Lee MacKay and Grant Beattie, who were also standing out in the corridor exchanging fumes of cigarette smoke, snickered as they watched Richard staring at the ladies walking down the corridor. They may have been wondering about Richard's motivation as well.

The next day, Richard arrived in the Saint Ignatuis Chapel a few minutes before the Wednesday morning confession was due to begin. He had wait for Father Barnes, Catherine having introduced him to Richard a couple of weeks previously. Late by ten minutes, Father Barnes stepped into the confessional, apologetically nodded to Richard before disappearing into the dark of the confessor's booth, no other penitent was waiting for absolution. It was Richard's turn to step into the confession. The screen slid open just as Richard knelt down to confess. The script for Richard's confession was almost identical to the admission he had provided a previous week to Father Cushing, one of the other Jesuits that provided confessional services before and during the Wednesday morning mass. By the time Richard received his pardon, mass had already started. Catherine smiled as he knelt beside her to complete his penance, a few decades of the rosary, a penalty similar to the one that he had previously received from Father Cushing.

Catherine and Richard sat through the mass without making any comments either to the altar, in the form of prayer, or to each other. Once the service was over and the congregation started to leave the chapel, Catherine remained in the pew and signalled Richard to remain there as well. It took several minutes for most of the parishioners to exit the chapel, the only other people remaining in the chapel were three elderly women who seemed to be rooting through their purses for something. Several minutes went by and Catherine asked Richard if he intended to continue to go to confession and take communion after the school year was over, the last class scheduled for the following Tuesday. Richard took Catherine's proffered hand and quietly nodded. She smiled, put her prayer book back in her school bag, and got up to attend French class at nine o'clock. She leaned down and whispered that she would see him on Friday afternoon at the cafe. It would likely be their last rendezvous of the school year.

As was his custom, he planned to head to the library to invest two hours or so before his history class was due to begin. He thought he would return to studying some of the more curious events that had befallen the church over the centuries, some with which he was already familiar. He was still interested in stories about indulgences, which the class had studied extensively over the past few classes. In addition, the students themselves, including Richard, discussed the church charging for the remission of sin through indulgences. He was particularly fascinated by a story about people called "sin eaters", individuals that appeared to have lived in Wales and in some other areas of the British Isles bordering Wales in the seventeenth and eighteenth centuries. Quite simply, a "sin eater" was a person who consumed a ritual meal in order to spiritually take on the burden of transgressions of a deceased person. The food consumed was believed to be the sins of a recently deceased person, thus absorbing the sins committed by that person throughout that person's life. In addition, "sin eaters" were said to also absorb the sins committed by living persons, to Richard meaning that "sin eaters" basically replaced the role of priests in confession. One particularly strange tale involved a "sin eater" compelled to absorb the sins of a dead person who had been was a "sin eater" himself.

As apparently agreed during their class two days ago, their appointment was fated to be their last meeting at the cafe. The theology class the previous Tuesday was to be their last with Father Breslin. As customary, Catherine was sitting at a small table in the corner of the room before a tea and a scone of unidentified type. She was reading a copy of the college newspaper, surprising reading material for Catherine, as Richard had never having seen her with any other periodical. As Richard sat down and signalled Brother Nelson, Catherine held up page 12 from the newspaper and pointed to a short article positioned in the right bottom corner of that page. The title of the article was simple and clearly indicative of its content: "Father Breslin To Retire". Richard took the paper from Catherine, quickly read the article, and understandably expressed surprise. "While the good Father is quite possibly the right age, he does not seem ready to retire. And besides, according to the article here, he only taught theology, our class, Theology 230 as well as Theology 330. That means he only had ten students, seven in our class and the same three in the other class." Catherine nodded slowly and then pondered, "Why didn't he tell us? Do you think he told any of his students? I mean, besides our class, doesn't Father Breslin have only three other students, the same three in the more senior class." Both Catherine and Richard sat in silence for a few minutes. Brother Nelson brought coffee and a chocolate chip muffin to Richard. Then, Catherine continued with her contemplation of Father Breslin's retirement asking, "I wonder if the author of the article asked the three senior students, all of whom are probably headed for the priesthood, for their opinions on Father Breslin's retirement. I wonder what they think." Richard shrugged, "Maybe. It would be interesting. Maybe he'll tell us during our class on Tuesday."

After considering Father Breslin's future, Catherine asked Richard about his future, stunning him into reflection for several minutes. Catherine sat quietly while Richard seemed to be quietly deliberating with himself. She then looked up and asked a surprising question, Catherine asked him directly. "What are you going to do this summer?" After an appropriate silence, during which Brother Nelson arrived to provide Richard with a refill of his coffee, Richard said that he intended to return to the factory that had employed him during the last two summers. Catherine made an observation. "That doesn't sound very pleasant." Richard laughed a little and asked her what she planned to do. Catherine answered,

"I intend to work for the Salvation Army Thrift Store just down Sherbrooke Street." Richard was not surprised one bit.

It was Tuesday morning and all registered students appeared in Father Breslin's last class. It was not a surprise, based on the article in the college newspaper, that Father Breslin announced that he planned to depart from his teaching career after that Tuesday morning lesson. A number of the pupils, after expressing regret with Father Breslin's declaration, asked about his plans for the future. Father Breslin offered up a grin and told the class that he planned to spend his retirement at the Jesuit Retreat in Guelph. In addition to prayer, serving mass and other priestly duties, he would be holding seminars and other opportunities for Jesuits seeking to recover their commitment to their faith. Father Breslin declared that he intended to write a book. The class looked at each other with mild astonishment on their faces.

Lee McKay, who was his usual inquisitive self, asked if Father Breslin intended to write a book on theology. He replied that he thought he would try his hand on a novel. The incredulity on the faces of his students stayed, if not grew. Father Breslin continued to grin and assured his students that he had not taken leave of his senses. "Mr. MacKay, I can assure you that while I don't intent to write a book on theology per se, years, if not decades of reading about religion may have given me enough characters and events to construct an acceptable fiction. So I thought I would give myself an opportunity to write something." Father Breslin then said that if he ever got published, he hoped that his students would purchase a copy. Everyone of the students listening to Father Breslin simply nodded.

After informing the group of his intentions to become an author, he reported that he had read their essays in order to finalize their examination results. During the first Theology 130 class, Father Breslin had informed his students of the scheme to determine their final marks. He then told them that he would ask each individual student to communicate to him and the rest of the class what the course had taught them about their own beliefs. He simply said that he would be interested in what they had to say. The students had anxious looks on their faces. So Father Breslin comforted the students. "Don't worry, I don't expect any of you to give me an explanation as if you're defending a doctoral thesis. I know that this is only a first year theology class and many, if not all of you didn't really want to register for this class. I know that theology, like the classics for example, is not a popular course in university any more. I'm the only professor in the theology department. I remember fourty years ago when I started here as an instructor, there was two other teachers in the department. On the other hand, the classics department had six teachers. Now it has half that number. So over the years, you can see that the university has become, if you'll pardon me saying this, apathetic about both theology and classics. So don't be embarrassed. You can say anything you want to say. And by the way, whatever you say won't have any effect on your examination results."

Father Breslin then looked at a list on his desk and announced the candidate for the first testimony. "I think we should call on Mr. MacKay whom I am certain will have something to say." Lee MacKay arose as if his seat had suddenly become hot. He faced Father Breslin with a certain confidence. He seemed to be without anxiety, unlike some of his classmates. He looked and sounded like he had rehearsed. He immediately went into an explanation of what he had learned during Father Breslin's theology class. He told the class that he was particularly enlightened by the class discussion of the church's history of corruption, particularly the use of indulgences, adding that he wished they had had the time to consider the possible recent involvement of government and the church. On the other hand, somewhat embarrassed, he gently informed Father Breslin and his fellow students that while he was not overly inspired by the class's consideration of matters of confession and the "Seven Deadly Sins", he did find the class discussion after the "Seven Deadly Sins" interesting, his opposition to Catherine's identification of pride as her deadly sin a highlight. But he did conclude his discussion by saying that Father Breslin made the class as interesting as anyone could. Father Breslin, who was now sitting behind his desk at the front of the class, offered Lee MacKay a thin smile and thanked him. Richard glanced at Catherine, who had taken up her customary seat in front of him, and noticed that a grimace had briefly appeared on her face.

Grant Beattie, who often competed with MacKay in expressing himself in class, followed. In his brief comments, he said "I'm all with Lee. Like him, I found the discussion on church corruption worth listening to although I wasn't that interested in the class talking about the "Seven Deadly Sins" although the individual identification by that class of sins was kind of entertaining, I mean interesting." Father Breslin then thanked Mr. Beattie for his comments. He then called upon Richard who nervously rose from his seat and addressed Father Breslin. He surprised the class and impressed Catherine Morris by telling Father Breslin and the class that the theology class inspired him to renew his faith in the Catholic religion, a development that Richard said he found surprising, claiming that he didn't really know that he had faith in any event, at least not since he was in elementary school and was a regular altar boy. He also said that he had returned to regularly attending mass and going to confession, changes in his behaviour that he said were related entirely to what he had heard in the theology class. Not only was Father Breslin impressed, so was Catherine Morris who was looking at Richard with nothing other than esteem. Catherine's friend Mary was also looking at Richard with a certain admiration. Father Breslin expressed, as sincerely as he could, his admiration for Richard's conversion from being an agnostic to a person of faith.

He then asked Mary for her views about the class. She admitted that she was skeptical at first about the course but registered anyway because her friend Catherine had been a student in an introductory course in psychology the previous scholastic year. Understandably, Father Breslin asked for her reason for registering for Theology 130 simply because she was in a same class the previous year. Mary said Catherine Morris was easily the best student in the class and she thought that if she registered for Theology 130, it must have have been a worthwhile course and therefore worth taking. "As it turned out, I enjoyed the course and I'm not a religious person. I learned things that I never knew, particularly since my only experience with religion was Sunday mass with my parents although I never paid much attention. And in primary school, I had to study the catechism just like every other kid but can't remember anything that I was supposed to remember." She then ended her explanation and looked at Catherine Morris. Father Breslin thanked Mary and then asked for Catherine Morris' comments.

She got up from her seat but not before she patted Mary on the arm. Father Breslin must have had a positive expectation about what Catherine Morris was about to say. She looked serious, neither nervous nor embarrassed. She was looking straight at Father Breslin who was looking back at her in a similar manner. "As you may know, I am a fairly religious person, Father Breslin, and I thought that this course would strengthen my faith somehow, maybe give me more of a justification for my beliefs. In fact, up until attending your course, I never thought about that, never examined my faith even though many, if not most of the people I knew questioned their faith not to explore its basis but to possibly abandon it. Besides, I did enjoy the discussions the class has had. I must thank you for teaching the class and by the way, I don't think you should retire."

Next up for a testimonial was Lorraine Laflame who, aside from a short interjection weeks ago, broke her silence. "I found most of your classes quite interesting. While I am not in any way religious," she turned and briefly looked at Catherine Morris, "my family is, especially my mother. So I would discuss specific subjects that may have come up in our classes. Of course, I would avoid certain issues that may have arose in our talks, like corruption in the church, but I used our class discussions to engage my mother in reflecting on religion and the church." Father Breslin seemed satisfied and thanked Lorraine Laflamme for her talk. Finally, Father Breslin told the class that the other two students, Judy Edge and Patricia Forsyth, both of whom had never spoke in class, had asked to be pardoned from giving the class their impressions about the course. No one seemed disappointed.

The good Father then declared that class was dismissed and he acknowledged his pupils for their attention in a course he said covered issues that were not very interesting to most students. With that, he made the sign of the cross and wished them luck in their future academic endeavours. As the students departed from theology class for the final time, Catherine turned back to look at Richard. She looked at him almost seductively, a most unusual gaze for her.

He wondered if he had made an error in ending their romantic relationship, however chaste it may have been. He returned Catherine's stare with a forlorn look on his face. He just stood there. She had gone.

FAITH RENEWED

He was now in his third year of college, having completed his previous five courses of second year without any apparent trepidation, convinced that he had done competently, if not well considering his previous record at Saint Ignatius. He was particularly pleased with his grade in Theology 130 that had been based on a one page essay on its influence, if not his more general experience in the class. His dissertation, as brief as it was, was based on his equally short speech during the last theology class. Essentially, his paper stated unequivocally that Theology 130 had changed his life, having added to that life a spiritual dimension that he didn't think he had. Richard's paper maintained that not only had the issues covered during the class inspired his spiritual growth but so did his own research as well. In that context, he also wrote that Father Breslin had contributed significantly to his religious development. He also asserted that his classmates whose frequent comments precipitated Richard's theological reflections were a factor as well. However, he did not mention that his daydream girlfriend and theology classmate Catherine Morris had likely influenced his sudden epiphany more than anything or anybody else. Nor did he include any suggestion that her influence in inviting him to the Wednesday morning mass in the Saint Ignatius chapel was more than enough to demonstrate to him his own salvation. And finally, he did not refer in any way to his original infatuation with Catherine Morris and the effect it almost certainly had on his religious conversion.

His father, who had been installed as a church warden at the Saint John Fisher church in the family's neighbourhood even though he was generally indifferent regarding matters of faith, did not notice any change in his son's behaviour as it pertained to religious belief. On the other hand, his mother Doris, who was doubtless as devote as any middle aged Catholic woman could be, became increasingly aware of modifications in Richard's conduct as it pertained to spiritual matters. She had noticed that since he had started as a pupil in Theology 130, he began to regularly attend church every Sunday, a practice that he had previously eschewed since he entered high school and no longer had to serve mass as an altar boy. While she thought that her son had allowed her to think that he was still regularly going to church, she had known for some time that he hadn't, an unfortunate habit that he had then abandoned after he had started studying theology with Father Breslin.

So his mother was understandably pleased while his father didn't notice a thing. Richard's religious transformation was sufficiently sincere as to motivate him to regularly accompany the family, which included his mother, his occasionally reluctant father and his two younger brothers, to Sunday services. Richard's mother was even more than pleased when she witnessed her oldest son actually receive communion practically every time he went to Sunday mass with his family. Fact was that his mother was almost astounded, in fact she thought it was a miracle, that a teenager who had abandoned his religious faith in high school despite the efforts of his parents to nourish it since he made his first communion, had renewed a faith that he probably deserted when he was entering the eighth grade. His mother became convinced that her son's faith was the consequence of prayer, specifically her daily recitation of the rosary the likely cause. Regardless of the source of her son's evolution, Doris could not stop herself from referring to the change in her son's spiritual disposition, either to her husband, who spent much of his time ignoring almost everything she said unless it was a command, her female neighbours and relatives, and her fellow parishioners at Saint John Fisher, the latter two groups almost obviously envious of the ascent of the son of Doris to heaven. Further, she even contemplated confessing her pride and maybe even her envy in the confessional until she realized that it would may not have been a sin. She actually considered asking him how his theology class had contributed to his transformation. But she didn't.

As for Richard, he didn't much acknowledge his mother's change in attitude toward him, at least not directly to her. Of course he had noticed that she was more congenial toward him than she had been previously. His father had also noticed the change in his mother's point of view, having remarked that he had also had noticed that Richard's performance at school had improved, not that college ever allowed parents to follow their students' performance. He therefore had no idea of the reason for his wife's change in view toward Richard. Neither did his brothers although they seldom had any idea about anything anyway. At least, neither parent was speaking harshly to Richard anymore. In fact, they were both were unusually pleasant with their son Richard.

That summer, he was working at the Lawrence Industries, a chainsaw factory that was block north of the Trans-Canada and just east of Saint John's Road in Pointe Claire. Every day, he would walk to the plant from his house which was less than a mile away. It was his second summer working there, having been hired the previous summer after applying at every company in the area. The previous year, it had to be maybe the tenth or twelfth place on which he had called before a man named Bergeron offered him a job. On the other hand, he had no trouble at all reclaiming a job at Lawrence Industries, a personnel officer named Mundy actually remembered him, although this summer he was placed in the press room as opposed to the paint shop, a definite promotion for which he would be paid twenty cents more an hour. He had reported to the press room the first Monday in May and was somewhat disappointed when he was introduced to the annoying noise level in that section of the plant, at least when compared to the relative silence of the paint shop. His new boss was an older man with the unlikely name of Arbec. He was always dressed in a faded white shirt, a thin grey tie, and a nicotine stained black suit. He walked around the press room with his head down, seemingly talking to himself, always smoking, listening for the voice of factory manager Tessier booming over the factory public address system. Richard's new responsibility involved standing in front of a clattering machine hoping not to lose a limb or his hearing.

It was not surprising that none of his new colleagues, four full time guys with cigarettes in their mouths and two summer students, seemed pleased with placing plain flat pieces of metal between two stamping presses to eventually become parts of a chainsaw for the $1.66 an hour they were making for doing a job that might have been regarded as highly skilled around the turn of the century. It was also a little frightening, thinking of losing a hand or finger to a punch press, a fate that had befallen a man named Albert two years ago. Most of the time though Richard felt that he was fortunate to be working at Lawrence Industries despite the dangers the machinery posed to him.

Interestingly enough, spending most of his weekdays standing in front of a punch press in a factory that manufactured chainsaws compelled him to generally overlook the changes that the renewal of his faith had precipitated in him during the school year. Sure, he continued to attend mass on Sundays, sometimes with his parents and his two younger brothers, sometimes on his own, which his mother suggested that perhaps he had resumed his previous habit of replacing church with sitting on one of benches that surrounded the main baseball diamond in the neighbourhood Valois Park. When Doris first noticed that Richard had returned to attending church, she wanted to question her son about it but didn't, thinking at first that it was an accident. When she realized that his return to church was not a chance occurrence, he having accompanied the family to church three successive Sundays in June, she wanted to question him about it but was reluctant somehow, as if her eldest son would be annoyed, if not suspicious of his mother's purpose in inquiring about his religious beliefs, whatever they were.

Over the years, Doris had always seemed to wonder about his participation in church, encouraging him to occasionally attend morning services, a practice that his elementary school often recommended, if not demanded, particularly during the months of October and May, months that the school regarded as particularly holy. He never knew why. She was also always asking him about his pursuit of prayer, particularly his sincerity in listening to various Montreal diocese bishops, monseigneurs, priests and even brothers recite the rosary to an appreciative audience on the radio. However, things had changed in high school. As his interest, if not his faith faded, his mother began to allude in their conversations, to previous religious events and memories, like Christmas, Easter, and his First Communion, hoping Richard would later speculate on and would somehow recover a belief that he had predictably lost at some point in the past. Along the same lines, Richard would later manage to convince himself that his parents, particularly his mother who basically instructed his father on all family matters, decided that Richard should be sent to a Catholic boys' high school to ensure that he would return to his previous state of grace, that is when he had no other choice.

Then, there was another intervening choice. He was told to attend a Catholic boys' school, Saint Ignatius High School being the obvious choice, Richard was disturbed, having tormented his best friend Peter after his father informed him that he was to attend his alma mater, the same Saint Ignatius High School. Richard wasn't alone in teasing Peter. He and another classmate named Harold were eventually slated to attend the school and therefore were the victims of taunts from Richard and the rest of the grade seven on the boys' side of Saint John Fisher. Earlier, his mother occasionally heard Richard tease his friend Peter and therefore criticized him, reminding him that he could also end up going to Saint Ignatius, a suggestion that he thought was so absurd that he almost laughed at his mother, a blunder that usually resulted in a stern look. There was therefore considerable confusion when almost a month after he heard from Peter that he was going to Saint Ignatius that Richard was told that he was going to Saint Ignatius as well, an irony about which he was to ponder until he actually knew the meaning of the word. When Richard reluctantly told Peter that he was about to attend Saint Ignatius as well, Peter snickered, slapped Richard on the shoulder, and then told him that he was pleased that he won't be alone riding the train into Montreal West every day. When asked, he admitted to Peter that he had been looking forward to attending Saint Thomas, the neighbourhood high school, a sizable portion of which were populated by girls. He did admit, however, that the Protestant high school in the area was co- ed, meaning of course that boys and girls were seated in the same class, just they were in elementary school.

Peter then pointed out that instead of girls, Saint Ignatius was populated only by boys, Jesuit priests and brothers, all of whom were teachers. That bit of information, of which he was barely aware, depressed Richard even more. He was definitely not looking forward to the next September.

Despite the fact that it was scheduled for a Thursday evening in June, Richard surprised his mother by agreeing to accompany her to the service observing the Festival of Corpus Christi. Although he wasn't really sure as to what the Festival of Corpus Christi was he intended to celebrate despite his mother's explanation that it had something to do with Pentecostalism and the Holy Spirit, he somehow wanted to demonstrate to her that he was still a devout Catholic. Although that was his reason it was not entirely evident to her, his inclination to accompany her to a unfamiliar, unusual church service was a mystery to her. For her son, who had abandoned his religious belief for almost a decade after escaping elementary school, to then resurrect that belief remained a puzzle to her. At times, his mother would think that her son Richard was not being honest with her. In other words, he was trying to impress her somehow, as if he wanted her to intercede with his father, who inexplicably disapproved of his son's recent conduct, his religious conversion occasionally mystifying him, a habit that his wife sometimes had to overlook, his quietly agnostic tendencies something that she pretty well had to ignore. Sure, his father regularly attended church with the family, was well respected by other parishioners, even serving as a warden for several years, and responsibly contributed to various charities. But, at least according to his son Richard's observations, his father was not like his mother. He thought that his father approached his religious duties as if he was employed to perform them. His mother didn't look at it that way. Besides, his father hardly ever went to confession or communion, at least Richard seldom saw him participate in either sacrament. It was understandable, therefore, that his father did not accompany Richard and his mother to the service for the Festival of Corpus Christi. He was at home watching television with Richard's two brothers, Jack and Allan.

Throughout the service, which basically consisted of Father Griffin reciting unfamiliar prayers in Latin and swinging incense about the altar, Richard did not pay much attention, pretending to follow the service in a prayer book that was always available in the church pews. Amazingly enough, at least to Richard who had never even heard of the Festival of Corpus Christi, the church was almost full, an unusual occurrence for a Thursday evening. As Richard and his mother left the church, they both reached the bottom step of the stairs, at which point his mother turned and anointed him with a peck on his cheek, a gesture he seldom received from his mother since he was in grade school.

They were standing on those bottom steps when she expressed her gratitude for accompanying her to the service. "Thanks for coming with me. I didn't expect you to come with me but I'm glad you did." She delayed for a moment and then continued. "You wouldn't have come with me to a special service like this a year ago. You've changed, at least as far as church is concerned. Don't think I haven't noticed." Richard stood motionless, momentarily contemplating his mother's observation. He thought that he should be surprised but wasn't. After all, his mother had always been observant about his behaviour, particularly when it came to church and school. That was the reason that she was so upset when he began to gradually abandon his religious convictions, frequently asking him for an excuse when she discovered that he had stopped attending mass on Sunday. He never really explained his decision, if it was a decision at all. It was more like a development.

But he had to say something to her. He could tell her of the influence that Father Breslin and his theology class had had on his faith, which for many previous years had simply evaporated, as if it was ever there in the first place. The two of them had drifted towards the parking lot and now were standing by their car. His mother was waiting for him to pronounce on the miracle that seemed to have inspired her son to return to the church, to her church. When he couldn't think of anything else to say, Richard basically repeated the explanation that he gave Father Breslin and his classmates that the theology class inspired him to renew his faith in the church. Richard told his mother, "It was a conversion, some sort of evolution that I admit I found surprising. I hope this doesn't upset you but I really didn't really know that I had faith, at least when I was in elementary school and was an altar boy. So, for some reason, I suddenly was regularly attending mass and going to confession. As you can imagine, I couldn't believe it." Richard looked at his mother. She had sort of a curious look on her face. He was glad that he hadn't mentioned the influence that Catherine Morris had had on the renewal, if not the inauguration of his faith. If he had told his mother that his infatuation, if not his unrequited passion for Catherine had made a significant contribution to his rebirth of his faith in his mother's beliefs, she would have definitely gotten the wrong idea, thinking that Catherine would have used her appeal — she was a woman after all — to convince her son to return to church. His mother was always suspicious of any girl or woman with whom her son had a relationship, no matter how innocent or chaste it was. While she was pleased with her son Richard's spiritual transformation, she remained mystified by it. She was still standing there wondering about how her son has changed and whether he was fated to change back.

It was during their drive home that Richard was reminded of the only other time that he had attended a service celebrating the Festival of Corpus Christi. It was also a Thursday evening on June 12. It was 1961. He was about to graduate from grade six and was looking forward to summer vacation. He was not, however, looking forward the family camping holiday that always began the day after June 24, which just happened to be Saint Jean Baptiste day, the last day of the school year being the previous Friday. This year, he was particularly disappointed since he had managed to make the roster of the Valois Yankees, the area's little league team, and would therefore miss four weeks of games while the family was somewhere in Maine on their vacation. Over the first three games, Richard played left field, authored five hits and made a couple of semi-spectacular catches in the outfield. But then, over his father's objections, his mother instructed Richard to accompany her to the

Festival of Corpus Christi service. Kay Gallagher, her usual companion to special religious events was ill and therefore could not attend the Corpus Christi with his mother and therefore required her eldest son's presence. Richard's father objected to the arrangement and offered his younger son Jack as a substitute communicant, his basic complaint being that Richard would have to miss Thursday's Yankee game against the Cedar Park Pirates. His wife Doris declined his suggestion, telling him that it would be inappropriate, if not pointless to send a ten year old to a special church service. Richard's father attempted an rejoinder, pointing out that Richard was only twelve. It was unsuccessful.

Once they got home from that Corpus Christi service, he headed straight to his room in the basement to watch on the old television set his father had placed in the playroom. He sat on the sofa while he recalled the events that happened after he missed that little league game. Two games after the game he missed, during which time he tried to perfect his strikeout theatrics, he was unexpectedly dropped from the team, asked to turn in his jersey and his pants although he was permitted to keep his cap, the one with the red bill. He was later told by a former teammate named Burgess that the manager of the team, an older man named Ray had been convinced somehow that Richard wasn't serious about his duties as a Valois Yankee when he missed a game because he had to attend, at his mother's insistence, a special church service. He thought that he may have considered shedding tears but didn't. Once he heard about his Richard's release from the team, his father offered sympathy and an increase in his allowance. His mother made no comment.

The next morning, as he sat at the kitchen table consuming a bowl of Cheerios, he looked up at his mother, his father having already left for the train at the Valois Station, and thanked him for accompanying her to the Corpus Christi service. Richard wondered why she she said anything. It was the second Sunday in August when he went to confession for the first time in a couple of months. In fact, it was only the second time he had visited confession since his third year at Saint Ignatius College ended the previous April, school having ended for him in the last week of April. He was worried that his newly discovered orthodoxy was slowly evaporating. He had pondered that possibility for a while. Maybe it was the change in circumstances since the school year ended, the fact that he was no longer listening to Father Breslin leading the class through the subtleties of theology, exchanging observations on faith with Catherine Morris or going to church with her on Wednesday. He began to think that maybe Catherine, Theology 130 or the both of them had had such an influence on his religious behaviour that without them, he had returned to the dull state he had found himself in before he registered for a theology class almost a year ago. In addition, starting again at Lawrence Industries for the summer returned him, at least as far as he could recall, to the habits of his previous summer. He did accompany the family to Sunday mass, along with his reluctant father, his devout albeit confused mother and his two brothers. As for Richard, he stood, knelt and sat with appropriate reverence, glancing every so often at his mother who didn't seem to be paying any attention to her eldest son. He even took communion even though he had not gone to confession in a couple of months and therefore was worried that the pastor or at least the priest saying the mass would know somehow. By the time the service concluded, Richard contemplated taking confession as soon as he could, possibly on Tuesday evening when Benediction was normally held and there would be a priest available to hear confession. By the time they arrived home and were preparing for breakfast, he had decided that he would definitely be going to confession two days from then.

Benediction was held on seven o'clock on Tuesday evenings. Richard insisted on arriving twenty minutes early, intending to visit the confessional. That unsettled his mother, who was also still a little surprised that he had volunteered to attend a service he seldom attended and then announced that his purpose was going to confession. As for Richard, he was a trifle frustrated to see that there were several elderly ladies waiting for Father Quinn, the designated confessor whose name was printed on a tag affixed on the door between the two penitents seeking forgiveness. Three others were kneeling in the pews in front of the confessional, obviously waiting for judgment. Rather than kneel, Richard just sat several pews back with his mother. He felt like he was waiting in a train station. He noticed that his mother looked like she was squeezing her rosary in preliminary prayer. He thought she would have looked bored, not expectant. Fortunately, the ladies expecting absolution from Father Quinn, the latter might have been asleep for all Richard knew, were able to enter and then exit the confessor's stall after ridiculously brief periods of time. The first old lady to leave Father Quinn almost stumbled out of the booth, almost bumping into another old lady who was rushing to unburdened herself of her own wrongdoings.

By the time he found himself waiting for confession to begin, he noticed that the screen that usually slid between the confessor and the contrite was open and he could plainly see that Father Quinn, who he had wondered might have been asleep, actually was in slumber, softly snoring with his chin down on his chest. He looked like he had been in that posture for a while. After considering the scene for a few moments, Richard concluded that his fellow guilt-ridden ladies expecting absolution from Father Quinn had simply provided their confessions to the sleeping confessor, waited for a few moments with doubt, struggled through acts of confession, and then left the dark cubicle without receiving a word from the sleeping Father Quinn. For his reaction to the curious circumstances that were now facing him, Richard wanted to simply state the list of sinful deeds he had planned to provide to Father Quinn, although even after his act of contribution, which he quickly realized was unnecessary given Father Quinn's condition.

As he left the confessional, he was slowly discouraged. He had planned to tell the confessor, whoever it was, even Father Quinn, that he felt that he was losing his faith, not like he did when he was younger, but more recently, possibly becoming some sort of apostate, renouncing faith that he had worked so hard to restore. He was seeking counsel, guidance somehow, a cleric's opinion on how he lost trust in a belief that he had apparently been born with, had gradually lost through years of slow neglect, then recovered somehow. Richard was not certain that it would be appropriate to discuss his spiritual confusion and misgivings with a priest in a confessional. He had come to the conclusion that while it may be more suitable to discuss any qualms he had about the loss of his religious convictions with a priest in his office, he decided as he was entering the confessional that he would bring it up with a priest, even if it was Father Quinn, who Richard did not think was particularly erudite about anything, including his supposed religious matters. Still, he didn't think he had much of a choice if he intended to broach the matter with anyone who might have expertise in faith. Father Quinn, if he was awake, seemed the only logical choice. But Father Quinn was asleep. It was obvious that he could not depend on the slumbering Father Quinn for any sort of opinion, useful or not. So he abandoned the idea entirely. He would have to struggle with his spiritual dilemma on his own.

After he disembarked from the confessional, he knelt down to complete his phantom penance and join his mother in following the service. By the time the congregation was preparing for the Eucharist, his mother had a pleasant look on her face. It was obvious that her son, whose recent relapse from faith had been troubling his mother for months, had somehow recovered, had taken confession and now looked like he was preparing to take communion as well. It was apparent that he had again restored his faith, at least for the present time.

LISTENING THROUGH
THE SCREEN

I t was a Sunday maybe a month after his most religious
episode when he happened to have a most unusual
experience during a confession that was being heard
by a visiting priest from Our Lady of Fatima, a parish that
was located off Lake Saint Louis in Lachine. He was ready
to beguile the visiting confessor with the usual tiresome
litany of alleged sins when he thought he heard someone,
likely an elderly lady, speaking in a loud whisper. Richard
did not even have to strain to hear the woman, her voice
so clear that he was able to hear practically every word
she said. On the other hand, Richard could not hear
a word from the visiting priest, who might have been
engaging in a conversation with the elderly lady but
wasn't speaking loudly enough to be heard. He suspected
he may be simply agreeing with everything she may have
been saying. In any event, he was able to ascertain that
the woman was relating a story about starting a rumour
about her granddaughter, whose name he thought was

Helen. He was not able to determine the precise nature of the rumour although it was his impression that it may have had something that could ruin her marriage. He immediately thought that it may have been something to do with adultery although he of course could not be sure about the details, whether she had been responsible for the something or the penitent lady had either invented or imagined the entire rumour, the purpose unknown.

Richard continued to kneel forward with his ear almost completely affixed to the screen between the visiting confessor and himself, waiting for his turn to confess. It must have been three or four minutes when he heard the talkative old lady rush through the Act of Contrition and totter out of the confessional. Before the visiting priest opened the screen on Richard's cubicle, he heard another older woman opened the door. Then the screen on Richard's side of the confessional slowly slid open, revealing the visiting confessor, who for some reason promptly introduced himself. His name was Andrew Firth, Father Andrew Firth. Although he should not have been surprised when he thought about it later, the visiting confessor was physically antithetical to Father Quinn, who Richard had assumed to be the confessor who was being replaced. He was much younger, much thinner and had a lot more hair than the confessor he was replacing. He looked through the grill, he crossed myself and followed the predictable script. "Bless me, Father, I have sinned. It has been two weeks since my last confession and I confess to the following sins."

Father Firth responded, a little more casually than Father Quinn would have, "And what sins do you wish to confess? You say it has been only two weeks. So how much trouble could you have gotten into?" Richard thought he saw Father Firth silently smile through the grill, an assumed grin, and referred to the previous penitent's admission about the rumour she started about her granddaughter. This time, Father Firth's grin became a quiet chuckle, something that it was obvious he intended to hide but couldn't. "Yes, I know she was speaking a trifle loud, not a usual volume for a confession. I tried to persuade her to keep it down but she obviously couldn't see me gesticulating with my hands through the screen, her head was down the whole time, like she was praying." He could see Father Firth nod though. He then went into his usual litany of transgressions, from the number of times he had taken refuge in self abuse, an admission that Richard previously submitted as "impure thoughts" as to avoid some degree of guilt, or so he thought, to excessive profanity.

By the time his relatively short exchange in the confessional was concluded and he had run through his penance of two decades of the rosary, he had almost forgotten about overhearing the old woman's confession. During dinner that evening, his mother, who was noisy about almost everything, asked if he had noticed the old woman who had gone to the confession just before him. Richard said that he had although at back of his mind, he was worried that she also had heard the old lady's confession. The fact was that she hadn't. She only observed that she seemed quite talkative. He was simply referring to the fact that anyone sitting anywhere her in the pews probably heard everything she said, including most particularly any prayer she recited and any aside she may have made to another old lady who happened to be sitting near her. At least, his mother wasn't aware of the fact that he had overheard the old lady's confession, something that could prove embarrassing if his mother knew that her son was aware of the lady's admissions to a confessor. Further, Richard was convinced that his mother might even consider such an intrusion a violation of church principles or rules, maybe even a sin. In any event, he was relieved, any guilt he may have been suffering had disappeared.

He thought about having overheard the old lady talking in the confessional while he was struggling for slumber that night. He invested a good deal of time speculating about that rumour the old lady had started and had been circulating about her granddaughter, gossip that was controversial enough to damage her marriage. He understood, at least from what the old lady may have said, that Helen, who was the subject of the rumour, had been having trouble with her marriage, infidelity an obvious possibility, whether on her side or the other. He had tried to imagine the scenario, a woman in her thirties or maybe even her forties, his estimates of her age a total guess, making clandestine hotel arrangements or, if she was some sort of homemaker, waiting for her lover to arrive. He had imagined the entire plot out of narratives created in novels or shown on television or in the movies. Or maybe an affair was not the subject of the rumour, or at least it was not an affair that involved the granddaughter. It could have been the husband of the granddaughter who was pursuing the illicit behaviour. In any event, there was a man involved or so he thought. On the other hand, there were a number of other possibilities that could have formed the basis of the rumour that the old lady had confessed to Father Firth. Perhaps the granddaughter or her husband were considering ending their marriage for a reason other than an affair, gossip of one of them visiting an attorney or sharing their doubts about their marriage with a neighbour or a friend or maybe even a priest but outside the confides of a confessional. Or maybe, just maybe her granddaughter or her husband had committed sort of transgression that could destroy their marriage or at least harm it, something other than adultery.

Finally, he gave up theorizing about the source and possible meaning of the old lady's admission to Farther Firth in the confessional and started to wonder about a confessor's responsibility in such a circumstance. He wished he was still sitting in the class of Theology 130 so he could pose that question to Father Breslin. Richard was fairly certain that there was an absolute confidentiality regarding anything said or heard in confession. According to his limited research, which was hardly as substantial as he pursued when he had access to the library at Saint Ignatius College, the secretiveness of confession was based on the conviction that it was a conversation between confessor and penitent, about the deepest realities of people's lives, their deplorable behaviour, their sins, a connection between God and a sinner. In that regard, he had read that it was understood by the partners in confession that any exchange in that blessed booth included the Divine as the major partner. In other words, anyone confessing anything in confession was basically talking to God through a priest. Richard recalled that he may have read a story in a book or have seen a story in the movies or on television in which a priest accepted the confession of an act that would normally be charged as a crime under the criminal code but could not be related to anyone who could take any action under the law. The narrative of the story covered the anguish of the priest who heard the confession by a sinner of an act so heinous that he felt that he would normally have no other choice but to alert the authorities. But he could not, the confidentiality of the confessional prohibiting him from telling anyone. Richard could not remember the finale of the episode so he guessed that it could not have been very memorable.

Although it was not a dream, it could have been. He awoke around four o'clock in the morning, restless to remember something about the confession that he overheard the other day. A song had been in his mind earlier that evening, a song that reminded him of a high school dance that had been held in a local high school which he did not attend but had dated a number of its female students. While he was rhapsodizing about his recollection of the song, the title of which he could not recall, the confession of the old lady who related her sin in an unexpected volume suddenly appeared in his mind. That prompted Richard to wonder about the reflections of confessors on the sinful admissions that penitents made in that dark booth. Did confessors remember every transgression they heard from every congregant who sought their absolution? Were all confessions by everyone seeking absolution genuine and complete?

Did they ruminate about the wrongdoings? Were they concerned about them? How did they agree with the penance that was allocated to former sinners now in a state of grace? And of course, he could discuss the issue of the confidentiality of confession with Father Breslin if he get in touch with him and if he did, would he be willing to talk about it? And then for some unknown reason, he found himself wondering if Jesuit priests went on summer vacations.

Richard did not fall asleep for at least another hour, which was a trifle exasperating since he usually awoke around six thirty weekday mornings in order to get dressed, have breakfast, which he prepared himself since his mother usually left for her nursing job just after Richard got out of bed. He then left the house just in time after bidding farewell to his father who took a later train downtown and to catch his lift to work with a guy named Steve who also worked on the assembly line at Lawrence Industries. That day, Steve, who was always cheerful no matter what time of day or night it was, greeted Richard by suggesting that he looked lost in thought, an observation that was entirely accurate. In response, Richard apologized, explaining that he was having difficulty in reconciling what he used to think at one time with something he may think now. Steve looked at Richard as if he had just removed his trousers. Steve obviously had no idea what specifically Richard was talking about. Neither did Richard. On the other hand, however, Steve had been right, he was in fact preoccupied, with his speculations about confession. He had considered raising the issue of confession with his mother who was devout as well as knowledgeable about Roman Catholicism. He was aware of his mother's interest, if not captivation with the renewal of his son's faith in their shared beliefs. However, he had come to the conclusion, after staring at the ceiling of his bedroom before he actually got up, that if he were to seek her understanding of a significant Catholic sacrament, his mother would change her opinion regarding his religious transformation. So he abandoned the proposal.

That left a possible approach to Father Breslin, that is if he was available and if he was willing to talk to him about the issue of confession. As he stood behind a drill press for the day, he could not resist allowing the various questions he had about confession to remain in his head like a remnant of another hangover. After weighing a number of possible approaches, he decided that the best way to contact Father Breslin was to write him a letter, a personal communication requesting an audience with an expert in ecclesiastical matters, the latter characterization anointed by a former student looking for further enlightenment regarding the Sacrament of Confession. Initially, he felt no need to explain his justification for seeking Father Breslin's erudition but after some reflection he wrote that he thought that his wisdom might prove helpful in research he was pursuing on confession. Although he did not provide any further explanation, he was prepared to inform Father Breslin that he was preparing a paper for a history course which he was planning to register for this coming year.

He realized that it was a strange plan but he thought

Father Breslin might be attracted by it. In addition, in what he hoped would be a final appeal to Father Breslin's academic interest, if not his self-esteem, his letter was written in fountain pen. Finally, Richard addressed the letter to Father Breslin, Society of Jesus, Saint Ignatius College, 7141 Sherbrooke Street West, Montreal, Quebec. He mailed the letter on a Friday. He thought that Father Breslin could receive the letter by the middle of the next week, that is if he wasn't enjoying a retreat, if not a vacation at the Jesuit sanctuary somewhere in the Laurentians north of Montreal. That is if the man had not passed away, which was a possibility when he thought about it.

He waited almost two weeks until he received a letter from Saint Ignatius College. It was a Tuesday and the letter was on the kitchen table in front of his mother, who was sitting behind a cigarette when he arrived home from work. She greeted him and then asked whether Saint Ignatius was being a little early in asking for tuition for the next school year, assuming as she did that Richard planned to attend Saint Ignatius the next year. His mother had a small grin on her face when she made her inquiry. She thought she was being witty although she sounded like she was being sarcastic. In response, Richard shrugged his shoulders and commented, "I hope not, I won't be able to pay for a couple of months." For a moment, his resentment over having to pay his own tuition lingered in his mind. His mother then picked up the letter from Saint Ignatius and handed it to him. He sat down and opened the letter.

Although the address on the envelop was typed, he

noted immediately that the letter itself was handwritten, scripted with a fountain pen although the ink was a green colour as opposed to the blue that Richard had used in his letter. The penmanship was elegantly awkward, as if Father Breslin had some sort of tremor but had made every effort to control it. The letter ran to almost two pages on letter paper with the crest of Saint Ignatius on the top of each sheet. Father Breslin's response was surprisingly cordial, predictable given the circumstances of their academic relationship. Truth was that his letter was written as if he and Father Breslin were more than former teacher and student but friends, actual friends. For a moment, Richard felt like reading the letter out loud to his mother, thinking that it would once again affirm her belief in his religious convictions. Instead, he informed her that the Saint Ignatius letter was an official notification of his choices of courses for the next academic year, not a request for tuition. She believed his story. He just did not want to share the letter with his mother.

He thought it was private, like a confession. He could have told her that but didn't. In his letter, Father Breslin asked Richard to get in touch with him by telephoning a Miss Chambers, the secretary for the Jesuit rectory office. His letter informed him that he understood from Richard's missive that he was working five days a week and therefore was not always available to speak to Father Breslin in person during the week. At first, therefore, they would have to speak to each other by telephone. The letter said that Miss Chambers would ensure that he could get in touch with him by telephone.

Richard spoke to Father Breslin after Miss Chambers

arranged for him to telephone the sanctuary office in Saint Sauveur at precisely three o'clock on Saturday afternoon, August 6, Father Breslin was waiting for his call. His conversation with Father Breslin was understandably brief, the cost of a long distance telephone call made from a payphone generally prohibitive for Richard, who was making $1.65 an hour at the time. Father Breslin surprised him by suggesting that they meet for a lunch the next Saturday at a restaurant on Sherbrooke Street near the Saint Ignatius campus. Father Breslin said that he occasionally took advantage of an automobile ride from a fellow cleric named Father O'Grady who visited the Saint Ignatius library every Saturday. The restaurant was called the Golden Moon and Richard had not frequented it since he was in high school, last time being more than four years ago. He was frankly quite surprised that Father Breslin choose to meet in a local restaurant frequented by high school kids, as opposed to, for example, in the library or even somewhere in the main building of Saint Ignatius, preferably he supposed the Jesuit rectory office.

Regardless, Richard immediately accepted the invitation for lunch with Father Breslin on August 13 at the Golden Moon. He wondered if the restaurant still featured tabletop jukeboxes.

As the day of his lunch with Father Breslin approached, he slowly came to the conclusion that he should limit his inquiries regarding the sacrament of confession to one question. Do confessors feel any responsibility for anything they hear in the confessional? Most of the other issues regarding confession that he had researched, the memories of the admissions they may have heard, whether the substance of the confessions they may have heard were truthful, whether they thought about the sins they absolved, how did they determine the penances they provided to penitents, and of course the confidentiality of confession. He had investigated those issues and was still left with only one question. Aside from allocating penance, usually the recitation of prayers and other invocations, do confessors ever take any action that would suggest that the sinner had liability for any sin that was forgiven. For example, he had in mind for the sinner an expression of regret, an apology for wronged behaviour to another, the return of property stolen or, most unlikely, insinuating that sinners involve legal authority if it seemed appropriate.

On the evening before his Saturday lunch with Father Breslin, Richard had attended services, specifically a novena at Saint Louis, an older church down by the lake of the same name. It was a few miles away on Lakeshore Road and had been host to a small congregation who had been worshipping there long before the suburban developments to which Richard's family had eventually moved were built. Richard knew, from the local community newspaper, that Saint Louis held novena services three evenings a week, including Friday. Richard assumed that the church would also hold confessions at the same time and therefore arrived well before the scheduled seven o'clock time for the beginning of the evening service. He had been correct about confessions and had more than enough time to visit one of the confessional booths, the doors to which both were open. Neither cubicle was lit. He entered on the left, the one closest to the altar, and knelt down in the booth. He looked through the drape, it was practically transparent, and noticed that the priest to whom he intended to confide his misdeeds was not paying attention. A prayer book was sitting in his lap, one hand holding the book, a rosary wrapped around the other. He was an elderly priest with a substantial paunch, a ruddy complexion, his hair sparse and almost white, and a forbidding expression on that face. Richard presumed the man to be the parish priest, the pastor.

Richard must have been kneeling before the elderly priest for several minutes when the latter came to attention, almost dropping both the prayer book and rosary beads. He turned and looked at Richard, as if he had been expecting him, and then sternly asked him for a rendering of his sins, actually using the word, which sounded biblical to him. Suddenly, he felt a little frightened. It compelled him to reconsider his confession, to take it more seriously than he had intended, his plan to casually run through his usual list of minor transgressions. He swept the curtain aside and stared at his confessor, contemplating a confession that he thought he would have to modify to reflect a sudden solemnity. He was staring at the suddenly serious confessor, and realized that he did not have a sin suitably mortal to confess in the circumstance. It was apparent that this priest was not interested in casual wrongdoings, but sins that could consign one to damnation. That's what he feared. After an appropriate period of ambivalence, he made an appropriate decision. He did not need to confess anything. He was already in a state of grace he thought.

Richard stood up and escaped the confessional, then certain that he was not confused. He escaped.

Aside from Richard, there were only seven parishioners in the Saint Louis church, five in the front pew and two right behind them in the second pew. Richard was in the fourth pew, three pews opposite the confessional inhabited by the elderly priest whose spiritual services he had just disregarded. Not surprisingly, the elderly confessor appeared from behind the altar to conduct the service. He was assisted by an acolyte who looked much too old for the duty. He looked like he had received the obligation as a penance, the disagreeable and pained expression on his face indicative. His only task that evening was to hold the censer, a silver container in which incense is burned throughout various religious ceremonies, and hand it to the pastor when it was time to bless the proceedings with sweeps of incense. Further, the acolyte would stand by the pastor and turn the pages to selections in the large prayer book used on the altar. For this service, the acolyte's responsibility was to ensure that the correct prayers for the novena were recited by the pastor who sometimes, if not most times, allowed his declining faculties to contribute to recitation of the wrong prayers. Richard knew, however, that any such error would not have made much of a difference to the congregation who were probably in a condition that was not much more alert than that of the pastor. Richard stayed in the fourth row of the pews in the Saint Louis church for the entire novena, a little more than twenty minutes. He did, however, feel a little guilty for having avoided confession. He had realized that he did not have to attend in the first place.

He arrived at the Golden Moon on Sherbrooke Street the next day just before noon. He had taken the 10:40 AM train to Montreal West. He disembarked about 11:15 AM and made his way up to Sherbrooke Street. Along the way, he dropped into Johnny's to check out whether the pinball machine that he had played incessantly when he was in high school were still there. Unfortunately, it wasn't, the pinball machine being replaced by a slot machine. However, Johnny, the diner's owner, was still working behind the counter, dishing out hamburger and french fries to a combination of construction workers and students. Feeling nostalgic, if not a little sad, Richard sat at one of the two tables near the door and ordered a coffee and a muffin from a waitress who looked old enough to be Johnny's wife or sister. He thought he should have recognized her but didn't, suggesting that the waitress wasn't really related to Johnny. The coffee and the muffin arrived, were consumed and were paid for by 11:45. He left the diner, walked across the street and was inside the Golden Moon before noon.

Aside from immediately noticing that the place still included tabletop jukeboxes, he also could not help but notice that Father Breslin was sitting in the one of the booths in the back, next to the washrooms. Father Breslin was smoking a Player's Plain cigarette, was wearing old looking spectacles, on which a piece of tape had been affixed, had a pot of tea sitting in front of him and was inspecting the menu, which still consisted of rudimentary Chinese food although it did include local fare, like sandwiches and hamburgers. He walked straight to Father Breslin's booth, greeted him as respectfully as he could and sat down. Father Breslin looked up, casually smiled and pushed the menu across the table to him. The menu was showing a fair amount of wear and might have listed the same items that it did four or five years ago. Father Breslin notified him with a slight smirk, "I think I've already decided. I'm going to have chicken balls and rice which to me is fairly exotic, at least compared to the fare I usually get at the sanctuary." Richard smiled, thinking that Father Breslin would have thought that the comment would have passed for wit in his lexicon. He replied predictably, "Thanks for meeting me, Father. I need someone who has a certain knowledge about confession for the research I am working on." Father Breslin then replied in a humorous tone, "And you think I have that certain knowledge." Richard nodded and then the waitress arrived. He looked at the menu, ordered a BLT, fries and a diet coke and then handed the menu back to the waitress.

As he had noticed, the Golden Moon still had tabletop jukeboxes installed in the restaurant's booths. He started flipping through the song selections, several of which seemed to be tunes that were originally on the hit parade maybe ten years ago. He was going to mention his interest in the songs but quickly realized that an elderly Jesuit priest who taught theology was unlikely to know anything about the past top twenty. For a moment, as he continued to examine the songs on the jukebox, he looked at Father Breslin, who was in the process of lighting another cigarette, wondering if he would know any of the songs on the jukebox unless they included hits from the 1940s. He doubted that the jukebox did.

Within a few minutes, during which time Father Breslin's chicken balls and rice and Richard's diet coke arrived and the waitress refilled the former's tea pot, the Father leaned forward and began their conversation on confession, basically the fundamental question that Richard was about to ask. Father Breslin had the idea that Richard, who had become he supposed his protege, had somehow summarized all his questions about confession into one request for enlightenment. So he asked it, "So what do you want to know about the blessed Sacrament of Confession that you don't already think you know? I would want to know such a thing if there was such a thing to know. I know it sounds like a mystery, a mystery of faith, but isn't forgiveness of sin always a mystery?"

As he looked across the table and listened to him philosophizing, Richard recalled the essential question he had intended to pose to Father Breslin, specifically do confessors bear any responsibility for any inquiry they may hear in the confessional and if they do, should they take any action beyond the principals established by the Sacrament. So he asked his own question. "Father, do priests hearing confession have a duty to rectify any sin they may hear and forgive in confession, beside the penance that the confessor may deem appropriate." Richard should not have been surprised when Father Breslin put down his fork and answered such a complex inquiry surprisingly simply or so he thought. "Well, I guess it depends on the priest and what sin or sins for which he seeks absolution. As you know, the situation is not described in the literature, it is not required by the rite, it is not part of the Sacrament but I would imagine that some confessors, not many but some may decide to apply additional judgments. And those judgments may not be spiritual but secular. I think that that might be what you had in mind with your question." Richard nodded and then seemed to be paralyzed for a moment, apparently waiting for inspiration as to any additional understanding he could gather from Father Breslin although he decided not to ask him about his own experience, thinking that he would not forsake the confidentiality of the confessional no matter what the purpose.

After the two of them discussed other elements of Richard's proposed research into the enigma of confession, which Father Breslin said a number of times was an unusual subject for a layman, he said that he was scheduled to meet Father O'Grady in the Saint Ignatius library around two o'clock for his ride back to the sanctuary. He told him that Father O'Grady, who was still working on a Master's Degree of Divinity at McGill University, would become irate if anyone was late anytime he agreed to drive them anywhere. A puzzled look swept over Richard's face, prompting Father Breslin to explain that Father O'Grady was one of the few who lived at the Jesuit sanctuary who had a driver's license. As a result, anytime anyone wanted to travel into Montreal or anywhere else for that matter they had to ask Father O'Grady or one of the two sanctuary custodians to drive them. When Richard asked how people who worked at the sanctuary got to work, Father Breslin told him that practically everyone who worked there also lived there as well. For a moment, Richard wondered where Father Breslin had lived during the school year.

Before Father Breslin left the Golden Moon, he sought an assurance from Richard that he would share his research on confession once it was complete.

CONFESSION RESEARCH I

It had not taken long for his experience of overhearing an elderly woman disclosing a sin and expressing her sorrow for it in a confessional to become more an occasional obsession. At times, usually at night when he was battling restlessness, he would ponder the possible basis for the old woman's apparent uncertainty about what she had disclosed so dramatically and apparently so publicly to Father Firth. Whatever the source of her dismay, a rumour she had spread for no stated reason or an incident or series of incidents about which she was reporting, Richard was seriously baffled not only by the motive for the old lady's revelation itself but also by the unknown reaction of the confessor to the curious confession. So Richard began to accompany his parents, particularly his mother, to the ten o'clock morning high mass at the Saint John Fisher church on Sundays. He managed to convince his mother to arrive at least twenty minutes prior to the commencement of the service. He had told her that the purpose of his early appearance was to take confession. It was, however, a ruse, a ploy, a stratagem to perform surveillance on elderly ladies having just left confession, currently taking confession or awaiting for confession, all ambitions based on little more than educated guesswork.

He had imagined, somehow hopelessly he acknowledged to himself, that the old lady would repeat what he thought may have been or become her practice when attending confession and providing her admissions in an easily audible volume. He would sit as near to the confessional venue as he could, usually one or two seats over from the edge of the closest pew and listen. He pretended to be praying, head down, hands clasped, though close enough to hear anyone speaking or anything said between the priest, who wasn't a visiting confessor named Firth but Father Quinn. It was the first of many attempts at rediscovering that inspiration that was prompted by overhearing that old lady confessing to a rumour that she may have started. It seemed impossible.

It was an impossible task that would begin in earnest the next Sunday. Within weeks, however, having visited confession at Saint John Fisher church on dozens of occasions, Richard contemplated an alternative approach to a possible resolution of a mystery that had bedevilled him ever since he overheard it. He had been convinced, and still was, that the rumour was damaging to the elderly lady's granddaughter, but had not been able to ascertain the rumour's details. For a reason that he could not justify even to himself, Richard could not forget about his pursuit of the details surrounding the rumour. He thought about it day and night, particularly the latter as he had trouble getting to sleep most nights. His continual meditations during his sleepless nights eventually led to an alternative solution to his dilemma. He would consult with Father Andrew Firth, the visiting confessor from Our Lady of Fatima parish who had been hearing confession that Sunday several months ago. The more he thought about it, the more he realized that he could think of no other way of determining the veracity of that elderly woman's confession. While unorthodox, he decided that he would have to approach Father Firth directly, asking him if he could remember the elderly lady confessing to a rumour about her granddaughter. That still left the question of why he was pursuing the strategy.

Father Andrew Firth was a priest in the Our Lady of Fatima parish. It was located in another suburban city on the West Island of Montreal. It was called Dorval, a little more than five miles east of the Saint John Fisher parish. The church itself was on Lakeshore Road, down by Lake Saint Louis. At first, Richard decided to telephone the rectory at the Our Lady of Fatima and simply ask for Father Firth. Ultimately, it was his intention to interview the priest, specifically to somehow convince him to discuss the admission of the elderly lady regarding a rumour she had apparently heard about her own granddaughter and that the rumour was serious enough to negatively affect her in some way. As far as the sanctity of confession was concerned, an objection that Father Firth would likely raise if Richard approached him about the overheard confession, Richard was prepared. After all, if Richard overheard the elderly lady's confession, or at least a substantial part of it, then Father Firth could hardly claim that he was prevented from discussing it with anyone else on the basis of some ecclesiastical privilege. In that event, Richard was hopeful that Father Firth could provide him with further detail on the elderly lady's hearsay, most particularly if Father Firth, or any priest for that matter, ever took action beyond assigning them penance. Richard was reminded of the occasional television police drama in which marital confidences were no longer relevant if a third party was aware of whatever secret had been discussed. He thought that the same principle would apply in the case of the overheard confession. It was worth a shot he thought. Besides, he did not think he had any other choice, at least in terms of explanations he could use to convince Father Firth to discuss the confession.

It was several weeks after school started for his final year at Saint Ignatius. Even though he had not made any decision about his future after college, he was relatively relaxed about it, entering the year without any trepidation of his coming studies or his future. In fact, he was looking forward to his classes, his interest in his major, English literature, almost a hobby, an entertainment. In addition, he had become friendly with some of his classmates, one of whom reminded, both in appearance and disposition, of that woman in a theology course about whom he had developed a significant infatuation, that was Catherine Morris who still appeared in his thoughts. The name of her successor was Linda Ryan, also a student in English literature. He had become friendly with her the previous year and found that the two of them shared an interest in the American novel, "Moby Dick" by Herman Melville, both having read the book several times. Further, both of them had seen the 1956 movie of "Moby Dick" on television, and had arranged to watch it together one evening when it was shown at a local repertoire theatre. In addition, each of them had submitted essays on aspects of the novel and its author to Professor Kirk, who taught American literature.

After several weeks of the new semester, during which time he had difficulty re- establishing his previous relationship with Linda Ryan, who apparently was currently smitten with an another economics student named George Hughes, he strangely found himself returning to his obsession with the so-called admission that he overheard in Father Firth's confessional more than two years ago. So he decided to telephone the rectory of Our Lady of Fatima church and ask for parish priest Father Firth, his cover story being that his devout grandmother was moving into the parish, a retirement home in the area being her new address, and that he wished to investigate the parish by personally meet with Father Firth. He claimed that the priest's name had been recommended to him by one of his friends in his parish. A woman named Gina introduced herself as the parish secretary and in response to Richard's request, said that she could arrange for an appointment the following Saturday afternoon even though she had expressed some confusion about the purpose of his request to meet with Father Firth. Richard agreed. He had three days to come up with a persuasive story for Father Firth.

After ruminating about the problem of attempting to convince Father Firth to share any recollections of a confession he may have heard two years ago, he decided that the truth or the truth that he had recalled was probably the best approach. So without any further consideration of his strategy, he arrived at the rectory of the Our Lady of Fatima to meet with Father Firth at two o'clock the next Saturday afternoon. Not surprisingly, Father Firth was neither dressed in a cassock nor was he wearing a cleric collar. He was dressed in a crisp sports shirt, tan slacks and loafers. He looked like he was in his late 20s, more like an affable elementary school teacher than a priest in his first parish. He introduced himself as Father Andrew Firth, shook Richard's hand and immediately asked how he could be of service. He led Richard into his office, a relatively small cubicle outside the larger office occupied by the pastor of the parish, Father Wallace Casey, Richard having seen his name plate on the desk in the pastor's office. As soon as they both sat down, Father Firth opened a small box sitting on his small desk and offered Richard a cigarette from it. Richard declined the cigarette and sat back as Father Firth lit his cigarette. He was waiting for the now smoking priest to inquire as to the purpose of his visit. Richard looked understandably uncomfortable and leaned forward as if he was about to whisper his explanation, having rehearsed to some extent a justification for a request for an interview with Father Firth. He first admitted that his original stated purpose for seeking a conversation with Father Firth, that was to investigate the Our Lady of Fatima parish for his grandmother which was fictitious. Father Firth then also leaned forward and asked Richard the actual reason for his request for an interview with him.

Richard responded by lowering his head, staring into his lap, shuffling his feet beneath his chair, and nervously clearing his throat. "Well, Father, and I must apologize, I went to confession two years ago in my own parish Saint John Fisher in Pointe Claire. Our parish had borrowed you to hear confessions and I was waiting for you to hear my confession when I overheard another one of the contrite, an old lady with a high pitched, loud voice, confessing to spreading a rumour that was somehow damaging to her granddaughter. I was immediately interested. I was attending a theology course in Saint Ignatius and the class was discussing the Catholic sacraments, including confession. You obviously heard that elderly lady's confession and so did I. For some reason, I became obsessed with the possibility that the confessor, in this case you Father, could have done something about it besides telling the penitent to recite some prayers. I then became fascinated with the doctrine of confessional confidentiality, that is that priests hearing confessions cannot divulge what is confessed to them to anyone." Father Firth nodded and confirmed Richard's account on the responsibility of confessors.

Richard then continued with his explanation. "But I also heard the old lady's confession. So I concluded that you could, if you wanted, tell anyone about it. You could also talk to the elderly lady about the rumour, about its details and about what, if anything, was true about it. In addition, more importantly, why the grandmother had made up the rumour in the first place. And maybe more particularly, you could also get in touch with the granddaughter." Father Firth, slowly, knowingly, understanding Richard's point, he responded. "Those are good points, Richard, but I am going to have to disappoint you. I didn't recognize the elderly lady who confessed to me regarding a rumour about her granddaughter. Don't forget that I was a visiting confessor that day in Saint John Fisher and therefore was not acquainted with the old lady. Quite simply, she was not one of my parishioners. And further, and maybe more importantly, I could not nor could any priest divulge the details of a confession."

Richard should have known that as a visiting confessor, it was quite possible, if not a certainty that Father Firth would not remember the elderly lady who used a loud voice in the confessional. In that event, Richard thought that he would ask the visiting confessor what he would do if he knew who the penitent was and had decided that the damage that the rumour, whether it be an extramarital affair or a financial misdeed, would do to the granddaughter could be prevented or ameliorated. Richard asked and Farther Firth declined to speculate. He was not surprised. He should have expected it.

CONFESSION RESEARCH II

After Father Firth choose not to speculate regarding what action, if any he would take if he could limit the damage that any person confessing to him could cause to someone else, Richard was momentarily stumped. With the second option of possibly solving the mystery of the overheard confession no longer available, Richard was left with no idea as to what he could do next, including abandoning the entire project. Aside from interviewing Father Firth, he had thought about possibly approaching other priests to determine whether any of them would or in fact could answer the question of whether any of them would attempt to take action that would limit any unfortunate consequences of anything people had testified to them in a confessional. He realized that it would likely be a difficult assignment to say the least, to find priests who had encountered the faithful in confessions involving transgressions that could damage other people, third parties who might be harmed by actions admitted in confessions heard by them. However, before even planning to search for priests who might be willing to discuss this scheme with him, he thought he might approach some of the Jesuit priests who still taught at Saint Ignatius, either at the university or even at the high school.

If this had been two years ago, Richard would have contacted Father Breslin, who taught him when he surprisingly registered for his theology class, an experience that he found surprisingly evocative and slowly led to the renewal of his faith in the Roman Catholic religion over the course of the class. He remembered asking Father Breslin for his views and advice on the parameters of confession in particular, his developed obsession with the sacrament the basis for his pursuit of Father Breslin's guidance. Fact was that he recalled his lunch with Father Breslin during which the latter told Richard that a priest could take action beyond the normal principles of confession, like penance, if he felt that such action was useful in any way. In other words, if Father Breslin was still available, he could make a personnel recommendation, that was if he knew any colleagues of the cloth who ever found themselves in such an unusual situation. If he wasn't available, he would have to find some other cleric to contact. But he thought Father Breslin was a good bet, considering the subject matter.

Richard's first step was to contact the Office of the Registrar of the Saint Ignatius University to determine Father Breslin's location, that is if they knew where he was. In this regard, during the year that Richard had attended Theology 130, Father Breslin had announced that he was retiring and therefore would no longer be on the faculty. Richard asked if the university knew where Father Breslin was living now that he was retired. The official in the Office of the Registrar he spoke to, a woman named Mrs. Lamb, told him that Father Breslin was no longer living at a Jesuit sanctuary. When Richard then asked how or where Father Breslin was living or doing, Mrs. Lamb told him to contact Father Emmett Graham, a colleague of Father Breslin who was the spiritual director of the Saint Ignatius High School. Richard was pleased with the news since he knew Father Graham, who held the position when Richard attended high school at Saint Ignatius five years ago. Richard should not have been surprised since, aside from Father Breslin, Father Graham was one of the longest standing members of the faculties at either the Saint Ignatius College or the Saint Ignatius High School.

He managed to get in touch with Father Graham, whose telephone number was easily obtained when he contacted the main office of the Ignatius High School. Although Richard knew Father Graham, he doubted that the spiritual director of the high school, a position that he still held, at least on an ex officio position, would remember Richard from his days as a high school student. Fact was that Richard had only visited Father Graham on the advice of his Class Master in Class 4A. The Class Master, whose name was Father Bradley, had suggested that most of the students in Class 4A seek advice from Father Graham who, as spiritual director, included providing occupational and spiritual direction to students who thought they didn't have any, which was applicable to most of them.

He met with Father Emmett Graham in his high school office the next week, in the middle of a Tuesday afternoon. He had explained to Father Graham that he was seeking the whereabouts of Father Breslin, his former theology professor. He could have interviewed him over the telephone but he would not have felt comfortable, particularly since he might have to tell Father Graham the reason for his search for Father Breslin, i.e. if he knew of any priests who might have heard confessions that could have motivated them to take remedial action after the confession was concluded. Richard recognized Father Graham the moment he was ushered into his office by Mrs. Lamb. His appearance had not changed at all. Surprisingly, in return, Father Graham also remembered Richard even though Richard's appearance had changed significantly in the last few years, his hair being much longer. That prompted Richard to ask Father Graham how he could possibly identify him so convincingly after meeting him only that once maybe five years ago. Father Graham reacted rather casually, his head shaking slowly. He grinned. He explained, "Well, I don't know if you ever knew this but every time I met with any student, I tried to find out as much as I could about them. So like every student that is referred to me for an interview, I got fairly familiar with your record — you know, your academic record, your extracurricular activities, that sort of thing. I spoke to your teachers, sometimes your friends, sometimes students with whom you played on school teams, sometimes students with whom you participated in other school activities. And finally, I also had your picture." At that point, Father Graham's grin turned into a broad smile. He then asked Richard the purpose of his search for Father Breslin.

As Richard had anticipated, he had to explain to Father Graham the reason for his enquiry, which he did. In response, Father Graham strangely informed him that Father Breslin was now accepted by the Jesuit Curia in Rome in order to study for his Doctorate in Theology, news that was not believed by Richard since he presumed that Father Breslin probably already had ample academic qualifications and was living in a local sanctuary. Aside from his opinion about Father Breslin's academic record, Richard thought it curious that a theologian of his standing would seek to enhance his scholarly achievements after retiring from teaching theology for decades. In any event, it was clear that it might be difficult, if not impossible to seek Father Breslin's guidance on unusual confessions, even if he could get in touch with him.

As Richard sat there with a disappointed look on his face, nearly placing his head in his hands, Father Graham volunteered to come to Richard's assistance in resolving his preoccupation. "I used to hear confessions. I did so for many years, both here and in Saint Monica's. I think I may have run into a situation that may fit the circumstance you describe. But I don't really understand your obsession with confessions in which certain penitents confess to serious transgressions. I have to admit I have encountered a few of such cases. I myself didn't take any unusual action following any such confessions. I tried to persuade those who confessed to take curative action for any such trespasses during the confession itself but never pursued it beyond that. In fact, I don't recall even considering it. But I really don't know what I could have done, if I could have done anything." Richard expected Father Graham to mention penance but he did not. That would come later.

Richard was surprised by Father Graham's admission. Having contacted Saint Ignatius with the purpose of finding Father Breslin, he had then been referred to Father Graham. But to then discover that Father Graham, who had apparently recognized Richard despite the fact that their previous contact had been five years ago, would offer to assist him in his project regarding overheard confessions, was almost inexplicable but it was welcomed nonetheless. So Richard gladly responded to Father Graham's offer, asking if he could provide an example of the phenomenon that Richard had been hoping to study. Father Graham smiled and leaned back. "I'm reluctant to disappoint you, not to mention myself, but I was never able, or at least I don't think I was ever able to convince anyone who had confessed to me something seriously unpleasant to take some sort of countermeasure. I can recall that there were at least three occasions in which people revealed actions that were wicked enough to merit corrective action, beyond the normal penance in a normal confession. He then said that it was difficult, if not impossible to determine whether the sinner had taken any action that could ease any guilt that he may have felt about his sin. The reality was, however, that I had no obvious way of apprehending any miscreant's action. In all three cases, I never got the opportunity to follow the sinners beyond the door of the confessional closet to determine whether they had sought forgiveness in an unusual way."

While Richard was interested, if not fascinated with Father Graham's explanation of his experience with confessions that were clearly unique, if not memorable, it was also evident to him that while he had found a confessor who was as familiar with the possible consequences of wicked transgressions as Richard was captivated by them. Still, Richard had asked Father Graham to describe the three confessions that had prompted his special interest in the first place. Although he was understandably unwilling to identify the contrite, he could and did share the three specific episodes. Father Graham then began with the most serious incident. "A man, sounding like a middle age man, confessed to me that he had poisoned his elderly mother by giving her too much medication. I told him to turn himself in to the police. I made it part of his penance." Richard then asked Father Graham what, if anything he could do to find out if the police were informed that an elderly woman recently passed away because she had been given too much medication." Father Graham shook his head. Richard looked at the Father and asked, "And? Were the police informed of such a case?" Father Graham shook his head again and answered Richard's inquiry. "Not really. You'll understand that I couldn't just contact the police department and ask. So I just consulted the newspapers for maybe a month and then just gave up. I concluded that the man who had confessed to me hadn't fulfilled the penance I had given him. So I had to give up the search."

The two of them stared at each other for a minute or so before Richard asked Father Graham to reveal the other two episodes of significant admissions. He answered.

"Both of them were comparatively minor but still detestable enough to be acknowledged outside the usual conditions of the ritual. In one case, a bank teller confessed to me that she had blamed the branch manager for stealing money that she herself had stolen from the bank. The bank believed her and the manager eventually lost his position with the bank." Richard immediately interrupted Father Graham with an obvious observation. "And of course you gave the bank teller an unusual penance?" Father Graham winked and nodded in the affirmative. "Yes, my penance to her was to have her admit to bank authorities that she had blamed the branch manager for the money that she stole. And again, there was no opportunity for me to find out whether she ever admitted her guilt to bank management." Finally, Richard asked about the third incident. "Actually the incident was similar to the bank teller's blaming the theft of money to the manager of the branch. In this case, a salesman in a department store confessed to forging his boss's signature for purposes of obtaining store refunds. Like the bank teller's situation, the manager of the salesman's department — it was the men's wear — got the blame and he was fired. Again, I had no way of knowing whether the salesman satisfied the conditions of the penance, which was basically the same as the bankteller's."

During the next few moments of silence, Richard contemplated whether he had any further questions for Father Graham who was now just sitting there with his head down, wrapping his hands together like he too was thinking about something to say. Finally, with a sympathetic look on his face, the priest looked up and summarized his observations. "I wish I had an opportunity to do something about these situations, to determine if those three sinners were able to return to a state of grace by making their good penances. It's too bad that I could never find out." In the meantime, while Father Graham was completing his conclusion about about the three sinners who had confessed to regrettable acts that had had calamitous effects on innocent relatives or colleagues, Richard asked if he had ever considered investigating the victims of the three sinful deeds by interviewing people who might have known or worked with them. "You might find a relative, a friend, a colleague, someone who could have given you a clue as to what may have happened after those incidents occurred. For example, one could have checked cases of poisoning at local hospitals around the time the man's mother died. But on the other hand, I realize that it would be more difficult, if not impossible to pick up any hints of bank or department managers being let go." Father Graham nodded slowly and then shrugged his shoulders.

Again, there was another delay in their exchange. Richard then asked a fundamental question, a question he slowly came to the conclusion he should have asked Father Graham much earlier in their conversation. "Father, why did you give those three confessing parties special penances? You had an idea that those attempts at atonement weren't going to end successfully." Father Graham smiled and gave Richard an obvious answer. "I just thought I seldom heard confessions involving wrongdoings which resulted in damage to other people in obvious ways. So I decided instead of prayers and maybe some charity work, I would give those three particular sinners penances I thought would somehow fit the sin, a repudiation of sorts that could compensate the victims, at least in two of them anyway." Richard was reminded of conversations he may have had with Father Breslin and some of the discussions that the theology class may have had a couple of years ago.

After discussing Father Graham's treatment of the unusual confessions he had heard from the three contrite sinners, Richard thought he might have found a way to finally abandon his obsession with Roman Catholic confession. In other words, he exhausted all possible approaches to his investigation. For several weeks after his meeting with Father Graham, the issue just faded from his mind, seldom occurring to him. His mother, however, prompted the resurrection of confession in his active contemplation. She had asked whether his interest in attending services at church was fading. Richard told his mother he went to Wednesday morning mass at the Saint Ignatius Chapel as he had a couple of years ago, first as a way of impressing Catherine Morris, whom he never identified to his mother, and then as something more serious and perhaps more spiritual in nature. Although his obsession with confessions also seemed to decline, it did not disappear entirely, vestiges of his fixation occasionally appearing, usually when he did not have anything else to contemplate. Further, maybe a month after their meeting, he ran into Father Graham in the first floor corridor of the main building of Saint Ignatius College.

That evening, having been reminded of his former interest, he began to reflect on it, particularly as it applied to confessions that prompted the assignment of secular penances. Maybe it was time, he thought, to reignite his interest, finally concluding, after several hours of serious contemplation, that he had invested too much time to simply discard it. Still, if that would turn out to be his plan, to return to a preoccupation had become and was now likely to remain an obsession, he would have to formulate another approach. He had exhausted several different approaches in pursuit of the implications of the overheard confession by an elderly lady. He had observed a number of old ladies waiting for confession, even going to great lengths to possibly identifying the elderly lady with a loud voice. He occupied the adjacent confessional to possibly overhear other sinners in the opposing booth. After the unsuccessful pursuit of that approach, hoping to pick up sinful testimony from maybe two dozen elderly ladies without hearing anything, Richard had turned to interviewing three priests who could provide insight into this strange rejoinder to confession.

First he had contacted Father Firth, who couldn't remember or didn't know the elderly lady who confessed to a false rumour that significantly damaged her granddaughter. Nor would he, or in fact could he, speculate on what action, if any could have been taken to ameliorate damage wrought by a rumour invented for unknown reasons by an elderly lady who confessed her sins in a easily audible tone. Another interview with Father Firth was not worth pursuing. Then after unsuccessfully attempting to contact Father Breslin for a second time, he coincidentally met with Father Graham who went on to provide him with three examples of circumstances that might have fit the scenario about which Richard had requested an opinion. Simply, he had asked him if he had ever provided any miscreants with penances that could remedy the damage their transgressions had caused. He thought he could have but didn't know if he actually did.

Confession
Research III

After all the time that Richard had invested in pursuing his preoccupation with confessions, he had finally come to realize that he could not abandon his struggle regardless the absence of result. That result would be a demonstration of the serious consequences to third parties that may have been harmed by actions admitted by penitents during confession. He wondered with considerable frustration about possible avenues that were still available to him, his motivation being to discover a confessor, any confessor who sought to make anyone confessing a grievous sin a penance of direct atonement. And then, that penance would be executed as directed by the confessor. He could not predict how he came upon the most recent scheme although it could have come to him after maybe watching a television show or a movie, although he also considered that it could have come to him in a dream, an unlikely possibility but a possibility nevertheless.

The plan seemed simple but was ridiculously elusive, therefore unlikely to achieve the intended result. Still, he thought he would attempt the plan anyway, even though its prospects were dim. Besides, he had fantasized that if he went forward with any proposal he could dream up, it might be enjoyable. It might turn into a game worth pursuing, even if that pursuit would not lead to anything substantial, the objective being confessions that would ultimately result in appropriate indemnification for actions seriously sinful.

The new plan that Richard had conceived was relatively simple. He would take confession and seek contrition for imaginary transgressions, for sins that, although seriously shameful had never taken place. Further, and more importantly, any sinful actions had to seem appropriately injurious to require a response that would go beyond a simple Act of Contrition and the usual penance of several decades of the rosary and perhaps several acts of charity. In other words, the confessed action had to necessitate penance that corresponded to the damage done by the sin confessed. In that regard, rather than require penitents to seek forgiveness through prayers of penance, confessors and those who confessed would be asked to receive absolution through reciprocating actions rather than the recitation of familiar prayers offered up as penance. It seemed like an advantageous plan, at least as it applied to the pursuit of his purpose.

Therefore, he had already decided that he would take confession and seek absolution for sins that he simply invented, his intention to prompt confessors to allocate penances that would rectify whatever damage the sins confessed had caused. His first objective was to formulate a sin to confess that would precipitate the priest hearing him to provide a penalty that would make appropriate amends for the sin he had admitted. That proved surprisingly difficult, unlike the three examples Father Graham had provided, as well as the unknown misdeed that he had overheard the elderly lady confess to Father Firth about her granddaughter's sin. Richard envisaged a scenario in which the confessor would not only request that the contrite consider action himself but would also follow up to determine if such action was taken. He had questioned Father Graham if he had ever pursued the actions that he had assigned to his three sinners. Father Graham responded by admitting that although he had thought about it, he hadn't investigated if any of the unusual penances he had given were actually accomplished.

Accordingly, this lead Richard to conclude that he would have to conceive of misbehaviour that could not only be confessed to a priest as a mortal sin but could also attract penance in the form of actions that could be verified as having been carried out. Of the three examples that Father Graham had given him, Richard was most persuaded that the poisoning of a sinner's mother was probably the most likely to be verified, principally by checking with the police, hospitals or funeral homes. Father Graham had, however, pursued verification himself by perusing newspapers for obituaries or reports of accidental deaths. He abandoned the search after a month or so, not finding any news even remotely indicative of a son who had confessed that he had poisoned his mother. A further difficulty was the certainty that if Richard went ahead with a scheme involving a similar action, an imaginary sin would be equally impossible to prove, regardless of whether through contacting authorities or through investigating the press, whether radio, television or newspapers. He would face a considerable dilemma.

Over the next several weeks, Richard invested a considerable amount of his time, whether trying to pay attention in his university classes or sitting in the library staring out the window with a book laid out before him, considering his predicament with his confession project. He came across several flashes of inspiration during his series of contemplations. Over a few beers at a local tavern named the Green Hornet, a friend of his, a relatively old friend named Peter who he had known since elementary school and saw occasionally even though he had little in common except history, made a suggestion that could solve the mystery. During their discussion of Richard's continuing pursuit of his conundrum about confessions, Peter said that he had seen a television drama about a priest who had heard during the provision of the last rites a confession regarding a previously solved murder committed by a man who was soon to pass away. Peter said that someone else had been convicted of the murder and had been languishing in jail for several years. The confessor, realizing that the man who had been convicted of the murder was in fact innocent, was faced with a difficult choice. To remedy the situation, a man innocent of an offence for which he was doing time, he would have to admit to the police or some other authority figure, like the innocent man's lawyer for example, that he had been given information about the guilty individual.

However, the priest was only provided with information that could disapprove the conviction of the innocent if it could be proved that the soon to be deceased had committed the crime. The priest who had performed the last rites and had heard the confession of the guilty party could not identify the actual murderer of the confidentiality of confession or because he was not identified in the first place. Either way, he could not give anyone a name. If the priest decided to provide police with the guilty party, they would have to investigate the circumstances of the murder with evidence. Richard quickly realized, however, that if the crime was fictional, the invention of his fertile mind, he would have to conjure up elements of proof of a crime, something that would necessitate more than just imagination. Despite his enthusiasm for the plan, he also realized that it was little more than a fantasy. At least in the television show, the priest had actual information that he could share with others. That left the two other examples that Father Graham had been given by penitents during confessions he had heard.

The remaining two examples that Father Graham had specified to Richard in identifying unusual penances that he may have assessed after listening to confessions involving forms of either theft or embezzlement. With respect to the penances, Father Graham ordered both sinners to admit their sins — admit their crimes which had resulted in the losses of the jobs previously held by a bank manager and a manager of the men's wear section of a downtown department store. In both cases, Father Graham could have either inquired regarding the whereabouts of the managers of both the bank and the men's wear section of a department store to determine whether the sinning miscreants had, as directed by Father Graham, admitted their crimes, reinstated their bosses and lost their jobs. Further, both sinners might have to reimburse the bank and the department store for the money that they had taken. Richard noted that Father Graham had overlooked one salient point: the sinners had not informed the confessor where either of them were working when they committed the sins about which they were seeking forgiveness.

On the other hand, if Richard was to employ a theft or a similar ploy in his theatrical confession, it was pretty obvious that he would have to contrive a misconduct that could actually be shown to be evidence of something. It was evident that unless he could come up with something tangible that was the result of an imaginary transgression, which seemed an obvious logical impossibility, Richard's project about discovering a confession that resulted in some sort of practical amends seemed stalled, if not finished completely. He sat there with his forehead on the surface of the library desk, almost daydreaming, straining to stay awake, wondering how he was going to continue to sustain his obsession. Either that, or as he had considered dozens of times, give it up. He felt like he did when he was conspiring with himself to telephone a girl when he was in ninth grade.

CONFESSION
RESEARCH IV

I t was obvious, alarmingly simple. He needed a partner, an associate who could be persuaded to assist him with his plan, however perilous it may turn out to be. In coming to that conclusion, which took him longer than it should have given his continued preoccupation, he had thought of a neighbourhood guy named Randy Novacheck with whom he had attended elementary school. He had run into him years later when they were both packing groceries at the Dominion grocery store. Richard was working part time while he was going to Saint Ignatius while Mr. Novacheck was a permanent employee, a position he had held since he dropped out of high school after failing grade nine three consecutive times. Given the complications of the plan with which he was left, Richard now deduced that if he was able to employ a partner, which now seemed the only option he had, it would require an associate who was compliant enough to go along with any sort of plan that

Richard could devise. His first step would be to contact and then convince Novacheck to agree to help him with his recently originated plan to prove that some priests would take unusual action if sins confessed to them did serious harm to others.

So on the first opportunity he had, a Tuesday afternoon in early November, Richard visited the Dominion grocery store in the neighbourhood shopping centre to re-establish his relationship with Randy Novacheck, somebody he had not seen or spoken to in more than six years. He walked into the store to look for employee Novacheck and noticed right off that he was not among four unfortunate individuals depositing groceries into tan paper bags. He then began a tour around the store, pushing a grocery cart up and down each aisle, placing an item in the cart every so often, just to ensure that no one got suspicious of his intentions. After covering the store, including taking the occasional glance in the back storage rooms, Richard left his cart in the dairy section and approached the administration counter, where two older looking employees sold cigarettes, newspapers, bus tickets and other sundry items. They waited with terminally bored looked on their faces. Richard thought they looked like they probably used to be cashiers.

He asked them if Novachek was still employed by the store, explaining that he had worked with him several years ago. The woman who had greeted him, she looked a little younger than her counter colleague, told him that Mr. Novacheck was still working for Dominion but in the fruit and vegetable department where she said she thought he was presently unloading a shipment at the back of the store. She then said that she would advise Novacheck that he had a visitor with an announcement over the public address system. She then asked him to wait, pointing to a chair by newspaper stand. As he sat there waiting, it seemed that a cavalcade of seemingly middle aged women walked by with curious looks on their faces. Richard had the impression that most of them might have thought that he was applying for a job, his general appearance presentable enough to imply his purpose in being there. Finally, with ten minutes having passed, Randy Novacheck put in an appearance. He waved at the women behind the counter with a goofy look on his face. He looked at Novacheck who physically did not appear much different than he did when Richard last saw him. He had gained a little weight, his hair was a little longer and he was now wearing a moustache. He still looked a little dumb.

"Is Mr. Gauvin mad at me again?" Novacheck asked. He was always taking hell from Mr. Gauvin, the manager of the store. He always thought that Novacheck was somehow disabled. That made him an easily target for frequent censure. Novacheck explained, "Peacock told me to come, I was in back helping to unload a shipment. Baxter was supposed to be helping me but he didn't he never does. He was just talking to the driver, who was smoking a cigarette and drinking from a bottle which could have been a beer. I came as soon as I heard my name over the PA." As Novacheck finished his unnecessary explanation, the desk lady pointed at Richard now sitting in the chair across from the administration counter and waved him over.

Richard stood up and offered his hand. "Remember

me, Randy, My name is Richard, Richard O'Brien. We used to work together, packing groceries at this place, five or six years ago. And we were also together in Mr. Clark's class in grade six in Saint John Fisher though I think you may have been in his class more than once." Randy Novacheck displayed that goofy smile he had in grade school and then held up three fingers in response to that remark. After displaying his three fingers, Randy shock his head. "I don't think I remember." Randy then allowed a quizzical expression to appear on his face and then asked. "Were you the only Richard in the class?" Richard answered. "No, I don't think so." There was then a delay in the conversation. Richard then continued with his explanation. "Anyway, I think we may have sat close to each other in grade six, not exactly beside each other but close enough for you to sometimes try to copy my answers when we had a class quiz. You may remember." Randy then laughed, saying he copied from everybody's quiz answers, unsuccessfully he supposed. Richard then sat there with a puzzled look on his face and then asked, "Did you ever steal my bike?" While it was possible, he could not remember if Novacheck had actually lifted his bike. He recalled that Bill McPhee would often take his bike but not Randy Novacheck who confessed nevertheless to such thievery. "No, I don't think I ever did but I used to like to steal bikes.Maybe I took yours but I just don't know." Then, the two of them grinned to each other.

During that ten minute conversation, Richard come to the conclusion that Randy Novacheck was probably just gullible enough to be convinced to partner in any scheme. Richard was close to graduating from university and Randy was working in a grocery store, not having shed his working class status, their differences significant enough to present Richard with a possible quandary. As appropriate as Novacheck seemed, in terms of being easily persuaded of practically anything, he might have difficulty understanding the plan, no matter how many times it was explained to him. Richard thought, at least for an instant, that maybe Novacheck was the wrong man for his plan.

Still, as he sat there in the Dominion store, conversing with Randy Novacheck, his reservations revolving in his head, he decided to invite him to the Mercury Tavern, a drinking establishment several blocks away from the store, for a few beers after Randy punched out. He agreed and Richard said he would back be in an hour. In the interim, Richard went to a record store called Arthur's. He knew it well. It was there that he had purchased most of his album collection, which had grown to more than a hundred LPs and a pile of 45s which he seldom played but kept for their nostalgic value. He looked through the bins for a while, both of new records and used ones, Arthur's being one of the few stores around that sold used records. He had come across several used albums that conveniently identified the previous owners, one of whom Richard recognized. The store also sold books, mainly about music. Most of the books were not sold in the university bookstore or available in the university library. He flipped through several of the volumes, including a couple about the Beatles, the Rolling Stone interview of John Lennon, a few pictorial books about popular bands, and surprisingly enough, a pocket book about Montreal rock bands. Before

Richard left Arthur's, he had purchased two used albums, including an early album by the Beach Boys, a musical preference that Richard had to hide from his hipper colleagues at university. By the time Richard arrived back at the Dominion store for his rendezvous with Randy, he only had a few minutes to wait.

Randy punched out and arrived as agreed to met with Richard. He first said that he had to make a telephone call, explaining that he had to inform his group home, a term with which Richard was not familiar, that he would be a little late for dinner. Richard overheard Randy informing someone that he would be home by curfew, suggesting to Richard that maybe Randy should not be frequenting the Mercury Tavern at any time. After hearing about the Randy's curfew, Richard started to wonder about his continued pursuit of him as a partner in his plan. In any event, the two of them were sitting in a corner of the Mercury Tavern within ten minutes. At first, Randy would not stop talking, describing in excruciating detail his duties in the fruit and vegetable department. He appeared to be as pleased with his current job as he was when they worked with each other as pack boys. In fact, he seemed to exhibit a certain pride with his current job, a transfer to a specific department an obvious upgrade from packing groceries. By the time a waiter arrived at their table, Richard felt like he worked in the fruit and vegetable department himself.

After they ordered three draft beers each, Richard asked Randy if he would be willing to assist him with a personal project that he had in mind. Before continuing with any description of his plan, Richard waited for the beers to arrive at the table, the waiter delivering the order being an older man who was obviously acquainted with Randy. The two of them engaged in a brief conversation with the waiter, whose name was Mike, mainly about sports wagering before they paid and started consuming their drafts. They both finished one draft each in silence before Richard began to introduce his proposition. He had decided to start with an obvious though unexpected question. He asked Randy if he was a practicing Roman Catholic. Randy looked at Richard as if he had just suggested something unfamiliar. Although his inquiry was based on the historical fact that Randy Novecheck had attended Saint John Fisher, a Catholic elementary school, he doubted that he ever went to any church, regardless of the denomination of his elementary school. Randy responded to Richard's question with an understandably stunned look on his face. That precipitated Richard to explain that Randy's religious beliefs, that is if he had any in the first place, really didn't have much to do with the project he was about to propose to him although he admitted to him that they would be helpful, a point that Randy didn't understand.

Richard then went on to provide him with a brief history of his interest in confession about which he asked if Randy had a working knowledge of it. He told Richard that his parents took him to church for years until he was an adolescent, after which point they began to ignore his developing agnostic, if not atheistic tendencies, worrying more about his potential for aberrant behaviour. In that event, he was familiar with confession, having been frequently compelled to visit the confessional when he was a boy. Richard smiled when he made that comment, an observation that did not make much of an impression on Randy.

Richard continued with an explanation. "I studied confession for a class in theology I took in university several years ago. I don't know why but I became fascinated with confession, so much so I decided I wanted to do further research on the subject. I decided I would conduct an experiment would require some assistance, mainly the participation of another person." explained Richard, hoping it would be adequately comprehensible to Randy. He then specifically indicated to Randy he was thinking of him as the assistant he required although he did not mention the reason he had chosen him. Since he couldn't tell Randy his possible gullibility was his qualification, fearing that he would take it as an insult, he decided to compliment him as indirectly as he could. "I remember that you used to get in trouble a fair amount. Face it, you were a bit of a delinquent and I kind of need someone who doesn't mind taking chances. And to be honest, I've never known too many guys like you.", Richard said. He was almost being honest.

Randy, who was almost finished his third draft, offered Richard a wide smile and then asked what he had in mind for him. "And what will you want me to do?" Richard did not yet have anything specific in mind for him, he just wanted just his agreement to help when Richard conceived the next steps in his plan, whatever that was. All he knew was that Randy would have to seek real absolution for sins Richard had confessed. He just hadn't thought of the transgressions he would confess yet, hoping to attract unusual penances. They then sat in silence for a few minutes. After a time, they both ordered a few more drafts, three by Randy and two more for Richard. Randy seemed to know what the waiter was talking about. So based on their brief discussion, Richard suspected Randy might be a regular gambler, suggesting maybe he might ask for cash to participate in his project. However, the thought faded and they went back to consuming their recently delivered drafts.

By the time they had finished their beers, Richard was relatively certain that Randy, regardless of any reluctance he may have and any shortcomings he might demonstrate in following whatever plan he would ultimately develop, would do. They left the tavern together and then went in different directions, Randy to his group home located several blocks away on Somerled Street and Richard along Sherbrooke Street the other way. Randy was a little late for supper and was worried that Ross, who was usually in charge at dinner time, would immediately notice that he had been drinking, which was normally allowed, at least in Randy's case, but not to excess, which again in Randy's case, probably qualified him with the six drafts that he had consumed with Richard. Richard was walking west along Sherbrooke Street to the Montreal West train station, confident that he would be on time for the 6:40 PM to the West Island, the last train of the day. His father, who worked at Eaton's department store on Ste Catherine Street, always complained of having to take the car if he had to work late on Fridays.

Fortunately, Richard managed to make the 6:40. It was pulling only four cars. The fourth car was practically empty, allowing Richard to stretch out on one of the two empty seats facing each other. He was considering resting his feet on the opposite seat but when he saw the conductor take a quick look into the window of the car, he thought better of it. There were only three other passengers in the car, two of whom were reading newspapers and smoking cigarettes while the third passenger was asleep, a state that inspired Richard to contemplate joining him in slumber. In addition to staring blankly out the train window, Richard took the opportunity afforded by the train trip to the suburbs to ponder a proposal that would allow him to prove that serious transgressions disclosed in the precinct of a confessional could be absolved by more than the penance of a series of prayers. Now that he presumably had the assistance of Randy Novacheck, he could devise the right kind of a scheme.

IMAGINARY
CONFESSION I

During the two days after his first meeting with Randy Novacheck, Richard spent much of his time attempting to devise an imaginary confession, the outcome of which would hopefully be the assignment of an unusual penance. Using the elderly woman's original confession to Father Firth regarding a rumour about her granddaughter, a middle aged man's poisoning of his elderly mother, the stolen money from the bank, and the bogus refunds from a department store as exemplars, he strained to discover an appropriate masquerade. He seemed to think about it almost constantly, unable to disconnect from one obsession to another. Finally, with his frustration exhausted, Richard decided that maybe he should consult with someone who was not familiar with his preoccupation of confession.

He thought of his former best friend Peter, with whom he had limited recent contact even though they still went to the same school, Peter being in his last year toward a degree in Commerce while Richard was still pursuing the study of English literature. Richard had concluded that he probably needed the advice of someone who was not steeped in the mythology of confession, was not aware of his old friend's fascination with a Roman Catholic sacrament usually pursued by old ladies and school children, and was an old friend. In other words, Richard was worried that his striving toward an answer to his continued perplexity about certain types of sins that would result in certain types of penances needed a more objective analysis. Someone who does not have any interest whatever in confession but had a particular and common history in confession, the incident with a priestly vestment years ago, might have an more appropriate opinion.

So he thought he would contact Peter and ask him for an opinion on the efficacy of researching unusual confessions. Two days later, Richard was able to reach Peter by telephone at his parents' place. Aside from exchanging predictable small talk about their families, the fates of their respective brothers Jack and Steven being of particular interest, they agreed to meet in the BVD, a well known tavern on Monkland Avenue further east in NDG, to discuss what he called "his project". When he explained rather clumsily the meaning of "his project", Peter understandably expressed confusion, if not complete mystification but admitted that he was still prepared to listen to him at the BVD next Thursday. Peter asked him not to smoke any weed that afternoon, which he falsely thought that Richard was addicted to. Richard agreed and then sought Peter's assurance that he would not make any reference to his studies during their meeting. While Peter was a trifled offended, he agreed to not to discuss anything even remotely related to the study of economics, which even he admitted, at least to himself, was occasionally boring. Peter then sought Richard's promise that he would not raise anything related to his studies, including most particularly anything to do with the works of any twentieth century American novelist. They both then laughed it up, with the two of them saying that left only sports and women to discuss. Richard added politics with Peter grudgingly agreeing.

The BVD was fairly crowded when he walked in and spotted Peter sitting in a small circular table in the middle of the room. It was three o'clock in the afternoon and maybe half the patrons in the place were Saint Ignatius students while the other half looked to be working construction. In any event, Peter had a pint of a recently delivered Labatt's 50 sitting in front of him and was reading a copy of the *Montreal Gazette*. Richard sat down and made a flippant remark about the golf shirt that Peter was wearing. Peter smirked, folded his newspaper, greeted Richard and commented on his shirt, which happened to be a t-shirt with a picture of the *Rolling Stones* on the front. His comment was equally flippant. Richard sat down and asked if Peter was missing any class to meet with him. Peter shook his head, Richard raised his hand and ordered three draft beers. While they both waited for the drafts to arrive before clicking glasses and getting down to business, there was a short exchange of the information about their respective courses which they had previously agreed not to discuss. Having dispensed with the scholarly stuff, Richard asked whether he was going out with anyone, his most recent recollection being that his steady girlfriend was someone named Beverly. Peter replied that he wasn't going out with anyone at the present time and asked Richard the same question. Before he could answer, a young waiter brought Richard's three drafts and they finally clicked glasses, just like their fathers would have.

Peter then asked not about anyone that Richard may be going with but why he had requested his audience as he put it. As he anticipated with some hesitation, it was now Richard's turn to explain what he thought might be inexplicable. "Well, though you might have had difficulty understanding me on the telephone the other day, I honestly have been working on a project regarding confession after taking a theology course..." At that point, Richard put up his right hand and then provided Peter with an explanation of his obviously peculiar decision to study the spiritual mysteries of confession. "Anyway, I was taking confession one day when I heard, or should I say overheard an elderly woman in the other confessional admitting to a priest, a priest named Father Firth as I was later told that she had spread a damaging rumour about her granddaughter. It occurred to me that Father Firth could have given the old woman a post-confession penance that was commensurate with the damage that her rumour had done to the granddaughter. I then become fascinated with the idea of the penance equivalent to the sin, you know like the punishment fitting the crime." Peter stared at Richard almost dumbfounded, then swallowed the remainder of his pint, held the bottle up in the direction of the waiter, and responded to Richard's elucidation. "You may have to explain your interest in confession again. I don't think I understand." With that, Peter brought a finger to his head with a confused look on his face.

Richard spread his hands out and then resumed the conversation. "I spoke to three priests who had been confessors, including Father Firth who had heard the original confession by the old lady. He said that he couldn't remember the confession itself and the other two priests, including a Father Graham who told me that he had heard three specific revelations of actions that could damage others. While Father Firth really didn't have an opinion about whether priests hearing confessions about such transgressions, the other two priests thought that exceptional penances were justified in the certain circumstances." Peter then brought his second pint to his lips, the bottle had remained on the table while Richard continued with the information on the history of his confession research. Although Peter's expression looked less confounded than it was several minutes ago, he asked Richard about his future intentions and the reason he had contacted him in the first place. Then Peter asked an obvious question. "So at least two of the priests you spoke with had an opinion that seemed the same as yours, that is that unusual sins can result in unusual amends. So you have an answer to the mystery that you has been pursuing for a couple of years. So why do you still seem to be chasing the subject?" Peter then delayed for a moment, took another swallow of his beer, and then asked in the form of an observation. "You're not making any sense. As one of my profs likes to say, it's counter-intuitive or whatever the hell that means." Richard laughed and asked, "Does that mean that I'm doing the opposite of what I should do? Or something." Peter answered, "Yeah I think so."

Richard leaned across the table with one hand on his forehead and expressed his thoughts, as muddled as they may have seemed, on his motive for continuing to pursue the mystery of an unusual type of confession. He admitted to Peter, as he had admitted to himself countless times, that he was inexplicably fascinated with the idea of a confessor telling penitents to atone for their sins by taking concrete actions instead of praying. Peter looked at him as if he had never heard of any such maneuver by any man of the cloth, no matter how egregious the sin confessed. They sat in silence drinking their beer, ordered more beer, and then Peter leaned across the table and simply asked what he currently had in mind, specifically why he had asked him to the BVD for a beer. Richard answered somewhat tentatively, in a low voice, as if he was confiding something to Peter, which he was. He outlined his plan, hoping that his friend Peter would have a suggestion or suggestions that would improve his plan. "Well Peter, I thought I would visit a confessional, give a priest an imaginary confession that might prompt the priest to give me an unusual penance. Instead of asking me to recite an Act of Contrition and parts of the rosary, the priest would then hopefully provide me with a penance that would force me to do something that would repair the damage that the act confessed may have done."

Peter again looked at Richard with a certain suspicion, a puzzled look having appeared on his face for maybe the dozenth time during their meeting. Richard responded by raising his hands in the air and asking what part of his plan he couldn't comprehend. Peter looked at Richard as intently as he could in the circumstances and asked a final question that pretty well summarized his own confusion. "Okay, a priest hears your imaginary confession and then gives you a real penance for your imaginary sin. I have one significant question. How will a priest who gives you this unusual penance know you and know whether you ever concluded the penance that he gave you? It doesn't make much sense to me when you think about it." Richard was ready for Peter's rejoinder. He answered almost immediately. "How does a priest know whether someone who just confessed to him fulfill the penance he just gave him? He just assumes it I guess." After a short delay, during which Peter looked like he was thinking about an answer, he offered a response, "This is a little different. A priest who gives a sinner an unorthodox penance might want to see if the sinner actually made good on the punishment he was given. I mean, prayers are one thing but any sort of other action a priest may have imposed as penance is an entirely different thing. And don't forget, the priest would have to know who was assigned the penance in the first place. Let's face it, the whole thing is weird."

Richard looked at him with a quietly thoughtful expression on his face. "As you may have guessed, I've already thought of those points. I just don't know how I could get that information. I mean, the first thing is that I don't know if most priests, if not all priests actually know the people who are confessing to them. A few might, that is if they recognize a face or a voice though the screen. But even if they did, how would they know if the penance was actually completed? That's what I have been thinking about it. That's why I called you. I just wanted to discuss my problem with you, to see if you had any suggestions. I should tell you that I convinced a guy named Randy Novacheck to help me with my project. Maybe you remember him, you know from Saint John Fisher. I also worked with him at the Dominion store. Anyway, I don't know what I'll want him to do. Maybe you'll have a suggestion or maybe you won't." He uttered a guilty laugh and looked at Peter who shrugged his shoulders and said, "I'll think about it.". Richard nodded and they sat in silence for a few moments. Then Richard spoke again, "I've thought about it many times. The only idea I ever came up with was to have the sinner who received a curious penance to send the confessor a letter. As if a letter could actually convince a priest taking confession that a penance he assigned was actually undertaken. It just doesn't seem credible. That's why I recruited Randy"

Again, Peter was able to provide Richard with another question. "Wouldn't it better for your confession project if we could find out if the confessor wanted to see if the sinner completed the penance rather than wait for the sinner to tell him that he had completed the penance." For a moment, he thought of Father Graham who may have had opportunities to determine if unusual penances in three specific confessions had provided the sinners with some sort of redemption. The opportunities did not result in anything conclusive although he did not pursue them, at least as aggressively as he should have. Richard agreed and commented with considerable reservation. "I guess you're right, it does make things a little more difficult. I mean, how I can press a confessor to look for actions further to any penances he may have allocated." They were both tired, the issue spent. They had both confused each other, the opportunity for clarification faded. They both placed cash on the table and finally signalled to the waiter.

It was the next week when he decided to contact Novacheck regarding the status of his project. He repeated the substance of his meeting with Peter to Randy and then informed him that he was planning an experiment at an imaginary confession in the Saint Ignatius church. He then asked Randy if he had any suggestions for his confession project. Randy said that he had not had any particular thoughts on their plan, Richard noting for a moment that he referred to the confession project as "their plan", a sign that at least he had made progress with his new partner. Randy responded by asking if Richard had any specific idea as to what imaginary sin he was planning to confess. Richard said that while he had considered several ideas, based almost entirely on the misdeeds about which two confessor priests previously informed him, he had not decided on any sin that could convince a confessor to assign any sort of unusual penance to him. Randy suggested that maybe one of those transgressions wasn't such a bad idea. Richard tentatively agreed and then added that he doubted that whoever heard his fictional confession would be familiar with any of them. It was a flash of inspiration that surprisingly enough came from someone who Richard did not think was capable of stoking inspiration of any kind. Maybe choosing one of those stories would not be a bad idea. He thanked Randy for his suggestion before promising that he would let him know if he could help in any way. Richard wondered if he could.

Of the confessions that Fathers Firth and Graham had related, the bogus refunds that were supposedly paid by a department store rose to the top of his list of imaginary admissions. He decided that he would visit the Saint Ignatius church for confession before the 10 AM service on the next Wednesday. That would give him six days to develop an appropriate script for his invented confession. Doubtless, he didn't have the complete details of the fictitious scam that ultimately led to a fictitious confession supposedly to be heard by Father Graham. All he had to do was to ask his father which he did. His father said that all department stores, there being five such stores downtown, had similar, if not identical bureaucratic practices and therefore could be counted to employ as examples. It was simple when Richard thought about it. A customer intending to seek a refund would get the attention of a salesman, explaining the reason for the refund, follow the salesman to the nearest register, wait for him or her to fill in the appropriate form with the appropriate signature, and then take the completed form down to the cash office, which in Eaton's was on the first floor, where the customer would receive the refund money. Suitably tutored, Richard felt ready to go to confession at Saint Ignatius on Wednesday. He was hoping that whoever heard his confession, his Jesuit training would somehow inspire him to a unique conclusion.

The priest was named Father McCallum, his bronze

title card attached to the door of the confessional. Richard entered the closest closet, Father McCallum's light went out, and the screen slide open. There was no other sinner waiting for absolution. The heavy odour of cigarette smoke wafted out of the darkness of Father McCallum's cubicle. He turned toward Richard. He squinted into Richard's booth over his spectacles and waited. Richard began with the familiar declaration, "Bless me Father, I have sinned. It has been several months since my last confession. I...." Before he could continue, Father McCallum interrupted to ask if he was sure about the timing of his last confession. A curious question Richard thought. What possible difference would the date of his last confession make? He wondered whether a temporal detail was always part of the ritual. Did the duration between confessions have some effect on confession itself, its absolution or its penance or both? In any event, Richard answered in the affirmative.

He then continued, describing what he called a counterfeit refund scam. Father McCallum, who usually listened to confessions barely awake, was obviously aroused, leaning forward with obvious interest, curiosity heightened compared to the usual litany of tedious wrongdoings. Richard then outlined the entire endeavour, beginning with an explanation of the supposed inspiration for the scheme, a co-worker in the T. Eaton department store named Fenwick who suggested during lunch in the cafeteria that someone who was familiar with store procedures could easily receive fraudulent refunds. He recommended that a sales position would be ideal. "He told me that all you need was a partner pretending to be a customer, the merchandise to be refunded, a sales receipt, which could easily be found in the trash near any register, and a cash refund form. You then bring the merchandise, the receipt and the form to a manager, get him to sign the form, and then have the partner submit the form to the cash office on the first floor. The cash office then hands the refund cash over to the partner who leaves the store and then the two of you divide the proceeds."

Father McCallum, whose concentration usually waned anytime a penitent's detailing of the sin exceeded a minute or so, was almost enthralled by Richard's admission. He had the temerity to actually ask how much money he and his unnamed partner were able to receive through the refund flimflam. Richard said around $500 although he said he wasn't sure. Father McCallum also asked about the partner in the scam. Richard offered a peculiar answer which he related in a barely discerned whisper that he had used several different collaborators, including a couple of partners who had not been asked to participate. He offered a strange through a fairly comprehensive explanation. "My friend Jack, who helped me with the first two refunds we pulled, went ahead and told a couple guys in the neighbourhood. The next thing I knew, three neighbourhood guys showed up on a Saturday when I was working and demanded that I help them getting a refund. They were sitting on a couple of clothing bins and said they weren't leaving the store until I helped them get a refund. One of them, a next door neighbour named Gary, was holding a jacket that he was looking to refund. It cost $150.00. Anyway, at first I refused but one of the other two guys, a guy named Doug to be specific, said that they would tell my manager about the refunds. So I pretty well had to agree, Father, I didn't think I had any choice."

There was a short silence and then Richard started an Act of Contrition without being asked. Father McCallum, who had been leaning forward to listen to Richard's testimony about the refund scam, moved back in his seat, or throne as some visitors called it, to consider his response, that is the penance that absolution which Richard deserved. Richard finished his Act of Contrition and waited for Father McCallum to pronounce his sentence. Expecting an entire rosary at least, Richard was more than surprised, if not stunned when Father McCallum asked him if he had any suggestions about his penance, admitting that the recitation of prayers did not seem a sufficient enough penalty for a transgression as significantly sinful as the refund scheme. As Father McCallum was contemplating the penance for Richard, he began to realize that someone senior in the men's wear department could get in trouble once the cause of the scheme was discovered. But with twenty salesmen, not to mention people who dress the mannequins, arrange the furniture on the floor, the domestic workers who clean the men's wear department, and the warehouse men who manage the merchandise, it would be difficult, if not impossible to pin the blame for the crime on anyone in particular. Therefore, since Father McCallum could not ask Richard to identify himself, the confidentiality of confession the grounds, he could only ask him to admit his serious crime to someone in store management. It was to be the penance that he planned to entrust to Richard.

His hands still together in prayer, Richard was waiting for his fate while Father McCallum gave consideration to his penance. Finally, the confessor spoke. "Thank you for a good Act of Contrition. Due to the sin your confessed, which I am sure you know is very serious, I have concluded it could result with someone in store management getting in a lot of trouble for allowing your refund scheme to happen. So as your penance, I am requesting that you take responsibility for what you and your friends did and admit the scheme to your manager. That is your penance. No prayers, just redress for your sin. I hope that you will comply with my request."

Before and During Confession I

It was predictable that Richard spent a good deal of time after his confession with Father McCallum analyzing the possibility of actually admitting to someone in the management of the men's wear department in the T. Eaton department store about potentially fraudulent refunds. However, it wasn't until he related the confession to his supposed partner Randy that he realized an imaginary confession could not be verified no matter what action the confessor took to confirm or deny the details of what he admitted. In fact, Randy waited until Richard was finished with his narrative to laugh and pointed out that it was impossible to support a story that was fictitious. Suddenly, Richard felt as dumb as Randy must have felt when he was repeatedly flunking those grades in elementary school unless of course he was failing on purpose, reason unknown. One thing was obvious. How he overlooked that fact was now difficult to believe. Even Randy pointed that out. They were sitting at the table in the Mercury Tavern preparing to start on their drafts, when Richard suddenly realized that he had known why he had recruited Randy for the project in the first place. He needed him to commit the deeds that he would subsequently explain to various confessors.

In other words, he would outline his idea to Randy, who would presumably execute the plan, after which point Richard would confess its details to a priest and hopefully receive a penance which would require him to seek absolution by making amends by admitting to the deed and providing some sort of restitution. He would have to convince Randy to undertake actions that, while suitable for his scheme, would not get in trouble outside the normal confessional penalties. He would have to assure Randy that he would have to get away with whatever exploit he would recommend. Richard thought that the counterfeit refund scheme, as inventive as it was, could not be employed for any sort of test of his theory regarding confession. That meant that he would have to conceive of an act that he could carry out, confess it to a priest, and hope that the priest gave him a penance that would involve some sort of compensation for the act.

Surprisingly enough, then Randy seemed to understand the circumstances facing Richard and himself. "So you're gonna have to have to come up with a plan for the two of us." Randy concluded and sort of laughed. "And you'll want me to act on whatever thing you come up with." Randy finished his third draft and started on his fourth, his hand up for another couple of beers. For his part, Richard was still working on his third draft. He had a seriously puzzled look on his face. He was flummoxed and Randy recognized his confusion. Randy was casually sipping from his fourth draft when he suddenly put his glass down and brought his right hand to his forehead, lost in thought for a moment. He then looked up at Richard and seemed to have a flash of inspiration. "Look, we both could think of a bad thing that could harm someone. You could then confess to it and hope that the priest gives you what you call a penance that requires you to seek forgiveness, you know like making amends to the person that was harmed by it." Richard just sat there, still puzzled but appearing to contemplate Randy's proposal. For his part, Randy then continued with his proposition, if not completing it. "Maybe we could then see if another penance was given, something that didn't involve prayers." Another interval and then Randy said, "And that I guess is what you are looking for in the end. Right?" Richard picked up his glass, had a swallow of his draft, and quietly responded. "I have to say you're right. That's what I'm looking for I guess." But what thing?

The partners, Randy and Richard, at the conclusion of their recent conference at the Mercury Tavern had agreed that they would continue to exchange ideas on sinful deeds that Richard could confess and seek unusual penances. Richard was particularly bewildered while oddly enough, Randy seemed hardly disturbed by a possible future undertaking with Richard. Strangely enough, within several weeks, it was Randy who was able to generate three or four suggestions that could fit Richard's scheme. He shared the concepts that he had developed with Richard who had not been able to come up with anything worth mentioning to Randy. He was somewhat embarrassed. After all, the confession scheme was his idea but he had been unable to come up with anything that could assist, if not guarantee its possible success. But on the other hand, Randy, who worked in the fruit and vegetable section of a Dominion Store and was not seriously familiar with Richard's confession project, was able to contrive several suggestions that could fulfill the requirement that Richard had set for the next stage of his project.

During the next meeting, six days later at the Mercury Tavern, it having become their usual place, Randy presented his suggestions. His first though probably most difficult proposal involved tampering with the medication taken by an older, if not elderly woman that would result in harm being done to the woman. The suggestion had a certain theatrical panache and could easily fulfill the objective of providing a sinful deed doing harm. But as Richard pointed out almost immediately, the plan was too dangerous, possibly resulting in serious illness, if not death. Further, Richard pointed out that it could be difficult to locate an appropriate target, that is a victim. Randy did not seem unduly disappointed, suggesting that they could also explore the residency of the two local retirement homes, the Stanley and the Park Place. Richard laughed, shook his head and then waited for Randy to share his second suggestion.

"I don't like the guy I work for, Jack Talbot. He's a complete prick, the only person in the whole place who can actually stand him is the store manager Jacques Choquette. So I thought that I'd make it look like he is stealing stuff from the store and hiding it in his house. But I would be doing the stealing, breaking into his house and leaving the merchandise in his basement." Richard smiled and offered a positive review of his suggestion. "That sounds like it might fit. And you would have to admit to the scam if my confessor gives me the right penance." Randy nodded, returned Richard's smile and began to tell him about the third suggestion. "I thought about stealing someone's car, using it for some sort of crime and then abandoning it so that the cops would find it. And" Richard continued Randy's explanation, "the car's owner would be charged with the crime even though he wasn't driving the car." Then, Randy took over the dialogue, "You confess the thing, the priest tells you to take responsibility, you admit that you did it, without allowing yourself to be arrested send the police a letter or something and we'll see what happens. Everybody's happy, right?"

The two of them looked at each other for a minute or so, presumably reflecting on Randy's suggested misdeeds and then Richard said that he preferred blaming the theft of store merchandise on Randy's boss as the act to be confessed. However, he did caution Randy not to steal anything from the store until he thought about it further. They then finished their beers, paid their tabs and headed out. They had agreed that they would continue considering possible deeds for confession and meet again in another week or so. Randy asked if Richard was still interested in the project, a question that was not unexpected. Richard said that he would hopefully have an answer to any doubts Randy had within the week. He hoped he would have an answer. In other words, something that would fit the scheme. He liked Randy's second suggestion.

It came to Richard almost in the middle of the night. It was behaviour with which he had been quite familiar and maybe quite proficient in his youth, particularly when he was twelve, thirteen and maybe fourteen. Shoplifting, it was shoplifting, something that was recreation for him and some of his friends during those years. He thought of several particularly memorable incidents of small time shoplifting, usually involving thievery of snacks and the like at local stores, including the Dominion Store where ironically enough his current partner Randy Novacheck has worked for years. One of their habitual pilfering activities concerned the theft of a selection of snack cakes, including most particularly the desert called Jos Louis. Regarding the latter, Richard and some of his pals, including Jack and his brother Steve, would regularly steal dozens of Jos Louis from grocery stores along with some large sodas, retire to an empty bus enclosure or train station, enjoy their stolen snacks and sodas until they were close to heaving and then go home, spattering whatever they hadn't consumed all over the walls of the enclosure or station. In reliving his career as a thief, he also recalled that he had attempted a number of times to convince his fellow burglars to expand their repertoire into breaking into neighbourhood houses. While they never undertook that particular career change, he had heard two younger boys from the neighbourhood, John McKay and his friend Jimmy, had started breaking into houses. Nevertheless, they were eventually picked up by the police when Jimmy tried to sell several television sets to a local pawn broker. He later heard that one of them, Jimmy obviously, drew six months at the juvenile detention facility. He thought that his pal John was still in high school. Jimmy may also be in high school although only occasionally.

In the event of that memory, a daydream appeared in his head, a notion that could have suited his confession project, certainly more appropriate than the three so-called acts that Randy had suggested. Richard could confess to a priest that he had broken into several houses, possibly remove items of value and then trash the place. When he was aware that someone, almost most likely Randy, would have to take action that would confirm somehow the iniquitous deeds his partner Richard had confessed to the priest. While he knew that he could provide a priest with an imaginary sin and precipitate an uncommon penance, without actual robberies that police could investigate and insurance companies could pay out, he would be unable to substantiate the theory he had about certain confessions. So he would have to convince Randy to break into a house, steal some of the owners' belongings and assume that any attempt to confirm the robbery would be successful, that is if the priest to which Richard confessed the robbery ordered him to admit the burglary and pursue some sort of remedial action. It seemed a gamble but it always had been.

Within six days of their last meeting at the Mercury Tavern, Richard and Randy got together again at what was becoming their customary haunt. Initially, Randy seemed fairly cordial, not his usual deportment when he first sat down, at least until he got two or three drafts into himself. Apparently, Randy had received a cheque from Dominion for the overtime he had done the previous month and therefore was quite happy. In that event, Randy ordered five drafts instead of his usual four and exchanged quips with the waiter. Richard ordered his usual three drafts and decided to take advantage of Randy's good mood to introduce his newly conceived plan. Randy had already consumed two drafts when Richard first raised his new plan with him. There was a lull in the proceedings, Randy had started watching golf on television, when Richard introduced what he thought was a good plan for what he was still referring to as the "confession scheme".

He started his presentation by describing to Randy the origins of his most recent proposition. "It just came to me during the middle of the night. I was just laying there in bed waiting for inspiration when it came to me. I was wondering about my shoplifting days, when my friends and I were eleven and twelve. You know, we would take snacks and sodas from grocery stores, including Dominion's, eat as many snacks and drink as many sodas as we could." Randy was obviously interested in the part of the story about stealing from the Dominion store. He snickered. Richard continued with his narrative, his shoplifting reminiscence then morphing into the history of his brief career as a B&E man. "In any event, it got me thinking that I could confess to a house robbery and then hope that the priest that I drew gives me a penance that requires me to pay for it somehow. That means that the deed would have to attract the attention of the police or an insurance company or somebody and that means that the act would have to be real, and not some figment of my imagination. So someone, I mean you, must break into a place, steal some stuff, tell me about it and I pass that along to a priest in confession."

Then Randy, who had been listening with obvious interest, interrupted him to finish his partner's thought. "And the priest gives you a penance that orders you to make it right, you know like admitting that the stuff was stolen or you are willing to return the stuff that was stolen." Richard nodded. Then Randy then continued. "You know we'd still have a problem. Are we going to actually volunteer that we broke into this house and stole some items from this house? I mean, what do you expect you or I to do? Turn ourselves into the cops? You're kidding?" And with that remark, Randy practically slammed his glass down on the table and went on to his next beer. Richard raised his hand and responded to Randy's apprehensions, "I've thought about that. I realize that it's a problem, a big problem. But I figure that we could either telephone the cops or send them a letter or something. Either way, you or I won't have to turn ourselves in. I think that will satisfy the conditions of whatever penance the confessor gives me. The priest has to know that the theft was real."

Randy looked confused, looking across the table as if he did not understand most of what Richard had just told him. So it was no surprise then when he asked Richard for further explanation, specifically that he was worried that he might get in trouble if they went ahead with the plan. Richard further clarified the details of his plan, emphasizing that it would highly unlikely that either of them would have to actually find themselves in the company of police. "As long as the priest who took the confession ends up believing that the sin was actually committed, my project would result in an outcome that might be worth considering, if not studying further. I know that you probably don't understand but I still think that the way confession is managed could be expanded." It is clear that Randy did not quite understand Richard's musings on confession, his comprehension of the theological implications of his deliberations minimal. He listened but had graduated to being only mildly concerned with whether he would get in trouble with the law if he continued to help Richard with his project. Now assured somewhat he wasn't risking anything, aside from the possibility he would have to select a house they would have to break into, be certain the place was empty and contained belongings worth stealing, remove some of those belongings, and leave the house with some minor damage, not major vandalism but enough to convince the residents that it had indeed been robbed of things worth reporting to the local police and the insurance company, that is if the things were in fact insured.

Appropriately assured by Richard, who was still at pains to convince Randy that his role in the confession project was secure, which in a way wasn't really necessary since Randy was in the end much more adventurous, if not more the sinner than Richard, the scheme seemed ready for implementation. Richard was, therefore, ready to begin his plan, prepared to visit confession as soon as he was able. He decided to continue to seek absolution from one of the Jesuit priests available to provide spiritual adjudication in the Saint Ignatius chapel. Before proceeding, however, Randy did caution Richard that he himself should complete the deed about which he intended to confess should any discrepancies arise between his confession and any eventual evidence that may be discovered. Richard immediately agreed, surprised that Randy rather than himself would remember to be so vigilant. Fact was he was understandably embarrassed although he did not allow Randy to be aware of his discomfort. He simply said that he would wait to take confession until he was familiar with the complete details of the deed he was about to reveal. Randy said that he would need time to break into a place and steal a few things. Maybe several weeks.

He had decided to target a house that was about a mile north of the Mercury Tavern. It was located on Broadview Street. It was a moderate three bedroom bungalow on a fairly large lot. After watching the family that lived in the house, a father, a mother, and three children, for a week or so, he discovered that they owned a small cottage on a lake in the Laurentians and would spend practically every weekend there in the spring, summer and autumn. Any weekend night therefore would give him an opportunity to burglarize the place. His surveillance activities also resulted in confirming that the family usually left for the cottage immediately after the father arrived home from work on Friday and came home on Sunday afternoon. In addition, to further improve his plans, three sides of the property were lined by spruce hedges that were at least six feet high and could therefore conceal anyone attempting to sneak onto the property. He also took note of the fact that the basement windows in the rear of the house looked to be vulnerable to anyone considering breaking into the house. One of the windows looked to be partially unlocked, making entrance even easier.

So he decided that he would enter the house the next Saturday night, obviously a late night entry would be the best approach, Randy having already assured himself that there were no lights on in any of the surrounding houses. Around midnight would probably be the most effective timing. He also thought it prudent not to share his plans with Richard, choosing to wait until he had successfully entered the house he had targeted and removed some of the family's possessions.

On the next Saturday night, maybe fifteen minutes after midnight, Randy entered the house he had selected, slipping through the frame of the basement window which he had removed, his initial impression that the window was partially unlocked not being entirely accurate. He stumbled into what appeared to be the father's workshop, stepping on a wooden table on which a variety of tools lay. A hammer had fallen to the floor. It made a fairly loud noise but he was confident that no one would hear it, the house empty. He stepped gingerly around a collection of paint cans, paint brushes, turpentine, unused wooden slats, a pile of vehicle licenses of previous years, a stack of old Eaton's catalogues and hanging from the ceiling a variety of Christmas decorations. Randy briefly explored the rest of the basement, locating a laundry room, a freezer, and a clumsily constructed playroom with a lumpy tile floor, a television set, a large Victorian era sofa, two equally ancient chairs, a coffee table with a multitude of gouges, and under the table a large glass ashtray holding a bunch of cigarette butts and two empty quart bottles of Dow's Kingsbeer. There was nothing worth liberating in either the workshop, the laundry room, or the playroom. He turned and started up the stairs to the first floor with the kitchen, the living room, the dining room, the three bedrooms, and the bathroom. Hopefully, he'd find something worth stealing.

He avoided the kitchen, figuring that there would be nothing of any value there and went left into the connected dining room/living room where he first noticed a chandelier over a polished antique oak dining table. Between the table and the window was a matching cabinet which predictably held more than a dozen bottles of various liquors and several types of glasses, including four crystal goblets. He then searched another set of drawers which contained dinnerware, silver cutlery and different coloured cotton napkins. Immediately adjacent was the living room where there was nothing of any real value or could be removed without difficulty: a sofa, three chairs, one of which was embroidered with wool and the other two were made of velvet fabric, a large colour television set in a wooden cabinet with the screen surrounded by books, a stereo system in another wooden cabinet, three mediocre landscape paintings and a light blue curtain over the front window. Finally, a wall to wall navy blue carpet covered the entire first floor except for the washroom. Richard limited his search to the two small bedrooms, which he assumed housed the three boys, one of them featuring a bunk bed, and a large bedroom which presumably housed the parents. He concluded that he would invest some time and effort in exploring the parents' bedroom. He looked out the parents' window. There was nothing to see.

He first started to inspect the mother's jewellery box, which was sitting on the smaller of the two dressers in the large bedroom, the one with a large rectangular mirror. Inside, he found several pieces of costume jewellery, a couple of necklaces, one a gold colour, the other maroon, two small black and white photographs that could have been pictures of the family taken in the fifties, a diamond ring that looked fairly expensive and a silver crucifix maybe a foot in height. Randy immediately pocketed the ring, his first trophy in his search, and thought that it may be enough to satisfy Richard's scheme. On the other hand, there was still more drawers of the mother's dresser as well as what he assumed was the father's dresser, which was a large and expensive piece of furniture that dominated the room. He thought that there could be other treasures that could be used by Richard in any future confession. So he searched the dressers. While he couldn't find anything of value in the drawers of the mother's dresser, Randy did come across a black leather album hidden under several sweaters in the bottom drawer of the father's dresser. The album was identified as a "Coin Collection Book" that was embossed in gold lettering on the front of the album. Randy lifted it out of the drawer and examined it. There must have been maybe twenty pages of antique coins that were inserted in slots, the coins divided by domination, from pennies to dollar coins.

Even looking at the first couple of pages of the album, which held one cent coins, Randy detected that many of the coins were presumably valuable, minted well before the turn of the century. In addition, most of them looked to be in pretty good shape, some of them almost pristine. Flipping through the album, about a quarter of which contained pennies, he counted that there were four pages of nickels and dimes respectively, three pages of quarters, one page of fifty cent pieces and a half page of dollar coins, three of the six also dated in the late nineteenth century. Randy immediately realized that the coin album would be enough for Richard to confess its theft to a priest. The crucifix, although worth not nearly as much as the coin album, could have a sentimental, if not a religious meaning to the mother, if not the family. It was, after all, a meaningful artifact. That could also have a serious impact on the feelings of the family, which alone could have suited Richard's conditions for a special confession. Consequentially, he deemed a search of the clothing closet as unnecessary. Finally, as he crept out of the parents' bedroom, he noticed that there were two large black and white photographs of who Randy assumed were the parents of the family. Both of the portraits appeared to have been taken by a photographic studio possibly twenty years ago, maybe before they were married. He quietly left the house through its backdoor. He never knew the family's name. Finally, he never bothered to vandalize the place.

Randy telephoned Richard the next day. They planned to met the next evening to discuss the theft of the mementos from the house he had burglarized the previous Saturday. Richard was quite pleased and congratulated Randy for his efforts. He told Randy that he intended to visit Saint Ignatius the following Wednesday to take confession. He also advised Randy to hold on to the possessions he had stolen from the house. Richard also suggested that he canvas the city's coin dealers to determine the value of the coins in the album that he stole.

After Confession I

As usual, they met at the Mercury Tavern. It was there that Randy informed Richard that the coin collection, which he brought into three coin dealers he had selected from the city telephone book, were valued at anywhere from eight to ten thousand dollars. One of the dealers, an older man who looked like he had just been released from jail had asked Randy about the origin of the collection. He had a slight sneer on his face. Randy said that he told the inquisitive coin dealer that his father was thinking of selling the collection, which he had been assembling since he was a boy, and wanted some idea of their value. Randy asked if Richard wanted him to canvas any other coin dealers, suggesting that perhaps there were other dealers in the city. He admitted that he had selected the three coin dealers because they were located in the west end of the city, the other dealers he had found were located in the east end. Randy commented that he had been informed that the east end was known, among other things, for both coin dealers and pawn brokers.

Regarding the latter, Randy then asked Richard for his opinion as to whether he should approach any of the pawn brokers with the diamond ring and maybe even the silver crucifix.

Richard said that while the latter could be a good idea, it was probably not worth the effort. Finally, Randy also assured Richard that he never personally introduced himself to any of the dealers. They were both into their third beers when Richard said that he was prepared to confess to the theft of the coin collection and see what sort of the result would occur. Further to Richard's question, Randy said that the coin collection, the diamond ring and the crucifix safely in the top drawer of the dresser in his bedroom. Richard remarked on the irony of the current location of the three items, a reference to where the stolen items were found. Randy had a blank look on his face. Richard raised a beer glass to Randy and toasted him. The recipient of the salutation returned the gesture and asked. "Are you sure that this is going to work?"

Richard replied in the affirmative, "I plan to attend morning mass at Saint Ignatius chapel next Wednesday. Like a couple of previous times I attended confession in the chapel, I'll visit the confessional before mass starts and hope that the Jesuit priest who hears my request for amends doesn't recognize me." Randy seemed surprised and wondered why any confessor could identify anybody who admitted their sins to him. He may have thought that the confidentiality of confession also applied not only to what penitents said but also how they looked. Richard answered with a shrug of his shoulders and explained his caution. "Well, you just can't be sure. There aren't that many Jesuits who hear confessions at the chapel. And most of whom teach in the high school and the college. I don't know, I just want to be sure." Again, Randy was still a little confused but did not continue to pursue the question of whether Richard could be recognized in a confessional in the Saint Ignatius chapel. He simply dropped the issue.

The two of them then discussed likely future developments once Richard confessed to whichever Jesuit priest was fortunate enough to hear his declarations. Richard explained that most, if not the entire scheme was contingent on whether the confessor decided to provide him with a penance that could substitute for the normal result of the sacrament of confession, generally the recitation of prayers, that being a measure that would compensate for the impact of the sin confessed. That would mean either demonstrating the transgression outside the confines of confession and then paying for it somehow. If such a penance and proof was not forthcoming, then the confession and theft would simply be seen a standard ritual of a Roman Catholic sacrament. Randy then asked how such a penance could be demonstrated. Richard explained that some sort of authority, like police, an insurance company, or even a neighbour would have to substantiate the deed. "In other words, the sin and therefore the penance would have to be real, not imaginary. We talked about it before. Remember?" Randy slowly nodded and then looked off into the corner of the Mercury Tavern with an empty look on his face. "So I guess we'll just have to wait.", Randy concluded. This time, it was Richard who did the the nodding.

It was the next Wednesday a little after eight o'clock in the morning that Richard ventured into a confessional in the Saint Ignatius Chapel. According to a small sign affixed to the middle door of the confessional, penitent revelations were to be heard by Father James Hodgins. Richard did not recognize the name although he hadn't been in high school for several years and Father Hodgins, who was young and for all he knew, was a recent addition to the high school faculty. Richard was alone that morning in seeking a hearing for absolution. Aside from Father Hodgins and himself, there were only three other people in the chapel, two elderly ladies accompanied by a younger women who was almost certainly one of old women's nurses. Richard approached the confessional, opened one of its ornate doors, and the light in the closet in which Father Hodgins sat was extinguished. Once Richard knelt down in his booth and the screen between he and Father Hodgins was slid open, the slight shadow of the confessor appeared. The scent of maybe cologne or perfume wafted through the booth. Richard thought that it might have been the residue of a fragrance left from a previous occupant of the penitent's booth, presumably an older woman. It was a distraction from the case of nerves that was percolating somewhere in his nervous system. Even though Richard was extensively experienced with attending confession, particularly since his confession plan had come to him, he was still anxious.

Father Hodgins leaned closer to the screen, obviously waiting for Richard the penitent to begin his confession. Richard greeted the priest with the Sign of the Cross and recited the expected words, "Bless me, Father, for I have sinned. My last confession was six weeks ago." His recollection of the date of his last confession exact given the requirements of his project. Father Hodgins slightly moved in his seat and waited. Predictably, Richard began his confession with the major and only action, the sole purpose of his visit, the breaking and entering into the house with the hedges and the theft of several items from that house. Father Hodgins then asked about the items which Richard had confessed to removing from the house. Richard told him, at least about the coin collection, deciding not to mention the ring or the crucifix. Father Hodgins then asked, his voice lower than its normal hushed volume, if Richard knew the value of the coin collection. He replied, relating that he had consulted three coin dealers and that at least one had provided him with an estimate, the figure anywhere between eight to ten thousand dollars. Father Hodgins leaned back in his throne, his head on the top cushion, appearing to do some thinking, his chin in his left hand. Richard was staring through the screen of the stall, expecting Father Hodgins to assign him a penance.

Finally, after a few minutes had passed, the good Father shared his thoughts. "As you probably know, a penance, any penance must support the spiritual good of the penitent. I know that you probably think that I will decide to ask you to recite several decades of the rosary if not the entire rosary. I can, however, assign you some sort of work of mercy, a service or sacrifice. In cases involving violations of the eighth commandment, that is "Thou shall not steal." I have in the past asked penitents to receive absolution by returning any stolen property.

I am therefore asking you, as your penance, to return the things you stole." Richard was mildly shocked when Father Hodgins issued the penance he was to receive. While it was generally along the line that he and the project he had conceived had anticipated, it was secular retribution, not involving prayers or any other spiritual action. Because the penance did not require the sinner to suffer harm in any way, like if Father Hodgins had required him to report the theft to either the authorities or maybe even the owners of the house which he had burglarized, it was not quite the penance he had hoped for. The other possibility would be to be seized by the authorities for breaking, entering and burglary. Richard was seriously disappointed, being told to return the items that his partner Randy had lifted from the neighbourhood house rather than face any punitive misfortunes.

Richard then recited an Act of Contrition, expressing as intended his sorrow not only for the theft his partner Randy had committed but also subconsciously for the penance which had resulted from his confession.

Two days later, Friday evening after Randy finished his shift at the Dominion store, he and Richard met at the Mercury Tavern to discuss his confession with Father Hodgins. Of course, Randy was eagerly looking forward to their meeting. Upon arrival, both quickly attracted the attention of their favourite waiter, ordered four drafts each before they ever found a table, and sat down. Once the drafts arrived, Randy expected Richard to immediately report his exchange in the confessional with Father Hodgins. Richard took a quick swallow and began his account, surprising as it was. After finishing his first draft and starting on his second, Randy leaned over the table to listen to Richard. It was almost as if Richard was whispering. He wasn't, his narrative being delivered in a normal tone.

"I have to admit that I was surprised, really surprised. The priest I drew, his name was Father Hodgins, listened intently as I confessed to breaking into the house and lifting a coin collection and the two other items left unmentioned. But instead of a normal penance, you know like decades of the beads or going to mass every morning for a week or more, Father Hodgins ordered me to return the stolen goods." Randy allowed some beer to dribble out of his mouth and lifted his head up to stare at Richard. Sounding mildly surprised, barely able to be heard over the clamour of the Mercury Tavern, he managed to comment on Richard's report, as difficult it seemed to believe. "Can't believe it. You almost got the kind of penance you wanted but instead of paying for a sin, you're asked to take action to show that it didn't happen in the first place." Randy hung his head for a moment, took another gulp of beer, and then commented again. "Return the loot! Difficult to believe." Randy then asked Richard what he wanted to do. Richard answered with a certain glum inflection in his voice. "I think the only thing we can do now is to follow Father Hodgins' instructions and return the stuff. I mean, it's probably the only thing we can do, the only thing we should do."

Randy silently exclaimed, as quietly as he could. "The only thing? The only thing? There must be another thing we can do. Must be." It was obvious that Richard had thought about the situation for at least the two days since he had been surprised by the penance that he had received from Father Hodgins. He then provided Randy with the results of his contemplation. "I don't think we have any other choice. I know we could get as much as $10,000 for the coin collection and maybe more for the ring and the crucifix but then you would be vulnerable to being identified as the thief. I mean, I would imagine that coin dealers are pretty good as remembering amateurs asking to sell old coins and sharing that information with the authorities. I don't think you or I can afford to be that vulnerable. At least, if the stolen goods are returned, they won't have any reason to complain to anyone. Maybe even they won't even know they're missing." Randy then asked about whether Richard would want to continue with his project. "Well, at least the confession with Father Hodgins proved that some confessors assign penances depending on the sin." Randy nodded and then asked whether Richard expected him to return the goods to the house from which they were stolen. He nodded.

Randy looked a little mystified. He then swallowed a full draft. He then signalled for another round. Richard wasn't ready. He was still sitting behind two drafts. The two of them sat in silence until three more drafts were placed in front of Randy who then continued to express his hesitation about Richard's plan to make good on the penance that Father Hodgins had assigned him. He observed. "Do you really think that the family has not noticed the items I took are missing? But if they have, maybe it will be more difficult for anyone to break into the house. You know — the instalment of new basement windows, that sort of thing." Richard interrupted, pointing out an alternative. "Well, if breaking into the house a second time looks too difficult, you can just leave the stuff by the backdoor or something." While still reluctant, Randy agreed with Richard's suggestion. "Weird but okay." They then went back to drinking their beers.

After confirming that the family still went to their cottage on weekends and after surveying the property long enough to assure himself that there would still not much in the way of danger in breaking into the house, Randy choose the Saturday evening in eight days to return the stuff to the house. On the appointed Saturday evening around midnight or so, he crept across the lawn toward one of the basement windows. He and a small navy blue bag which carried a diamond ring, a silver crucifix and a coin collection in a black leather album. He was compelled to crawl rather than walk towards the rear of the house, noticing that someone was still awake in the second floor bedroom of the house on the street behind the house he was about to enter. Randy was relieved when he realized that the window through which he was about to enter the house was even easier than previously. The window frame which he had removed when he first entered the house had not been replaced. He was then standing in the father's workshop which seemed to be in the same ramshackle shape it was when he entered the house two weeks ago.

It didn't take Randy long to enter the parents' room. He took the mother's diamond ring and silver crucifix out of the navy blue bag and placed them in the top drawer of her dresser, wondering again whether anyone had noticed that they were missing. He then turned to the father's chest of drawers and carefully put the black leather album with the coin collection into its bottom drawer. His mission accomplished, Randy started out of the house and was out the unlocked back door in minutes. The light on the second floor of the house facing the backyard of the house was still on.

BACK TO THE CHURCH

After Randy fulfilled the conditions of the penance that Father Hodgins had given Richard, he found himself again bewildered by the circumstances facing him in the pursuit of this study of confession. After the results of the first experiment with seeking absolution from Father James Hodgins, in which he received an admittedly unusual penance, specifically that three purloined items be returned to the house from which they were stolen, he didn't know what to do next. The episode, with the assistance of his associate Randy Novacheck, was able to demonstrate that certain confessors assign unique penances for otherwise sinful acts. That left Richard to face a serious dilemma, specifically how to test any theory that may emerge if he were able to persuade an individual priest or more than one individual priest to assign penances to penitents that would somehow cause as much damage to themselves as they had caused to others by the original transgressions. The only incident that Richard had to interpret involved a penance that did not cause damage which had have been caused by the transgression itself. It was obvious that Richard would have to devise a scenario within which the punishment was somehow equivalent to the sin that precipitated it. He was profoundly confused. He was thinking too much.

He could have employed one of the examples that he had been given over the time he had been working on the confession scheme, using examples involving thievery at a bank and a department store. In those cases, the penances specified penalties that had nothing to do with prayers or any other religious measures. So Richard faced a question of formulating a deed that would lead, if it were to be confessed to a compliant priest, to a penance that required the penitent to obtain contrition by taking action that would somehow reverse the original sin. The difference between the examples that Richard had been given by Father McCallum and the example of home burglary committed by Randy Novacheck was that there was no negative effect on the victim of the robbery. In fact, following the penance handed out by Father Hodgins, there was no effect whatsoever.

Richard had to come up with an offence that definitely caused harm to the target of the misdeed. In other words, whoever ended up being victimized by the sin would have to be absolved by action required by any penance that may eventually be assigned by an perceptive priest. The examples provided by Father McCallum involved individuals who lost their livelihoods due to accusations of misconduct committed by others. As penances, Father McCallum required the two sinners to admit their sins so that the falsely accused could be exonerated. In both cases, however, there was never any evidence that the falsely accused managed to get their jobs back. Father McCallum had told Richard that he expected the penitents to either approach the bank or the department store or the police or even the press to admit their guilt and by implication exonerate the two individuals who lost their jobs because they were falsely implicated by the sinners who had visited Father McCallum. In other words, the entire confession project was getting unduly complicated.

Another obstacle standing in the way of continuing with the confession plan was the developing reluctance of his partner Randy Novacheck to persist with his participation in the project. It had been almost two months since the two of them had first discussed the matter, as usual over draft beers at the Mercury Tavern. At that time, Randy said that he did not intend to talk about confession until Richard could convince him of the project's purpose. Richard eventually did but he began to admit that the project began to look progressively pointless. He admitted that he had to find a strategy that required the penitent to repent for his sin by taking action that would repair any damage suffered by the victim of the sin. Richard agreed with Randy that there could never be a guarantee that such a penance would be assigned by a specific confessor no matter what kind of transgression was confessed but he said that another plan would have to be considered. Randy suggested that they delay their next meeting until either of them could come up with another idea.

Richard asked Randy if he had any suggestions. After all, Richard pointed out, the two of them had been discussing the confession plan for more than two months, if not longer. During that period, Richard must have introduced or at least thought of a number of proposed strategies for actions that could be portrayed as sins for purposes of confession and more importantly for the inevitable result of penance. Randy shrugged. "Hey, you're the guy in college and I'm just a guy who works in Dominion. You're the guy who should have the ideas. Besides, this whole confession thing is your scheme. You're the one who should have ideas as to how to prove whatever it is you want to prove." Randy then almost started to cackle. In response, Richard emitted a quiet chuckle and then maybe a snicker. There was a pause and then Richard began to explain the reason behind his apparent laugh. "I have almost forgotten what it is that I'm trying to prove anyway." Randy joined Richard in faintly laughing. "Well, I kind of understood what you were trying to do but like you, maybe I kind of forgot, that is if I ever knew in the first place." Randy downed the rest of his draft, let out a satisfied belch, and again laughed. Richard joined him, although without the belch. The two of them then faced each other over their beers, silently quaffing for a few minutes. The evening was coming to a close.

The two of them paid their tabs and got up to leave the Mercury Tavern. Richard reached out and grasped Randy by the forearm. The former looked at the latter with more than a glance. Randy turned over his shoulder and waited for comment. Richard then provided that comment. "I let you know when I can come up with something. I'll try to make sure that it is foolproof. Word of honour." Despite that vow, Randy offered him what may have looked like a smug smile and a slight nod of his head. Richard wondered when he would next talk to Randy. As for where, he would know. The two of them walked out of the Mercury Tavern together.

Over the next several weeks, Richard spent a fair amount of time pondering another strategy for prevailing on a priest to assign him a penance that would balance the harm caused by the sin. He had known for some time that he had to devise a wrong that would prompt the confessor to consider and possibly assign the right penance. In that regard, Richard was suddenly encouraged by a thought that had occurred to him while he was again bemoaning his unfortunate fate sitting in the college library. What if, he thought, he were to provide a sin that had an unfortunate impact on a diocese, a church, or an individual priest for that matter. Connecting the damaging action to any element of the institution of the church could have produced the kind of outcome that Richard wanted in terms of penance. He concluded that once confessed, a sin that was an affront to the church or some individual from the church could culminate in that result. Such a misdeed, once confessed, could lead to that result.

In that spirit, Richard recalled the theft of a priestly garment, an article of clothing called a chasuble, that he and a couple of his friends accidentally engineered many years ago. Aside from an unsuccessful attempt to pawn the garment, he visited confession in a downtown church, Notre-Dame de Lourdes. The priest who had heard the confession suggested that he return the garment to the priest that had worn it. He was kidding or at least Richard thought he was kidding. He immediately settled on a penance of several decades of the rosary. On the other hand, further to his request, he did allow him to leave the garment in one of the pews in the church. In other words, Richard's confessor was facetiously suggesting a penance that was similar in effect to the penance that had been assigned by Father Hodgins resulting from his confession about the Randy's theft of the coin collection, the diamond ring and the silver crucifix. It was unfortunate, therefore, that he could not consider asking Randy or anyone else for that matter to take any sinful action that could as a consequence led to a penance that was adequate compensation for a transgression, no matter how serious.

Richard still thought, however, that accusing someone associated with the church in some sinful act was still worth pursuing, given the likely sensitivity with respect to anything that could bring shame on it. Since stealing articles that belonged or could have belonged to the church in any way was not likely available for his scheme, Richard would have to come up with some other endeavour. After continuing to draw a blank about any new proposal for a couple of days, Richard had a notion that unexpectedly came to him while he was barely watching a detective show on television called *Columbo.* He was alone, smoking cigarettes, drinking pints of Labatt Fifty and wondering about his continuing lack of inspiration regarding the confession scheme. Fact was he was close to abandoning the entire project, despairing of any expectation that he would be able to come to a decision about another scheme that would convince a priest to assign to him a penance that would be unusual enough to support his interest in possible confessions that could go beyond the normal religious retribution.

It was undoubtedly predictable. Although he could not be certain about the basis, his mind drifted away from the television to his now continuing obsession. He again recalled the theft of the church vestment. Almost reflexively, he thought of the simple penance that Richard received from Father Hodgins when he confessed to the theft that Randy had successfully arranged: return the items that were originally stolen. He then started again wondering whether a sin involving the church, once confessed, could precipitate the kind of penance that Richard was looking for. The *Columbo* episode was over and a few scenes from next week's show were shown. Richard turned off the television and hoped that something useful would come to him.

Richard got up the next morning with a notion that had never occurred to him before. He had previously concluded that churches had a particular interest, if not sensitivity to anything that could be interpreted as a sin against them. It was likely that had Richard and his co-conspirators been aware of any reaction that their church would have exhibited to their theft of the priestly vestment from its sacristy, they would have realized their assumed sensitivity. Richard concluded therefore that if an action he intended to confess was connected in any way to the church it would result in the kind of penance that he was likely searching for. So he could ask Randy, if he was agreeable, to steal a church article and hope that a penance following Richard's confessing to the theft did not require him to return the item or items to the church. Regarding the latter concern, he pondered the possibility that a penance could not result in the outcome for which he had hoped. Accordingly, he concluded that he would have to determine some other kind of transgression to commit and confess.

Rather than outright theft, a tried and true violation of a commandment, Richard began to consider other violations serious enough to merit significant attention from church authorities. He considered embezzlement or larceny of church funds, similar to the recalled example that he had heard from Father Graham about the bank or department store managers who were fired after being accused of certain acts of culpability. Richard theorized that if he were to somehow incriminate a priest of a blameworthy deed, that might create circumstances that would significantly interest him when it came to his confession. It was obvious, at least to Richard, that a confession involving misconduct by a member of the church might result in, if not guarantee an unusual penance. It would be a convenient fiction.

Although he thought he had established a method by which the confession of a sin would result in a penance that would likely require extraordinary action, that is, something to do with the theft of church possessions or church funds, Richard doubted whether either of the two churches he had in mind, either Saint John Fisher where he lived or Saint Ignatius where he attended school, were prosperous enough to provide enough possessions or funds to provide opportunities for theft. In other words, it would probably be more advantageous to select another example of misconduct that could precipitate priests from either church to take particular notice. So he decided to consider accusing a priest in either church of some sort of sexual impropriety, serious malfeasance regardless of either the specific circumstances of the sin accused or its victim. Aside from a possible confession, such an allegation would have to be reported to police authorities, regardless of the evidence offered in the confession. Such a circumstance could easily discourage church officials from handling penalty or punishment within its own authority, meaning that penance, if any was assigned, would be handled by civil rather than religious officials.

ANOTHER PROPOSAL

I t could have been more than a month, during which time he frequently pondered, and obsessed about the folly of his previous failures of imaginary confessions. He fantasized about future projects that would somehow satisfy his aspiration for a different kind of absolution for a formal declaration of sin to a priest. The apparently unexpected sins he thought he had envisaged for his project were on reflection predictable and therefore not likely to result in the kind of sentence or sentences that he had hoped for. He had thought that the transgressions he had provided to the selected confessors were profane enough to result in more than the predictable ways of restitution. Instead, his objective remained to determine if any confessor assigned any penance in any confession that directed the sinner to suffer penalties that harmed the transgressor. It was starting to seem impossible.

He realized that he had been attempting to fabricate and confess misdeeds that would give rise to exceptional penalties, like the kind of measures that civil authorities would provide in event of such misdeeds, some of which could even approach major crimes. Aside from possibly going beyond relatively minor criminal activities, Richard began imagining the kind of action that could attract serious police interest. Maybe he would have to involve a collaborator other than Randy Novacheck. Fact was that he had begun to believe that he was empty of alternatives, having exhausted the two lists with which he had to conjure, the ten commandments and the seven deadly sins. He had either made use of violations of those commandments with which he was well familiar, bearing false witness and stealing for example, or considered several of the seven death sins, most of which seemed wicked enough to merit serious recrimination. Besides, if he were to confess to behaviours like gluttony, greed or sloth, he would have to demonstrate to certain actions that had originated in such sentiments, such notions giving rise to actual sins, sins that could result in penance being meted out by interested confessors. Regardless, he was generally bewildered by his predicament. Again, he was prepared to abandon the project. It was within that same month that his next inspiration arrived like it had originated somewhere in the outer limits of perdition. At first, he thought he was having a bad dream, a nightmare reminding him of the the most forbidding confession he had ever attended. It was the ultimate in transgression. Or so he thought. He realized that he was to admit in a confessional that he had committed a fundamentally immoral act that violated the highest doctrine, the most serious precept of the Catholic faith. So it was that he was thinking of confessing to a murder, whether it was fictional or not, concluding that and that alone would provoke an extraordinary response. He had considered the prospect previously, rejecting it as too radical, too extraordinary, too difficult to be heard, let alone to be believed inside a confessional by a member of the clergy, no matter how experienced he may have been with sins confessed. He contemplated the ambition, no matter how eccentric, no matter how unusual, no matter how unlucky to result in any sin as grave as murder.

At first, that is by the time he had been contemplating the possibility of confessing to a murder, it occurred to him that he would likely have to convince his erstwhile partner Randy Novacheck to assist him in such a scheme. He came to realize that there would have to be a corpse to possibly convince a confessor that a penitent who might have disclosed an actual killing in confession was not prevaricating for whatever reason. On the other hand, Richard might have researched the press looking for unidentified dead bodies that could be associated with such a revelation. That would be a much less perilous alternative if he was to decide on such a confession. While an unlikely possibility, given Richard's research of newspapers over the previous six weeks or so not resulting in any remains that were suspected to have come to an unnatural end, it still seemed a more favourable opportunity than waiting for Randy Novacheck or some other homicidal collaborator to provide evidence of a murder that Richard would confess to a priest.

So as reluctant as he was about the alternative plan, he decided that he would investigate local murders in the college library until he came across any appropriate stories reporting murders. He would try to ensure that any suspected murder that was reported would be recent enough to be a credible admission in any confession. In that context, he came to the conclusion that any story about a suspected murder victim that Richard could reasonably connect to not just to himself, as the perpetrator but also to having knowledge about the circumstances of the murder itself. Within hours of concluding that the latter scenario was a reasonable alternative to an actual murder, he realized that it was a direct plagiarism of the plot of a television show. He was faced with the confidentiality of the confessional and therefore could not reveal the contents of the confession to the authorities despite the fact that it would exculpate a man falsely punished for a murder that he did not commit. While Richard was mildly concerned with the ethics of using a story, which fictional, was not his to use, whatever qualms he may have seemed irrelevant once he pondered the matter for a time.

It took more than a month before Richard came across a short article in the *Montreal Gazette* relating the story of an unidentified middle aged man who was found dead past midnight in the doorway of a shop in the Little Burgundy area by two police officers. The deceased man, who looked like he was killed within hours of when he was found, was likely beaten with what could have been a piece of lumber or steel rebar. The press article, which was comprised of four short paragraphs, reported that the man was likely indigent, at least according to the police who found him. They made that judgment based on his clothing and where he was found, a known location for the homeless, on the corners of Delisle and Vinet Streets. They also said that the homeless man's death was officially pronounced a murder. Richard surveyed editions of the *Montreal Gazette* for the next six weeks but did not come across any further reference to the murder. Richard contacted the police to determine whether they had any further information on the murder. Although the police had scant comment on any investigation that may have been initiated, noting that the only clue they had was that the dead man was wearing an artificial leg.

Nonetheless, Richard had the impression that the police, at least according to Constable Bouchard who spoke to Richard when he telephoned the Parc-Extension police station, weren't particularly interested in the fate of the homeless man. It was easy then for Richard to conclude that the dead homeless man was a plausible victim for any phony confession about a murder that Richard could concoct. After all, it was clear that there had been a murder in the city in which the police had neither interest nor motivation. Richard could therefore include almost anything in any confession he may decide to invent. He was prepared to commerce his most recent plan to precipitate a certain reaction to an unusual misdeed. He had managed to convince himself that this was the most likely scheme. He was feeling fortunate.

Like a couple of previous trial plans, Richard had decided to visit the Notre-Dame de Lourdes cathedral on Berri Street to have an anonymous priest hear his latest confession. He was concerned that if he were to have one of the priests at either Saint John Fisher, his parish church, or the Saint Ignatius chapel, they would recognize him, so well acquainted many of them may have been with Richard, his visits to the confessions in both buildings being surprisingly frequent. He thought that any priest recognizing Richard would cast doubt on the authenticity of his most recent confession. That was possible he suspected, particularly given the provocative nature of what Richard intended to confess. In other words, relating the story of a murder with which he was familiar due to a drunken revelation made during an evening spent in a local tavern. A curious aspect of the discussion Richard was prepared to construct was that the man who was to confide to a murder was that the latter had not bothered to introduce himself. In other words, neither Richard nor his late night conversationalist knew each other's names. It was an interesting attribute to Richard's planned fiction. He didn't read it in the paper. He made it up.

After some investigation, Richard was able to ascertain that Notre-Dame de Lourdes provided confession to potential penitents weekday evenings from seven to nine o'clock. He selected a Wednesday evening to evaluate his planned imaginary confession. He arrived in the cathedral around eight o'clock. There were three confessionals in operation. Only one of them was hearing a confession, the other confessional doors were partially open, soft lights glowing. In addition, there were several dozen congregants in attendance, most of whom were worshipping in the first few pews from the altar. Richard took up a spot on the left side of the church close to the three confessionals that were receiving customers. Richard knelt for a few minutes, made a sign of the cross, and then advanced to the confessional on the left. He opened the door to the right of the confessor's stall, noticing that he

was announced with a small name plate as Father Paul
Monfils. The light in his confessional went off. He also
noticed that Father Monfils was elderly, with white hair
and a face decorated with a mass of wrinkles. Richard
immediately had the impression that he had selected the
wrong confessor. He was elderly and probably hard of
hearing and light on curiosity. His contrived confession
would not likely be well received by Father Monfils. So
Richard concluded that he should exit Father Monfills'
place of business and try another confessional. He quietly
closed the door to the latter's confession and opened the
door to another, which was situated several feet away. A
confessor named Father Cartier was waiting there alone,
no other penitent in either of his booths.

As he knelt and began the proceedings, Richard
thought that he had caught sight of Father Cartier
holding a magazine in his lap. He casually put it aside,
slide the screen open and turned toward Richard. Hardly
into a normal confession monologue, he brought up the
objective of his visit, the testimony about a murder that
had been supposedly revealed to him during a drunken
chat with a fellow patron of a local tavern. Richard
took care to confide to Father Cartier that neither he
nor his drinking companion had bothered introducing
themselves to each other. Richard admitted that it
was curious, that two drinkers well into beer induced
inebriation would avoid or perhaps forget introducing
themselves to each other. Father Cartier offered a short
observation, "That seems strange, wouldn't you say?"
Richard responded by commenting that an obvious lack
of social graces was a minor indiscretion compared to

admitting to the murder of a homeless man. There was then a silence, the only sound the low murmur of elder congregants whispering prayers to themselves. A service was about to begin, so Richard thought. Some of the ladies had started to stand.

Maybe Father Cartier should have expected it, maybe not. He had never heard anyone confess to a murder or hearing about a murder, most, if not all the confessions he had ever encountered involved pedestrian acts revolving around sex or dishonesty. So it came as no surprise that Father Cartier was speechless, searching for a response. Richard broke the silence by then coming to the objective of his visit with Father Cartier, seeking penance further to his confession. He felt he had to prod the confessor. "I don't know if this is proper, Father, but rather than a penance, I would like you to give me any advice you may have for me following what I was told about a murder." Father Cartier leaned closer to the grating, the faint scent of an inexpensive aftershave now evident, the sound of his whisper lower. "You will forgive me but I have never had to consider a penance or any advice following a confession like the one you just provided me." Father Cartier paused for a moment and then asked with a certain mild bewilderment, "Why didn't you just contact the police? I would think that the police would be interested in that man's story." It was an understandable observation. Richard actually had contacted the police twice and had thought about continuing to contact the police a third or fourth time but an obvious lack of interest by the unidentified police officers who answered the telephones at the Parc-Extension, the police station that supposedly was investigating the alleged murder caused him to give up his pursuit of the police.

After explaining his reluctance to continue to contact the police, Richard had to admit, at least to himself, that he was surprised, if not astonished when Father Cartier imparted to him a penance that would return him to his pursuit of the police with respect to the murder of a homeless man. "Instead of reciting prayers, I want you to continue to try to convince the police to pursue the investigation of this man's death, this man's murder." Richard's voice rose a bit when he replied to Father Cartier's order of atonement. "As I told you, Father, I already have contacted the police about the case. They didn't...don't seem interested in the case, that is if a case." To give Richard some sort of hope, a kind of ecclesiastical form of optimism perhaps, Father Cartier gave him an unusual assurance. "This time, you can tell whoever you end up talking with, whichever police officer, that a priest required you to contact the police about the murder as a condition of a confession. In other words, that condition was a prerequisite of the penance that I gave you. And you can, in fact I urge you to tell the police that you are pursuing a penance that I gave you."

Again, a mysterious silence quietly emerged between the two of them, Richard in particular obviously stunned by Father Cartier's guidance. It was a notion that was so far out of any range of expectation that Richard was rendered speechless. He didn't know what to say. Within moments, however, Richard began to realize that Father Cartier's penance was the kind of atonement that his plan may have been searching for ever since an idea about confession and penance had occurred to him. Once recognized, he understandably developed an obvious enthusiasm for the penance provided by Father Cartier. Once Richard came to that conclusion, he thanked his confessor and quickly closed his confession with his Act of Contribution. He believed that he finally had an achievable objective. So he thought.

FINAL PROPOSAL I

I t was the day after his confession with Father Cartier. He was not able to sleep the previous night, the predictable tossing and turning with the occasional glance at his alarm clock. He was now faced with a penance that could not have been less fortuitous. Father Cartier had directed him to continue his search of the true circumstances of the death of an unknown homeless man. After coming across that short article in the *Montreal Gazette* about a month ago, he had contacted the police at the Parc-Extension station to determine whether the police had made any progress in the investigation of the man's manifest murder. After one telephone conversation with a Constable Bouchard of that station, he was to discover that the case of the murder of the homeless man was not being researched at all. In fact, Constable Bouchard initially was unable to claim any familiarity with the case, which involved a victim who was and remained nameless. After asking Richard to give him a few moments, the constable returned to the telephone to admit, with a certain embarrassment, that the only information the police had on the victim was already in the paper. Several weeks later, Richard telephoned the police station a second time, again asking for Constable Bouchard who was not available. When Richard asked to speak to another officer, whoever had answered the telephone in the first place said that there was no one else in the station to give him information on "A drunk who died without a name and without a home." However, before hanging up the telephone, the unnamed officer said that if he were to guess, the body of the nameless victim was probably unclaimed in the Montreal morgue. In the second telephone call to the station, a call that lasted less than three minutes, Richard did not acquire any additional information. Father Cartier was now requesting that Richard make more telephone calls.

He didn't know whether he would continue to purse his fascination with the circumstances surrounding the death of a homeless man when the police evidently had no interest. But now, with Father Cartier's liturgical retribution to resolve the mystery of the murdered man that troubled Richard even since he read about the man's death in the *Montreal Gazette*, he had another reason, another reason aside from his curiosity, if not his guilt, to seek resolution to that puzzle. At first, while he was prepared to telephone the Parc-Extension police station for a third time, he eventually realized that there might be a more effective way to encourage the police to conduct an investigation. After pondering his uncertainty regarding Father Cartier's penance, considering at one time simply forgetting the penance, he concluded that his preoccupation with the mysterious sacrament of penance was such that he could not simply discard his pursuit of the mystery of the nameless man's death. Given his absorption in television police shows, it come to Richard that he might consider engaging a private detective to look into the nameless man's killing. He realized, however, that hiring a private detective would be a complicated assignment.

Not surprisingly, it come to him while he was watching one of the many police television shows with which he normally sought entertainment. In this particular episode, a man was looking to hire a relatively affordable private detective to find his wife who was missing. In any event, the show had the man hiring the detective by seeking the listing in the telephone book, a comic aside for a television show that was usually action oriented. Consequently, Richard decided to consult the telephone book as well. Two days later, he consulted the city telephone book in the Saint Ignatius library, noting that there were more than four dozen detectives listed. Many of them were registered as security consultants, an occupation that sounded a lot more sophisticated than private detective. For a moment, he wondered whether less formal terms such as private eye, private dick or gumshoe were ever listed in previously published telephone books. In any event, he located listings for several private detectives, so registered in the tougher neighbourhoods, areas where the dead man was found. It was Richard's opinion that such detectives should be in a better position to investigate the circumstances that he sought, their familiarity with their neighbourhoods obviously relevant.

Richard decided to further eliminate at least one category of detectives that were listed as working in the selected neighbourhoods, i.e. detectives that were advertised as specializing in matrimonial situations. Otherwise, he had a list of eight individuals, including a woman named Margaret Buckley, a surprising occupation for a woman, the only female detective that was listed in the Montreal telephone book. Regardless, Richard selected three detectives from the list, all of whom had offices in the general area of Parc-Extension, where he approximated the murdered man was found. There was John Greenberg, whose office was on Beaumont Street, Guy Talbot who had an office on Saint Michel Street, and a detective named Claude Tessier who saw clients from an office on Jean-Talon. He chose the three detectives after consulting a map of the specific area of Montreal in which he had the specific interest. The three offices were all located in the middle of the specific area. He decided he would telephone the three detectives to request detailed information regarding their practices and to possibly request appointments.

The first candidate he interviewed by telephone was John Greenberg on Beaumont Street. He was able to talk to him on a Tuesday afternoon. Greenberg answered the telephone himself, explaining that he shared a secretary with an accountant on the second floor of the building on Beaumont Street. Richard asked after the kind of cases that Mr. Greenberg normally took. Greenberg said that he normally worked on workman compensation cases, involving injured workers contesting the financial judgments given to employees injured at work. When

Richard reluctantly told Greenberg that he wanted a detective to investigate the murder of a nameless man found more than six weeks ago, the detective lightly laughed and said that not only did he not have any experience with police cases but would not be bothered in any event, pointing out that if police had not shown any interest in the murder, there was probably nothing worth investigating in the first place. That was enough to convince Richard to contact one of the other two detectives.

Next up was Guy Talbot who occupied a relatively small office on the ground floor, next door to a Couche-Tard convenience store on Saint Michel Street. Like Mr. Greenberg, Detective Talbot did not have a secretary nor did he seem to share one. Richard quickly rejected Talbot for a reason similar to the conclusion he had reached with respect to Detective Greenberg. Guy Talbot said he worked for small retail stores where he provided surveillance and advice to prevent shop lifting. While Talbot likely had more than occasional contact with the police, Richard judged that any such exposure would not be investigative in nature but as a witness to potential petty crimes. In Richard's opinion, Guy Talbot was not suitable for the kind of inquiry he had in mind. That left the other candidate Claude Tessier.

Two days later, he visited Mr. Tessier in his office on Jean-Talon. Unlike the other two detectives, Claude Tessier had a secretary sitting outside his office, a comparatively young woman who seemed to have the demeanour of a cocktail waitress, all pleasant smiles and a certain affability that made him feel like ordering a drink. Richard recognized her voice from the telephone call they had the previous week. A nameplate on her desk identified her as Louise Goudreau. She got up from her desk, walked around it, and then led Richard into Claude Tessier's office. He was impressed with Tessier's office. It was certainty better appointed than the office occupied by Mr. Talbot. Richard was in touch with presumably Mr. Greenberg with whom he had been by telephone. So it was evident to Richard that Mr. Tessier had a fairly successful practice as a detective. Tessier was standing in front of his desk when Richard entered his office. Louise introduced him to her boss who smiled and asked Richard what he could do for him. Richard was taken aback somewhat, having questioned the previous two applicants on their qualifications rather than indicating his requirements. He realized, however, that determining his qualifications was likely unnecessary, in view of the impression that Tessier had already made in the opening moments of their conversation.

Richard then outlined his interest, if not his fascination with the circumstances of an indigent found by the police apparently beaten to death in the middle of the night in the poor area of the city. He had no name, no home, and no reason for his death. Aside from determining that the man had been murdered, an assessment made by a couple of policemen from the Parc-Extension station based on the marks made on his body by a piece of lumber or steel rebar, the only information anyone had on the man's fate was contained in four short paragraphs that appeared in the *Montreal Gazette* several days after the deceased was found. Richard also told Claude Tessier that he had pursued, without success, further commentary from the Parc-Extension station. He ended the history of his pursuit of the story of the murdered man by telling Claude Tessier that he could not explain the reason for his fascination. He then stated that he was seeking the assistance of a private detective in unravelling the mystery of that man. Richard did not reveal that he had been given the penance of resolving the mystery of the murdered man. He was worried that Tessier would not believe him.

It did not take Claude Tessier long to react to Richard's narrative. At first, he shook his head and nodded with a certain resignation, as if he had expected to hear the story. He even laughed. He then went on to explain himself. Richard was gratified. "I have to admit that you're telling me an interesting story but I also have to admit that I've heard these kind of stories before, you know like from other people although I have to admit that they were related to people who were killed, people who disappeared, people who went missing. You'll understand that some of them, in fact many of them ended up as clients." Richard was more than gratified, he was relieved. He was pleased that maybe he hadn't been wasting his time, thinking about whoever the nameless dead man was and what he had happened to him. He also thought about the atonement that Father Cartier had directed him to seek. It was clear that Claude Tessier might agree to take Richard on as a client and investigate the circumstances surrounding the nameless dead man.

Before they concluded their conversation, Tessier said he expected an important call and would therefore have to cut the meeting short. He did assure Richard that he was interested in the unknown man's story and would consider taking him on as a client, if that was something he had in mind. Richard answered enthusiastically, "Yes, that was the purpose of my request for an appointment with you. I was hoping that you would take me on as a client." Tessier offered a smile and nodded. "Louise or I will be in touch." They did not discuss Mr. Tessier's fee.

Richard had not contemplated the issue of how he would pay Tessier's fee, whatever it may turn out to be. He recognized that Father Cartier was probably the only source of finances that Richard could use to pay Tessier's fee. He had little money himself, his savings from his summer job at the chainsaw factory hardly sufficient he estimated, no matter how little or how much he would charge for whatever he could dig up. He could not approach any of his friends, none of whom likely had any money they could give or lend to anyone anyway. For obvious reasons, his family, particularly his parents were out of the question as well, leaving only Father Cartier as a most likely source for money to hire Claude Tessier. So he came to the decision that he would approach the confessor. Where and how Father Cartier would be able to underwrite any Tessier investigation and, more to the point, whether he would agree to help him were essential questions. That left him to formulate a plan to approach Father Cartier to ask for financial assistance to help him fulfill the unusual penance that the latter had specified for him. After all Richard surmised, Father Cartier was responsible for the penance in the first place and maybe he should contribute to the solution of any mystery associated with it. He thought of his lunch with Father Breslin a couple of months ago in which they discussed abnormal or unique confessions. Perhaps he thought Father Cartier would be prepared to provide a special penitent with the means to assist him in looking for an answer to a mystery that he had related to him.

So he decided to attempt to arrange an audience with Father Cartier as soon as he could. The most convenient, if not the most likely venue for such a meeting would be another confession with Father Cartier. While unconventional, if not awkward, Richard did not think that Father Cartier was uncompromising enough to refuse to discuss Richard's request, as perhaps outlandish as it could have seemed. He would visit Notre-Dame de Lourdes for confession on the next Wednesday night, hoping that Father Cartier was available, on duty to hear confessions along with a couple of other priests. If Father Cartier was hearing confessions, he would wait until his stall was available and use the opportunity to ask him for financial assistance to hire a private detective to help him to fulfill the penance that Father Cartier had given him. He had concluded that he would not pretend to confess but to directly and simply raise his request as soon as the screen slid across the window between he and Father Cartier.

It was a week later on a Wednesday evening when he went downtown to the Notre- Dame de Lourdes church to visit whatever confessional Father Cartier happened to be occupying, that is of course if he was in attendance. When he arrived in the church, he immediately noticed that there were maybe four or five dozen devout communicates knelling and sitting in the several pews near the altar.

There were three confessionals in operation, all of which were of left side of the church. A lamp was on in one of the three confessionals while the other two were dark, obviously in spiritual operation. He then surreptitiously walked by the three confessionals to examine the three name plates affixed to their ornate doors. The booth occupied by Father Cartier was currently hearing the admissions of one contrite penitent, the other confessional empty. Richard opened its door and crept into the enclosure. While he tried, he could not hear a word of the confession that was being conducted between Father Cartier and presumably the elderly lady, the faint sound of murmuring the only signs that there were individuals consulting in the other side of the confessional.

When Father Cartier and the penitent had concluded their business, there was a brief delay before the former was prepared to hear Richard. Father Cartier opened the screen between he and Richard. Expecting to hear the normal introduction to the ritual, Father Cartier was somewhat surprised when Richard immediately went into an explanation of the purpose of his visit to the Notre-Dame de Lourdes church that evening. "Father, you may remember that I confessed to you that during a drinking session at a local tavern, a man who I have never met before, a stranger really, told me that he had heard about the circumstances of a murder of a homeless man found dead one night downtown in been made aware him. I asked for your advice." There was a brief silence. Then, Richard continued with his request. "I am now asking you something else. It is more a favour rather than advice." Richard could see Father Cartier nodding through the screen and then heard him ask him about the so-called favour. "Favour?" Richard answered Father Cartier's inquiry. "Well, as a penance, you told me to continue to pursue the mystery of the death of the homeless man. As I think I told you, I was pretty sure that I couldn't come up with any further information. So I've decided to hire a professional, a private detective to investigate the homeless man's death. You know, the man's name for one thing, the circumstances of his death, who may have killed him. That sort of thing." At that point, Richard delayed, apparently lingering over the right way to ask Father Cartier for financial assistance. Although he had thought about it a fair amount, he had always arrived at the same conclusion. He would request assistance from Father Cartier directly. He didn't think he could find any other way.

He cleared his throat and leaned even closer to Father Cartier, his nose practically resting on the screen between them. As one could expected, Father Cartier seemed to sit back in his place. Although Richard could not see the expression on his face, Richard guessed that he would have likely allowed a startled look to come over it. He continued with his plan. "I need money. As you can imagine, private detectives are not free and I can't pay them. You can imagine that a student who depends on the money he made from a summer job or a part time job at a grocery store does not make enough money to pay anybody anything, particularly a private detective. So I'm asking you if you can help me." Understandably, Father Cartier was initially speechless, disconcerted by what only could be considered as an unusual request from anyone on the other side of the screen. The two of them were dormant, both immobile, staring at each other, Father Cartier wondering how to respond to what only could be said was a strange request from someone who confessed to a strange situation and to whom he had provided a strange response.

It required the contemplating confessor almost five minutes to come to a decision to Richard's request for financial assistance. In addition to an answer to that question, he also would have to come to an opinion as to how he would be able to help Richard hire a private detective to fulfill the penance he himself imposed on him. Father Kenneth Cartier did not earn a salary. He did not receive an income. He therefore did not and could not have a way of loaning Richard any money. He finally gave Richard an answer. "I'm going to have think about it. As I hope you can understand, it is not a standard situation. In fact, I'm sure that I've never been asked by anybody for money. And I don't know where I would get any money even if I wanted to give you any." Richard wasn't really surprised. He should have expected Father Cartier to be appropriately indecisive. After all, he doubted that Notre-Dame de Lourdes would allow Father Cartier access to the cathedral's financial affairs, which Richard figured were probably fairly complicated. In the moments he had while Father Cartier pondered his response to Richard's plea for a financial favour, he wondered where the good father would find any money even if he wanted to help Richard.

So after five minutes or so, Father Cartier finally settled back in his throne, exhaled, stared at the ceiling one last time, and gave Richard an answer, such as it was. It wasn't really an answer. "You'll have to give me some time. As I already told you, I have to think about it I think you'll have to give me a week." For the first time, Richard's voice rose above a whisper. He was expressive enough to be concerned that he may have interrupted the devotions of some of the few congregants outside the confessional, "A week!, you sure?" Richard exclaimed. Father Cartier nodded. Richard then gave him a more definitive answer. "I think I can wait a week. I guess I can." Then Richard hesitated for a moment before thanking Father Cartier and then asking him if an Act of Contrition was appropriate in the circumstances.

For the first time during their meeting, Father Cartier smiled. He shook his head and assured Richard that it was not. They could neither agree on the timing of their next conference nor its location. Richard was certain, however, that it would be held in a confessional in Notre-Dame de Lourdes. For a moment, in the interval, Richard again thought of his lunch with Father Breslin in the Golden Moon. The evening after his confessional conversation with Richard, Father Cartier made an appointment with the prelate of Notre-Dame de Lourdes, Bishop Emile Bergeron. As the clergyman with jurisdiction over its finances, Bishop Bergeron was unquestionably the most important individual he could consider in selecting an individual to approach for money. He would have to make an appointment with the bishop's assistant, that is if he could convince her that the purpose of the appointment was sufficiently legitimate.

Accordingly, Father Cartier would have to fabricate an excuse for wishing to meet with Bishop Bergeron, a request that he would not normally make in any circumstance. And this circumstance was obviously not normal.

FINAL PROPOSAL II

F ather Cartier knew virtually nothing about Bishop Bergeron and therefore was in no position to proceed with an approach to convince the bishop to assist him with engaging Claude Tessier or some other private detective to investigate a death about which he was told he must explore. For example, Richard was comparatively familiar with the spiritual consciousness of Father Breslin, an insight that had allowed him to discuss ecclesiastic complexities with him, involving most particularly the history and true meaning of the sacrament of reconciliation. Perhaps Bishop Bergeron was more an administrator of the diocese/cathedral/church than any sort of spiritual advisor or confidant. If that were the case, it would be doubtful that the Bishop would be sympathetic to any request for financial assistance from a parishioner seeking to satisfy a penance for an admission about a serious misdeed that the parishioner did not commit. Still, he didn't seem to have any other choice unless he was able to come up with an appropriate alternative explanation for his request for funds. In other words, a believable fiction.

On the other hand, while Richard was pondering another explanation for his request of Bishop Bergeron, he conjured up another approach to his problem. It was alarmingly simple. He would ask someone else. That someone else had crossed his mind several times as he contemplated his indecision about the money he needed to hire Claude Tessier. It was Father Breslin, the Jesuit priest with whom he had discussed the ideology and doctrine of the sacrament of penance. Based on their previous meeting, he thought that maybe Father Breslin would be agreeable to discussing his project with him, as unorthodox as it could seem to him to be. He could simply get in touch with him by arranging with Miss Chambers, the secretary for the Jesuit rectory office, another telephone call or luncheon with Father Breslin at the Golden Moon restaurant being the objective. He would once again attempt to find out whether confessors felt they had any responsibility for anything they may hear during confession, specifically if they have a duty to rectify any sin they may forgive in confession.

During their previous lunch, Father Breslin had equivocated, basically explaining that the answer to that question dependent on the priest hearing the confession and the sin being confessed. Since the issue that Richard was pursuing approximated the request that he intended to pursue with Bishop Bergeron, he thought that he could explore it with Father Breslin. Furthermore, Father Breslin could help him by actually making a donation to

Claude Tessier himself. As unlikely as it seemed, Richard allowed the possibility to remain in his mind as long as the issue was relevant to the discussion with Father Breslin, that if he managed to convince Father Breslin to meet with him to discuss his current dilemma.

He spoke to Miss Chambers, asking her if she could arrange another meeting with Father Breslin. She responded positively, remarking that she had heard that Father Breslin had enjoyed their lunch. That said, Miss Chambers then assured Richard that she could most likely convince Father Breslin to meet again with him. Before Richard made any suggestion as to where or when he and Father Breslin could meet, Miss Chambers recommended that the two of them get together for lunch at their previous meeting place, the Golden Moon restaurant. Richard suggested that they get together the following Monday, in four days. Miss Chambers then agreed to get in touch with Father Breslin to confirm the date and time for their meeting. She assured him that Father Breslin would most likely be available on Monday for lunch, commenting that the only obstacle to his agreement would be that there was no one to drive him to the Golden Moon for lunch with Richard. The next day, Miss Chambers reported that a Jesuit Novitiate named Hanley had volunteered to drive for Father Breslin.

He arrived at the Golden Moon to see Father Breslin seated in a booth. Richard noticed that his lunch companion was wearing a different set of glasses than he wore the only other time they shared lunch at the Golden Moon. He was seated behind a pot of tea, a package of Player's Plain cigarettes, a gold lighter, and an ash tray.

Father Breslin greeted Richard with a sly smile, as if he was still a pupil in his theology class. At first, Richard looked a little reticent, as if he felt a little embarrassed about requesting the meeting. Despite having thought about his proposed appeal to Father Breslin fairly seriously for at least a week, he started feeling a little unsettled about his plan, which probably explained the fleeting doubt on his face. Father Breslin did not waver. Richard sat down and reached out to shake his hand. Father Breslin's smile brightened.

"While I was somewhat surprised to hear from you again, I was pleased." said Breslin and then asked an obvious question. "Are you still investigating the conundrum of the sacrament of penance?" With that inquiry, the Father offered a slight laugh, more like a chuckle. Richard answered, telling one confessor about his deliberation with another. "I went downtown to the Notre-Dame de Loudres cathedral and went to confession. I confessed to being told by an anonymous companion in a tavern that a homeless man, whose identity no one seemed to know, had been killed one night in the Little Burgundy area. I read about the death in the *Montreal Gazette* and I used that story as my admission to a priest named Father Cartier who was hearing confessions in the cathedral that day. I wanted to determine that confessor's reaction. So I told the confessor that while I was fairly certain that having that knowledge was not something that I should confess, I wanted to get a priest's counsel about what I should do, if anything. I just felt guilty about knowing about something like that. I just wanted to know what a priest would advise."

Father Breslin then signalled for the waitress. "I think I would like to order lunch before I make any comment. Egg rolls always bring out the wisdom in me." Father Breslin laughed lightly again. The waitress, the same older woman who served them the other time they visited the Golden Moon, arrived to take their order, egg rolls and rice for Breslin and a western omelette and a coke for Richard. Once the older waitress took their orders and walked away, Father Breslin leaned across the table, clasped his hands together, as if he was about to pray, and started to comment to Richard. "I have to admit that is one helluva of a story. First of all, what did your confessor advise?" Richard then provided Father Breslin with Father Cartier's response. "He didn't give me a standard penance, which I sort of expected, but instead said that he wanted me to convince the police, which I had been trying to do even since I read about the man's death."

Understandably, Father Breslin looked more than a little surprised. In fact, he looked like he couldn't quite believe what Richard had just confided. "I must admit that I have never heard of any of my colleagues in the clergy giving a penance of that nature. I know I haven't. I remember telling you that priests sometimes have a duty to rectify sin rather than absolve it. It depends on the priest and the sin I guess." Father Breslin paused for a moment, waiting for inspiration to provide Richard with additional enlightenment on what he had to recognize was a unique situation. He could not find any. "Let me ask you. Have you taken any action following the Father Cartier's quote penance unquote?" With his question hanging between the two of them like cigarette smoke, their luncheon orders arrived. Father Breslin started on his egg rolls and rice almost immediately. For his part, Richard sat just looking at his western omelette.

After a few moments, Richard finally answered Father Breslin's question. "Well, Father, I have contacted the police about the case on two occasions. They didn't seem at all interested in the man's death. I even told one police officer that a priest required me to contact him about the man's death as a condition of a confession. But it didn't seem to have much of an impression on the man although he gave me a clue that he had an artificial leg. Still, while it was a worthwhile hint, I realized that I couldn't solve the case on my own. I would therefore engage someone, a professional, a private detective or maybe a retired police officer for example, to look into the man's death." Father Breslin sat listening to Richard with a extremely attentive expression on his face, so much so that he had placed his fork down and had stopped eating. He asked Richard whether aside from being told about the man's fake leg, had he made any progress in his investigation.

Richard had relaxed and sat back in his chair. It was evident that Father Breslin was prepared to continue to listen to his former pupil, no matter how improbable his story. Richard then related his efforts, which resulted in his selection of an investigator named Claude Tessier who operated from an office on Jean-Talon Street. "The problem is, and this is why I contacted you, Father, is that I assume Mr. Tessier's services are not free. I have no idea how much he charges and how long he will need to investigate until he discovers who the homeless man was and why he was killed. But, as maybe you can

imagine, I do not have any money to hire Mr. Tessier."
Father Breslin looked at Richard sympathetically and
then, maybe strangely enough, speculated. "And you've
come to me for help, maybe financial help.", he said.

Despite his surprise, Richard managed to settle himself
down quickly enough to agree with Father Breslin's
conjecture. "Yes, that was, that is my intent. I was going
to ask you to help me with money." Father Breslin had
gone back to finishing his lunch. He put down his fork,
drained the rest of the tea from the pot into his cup,
took a sip, straightened up, stared at Richard across the
table with a firm conviction and responded to Richard's
most recent admission. "I am sure you realize that as a
retired Jesuit priest, I'm not flush. In other words, even if I
wanted to, I couldn't help you financially. I just don't have
access to any money. But, just sitting here having lunch
and listening to your request, I'm thinking that you might
consider asking the priest that gave you this most unusual
penance to help you financially. I mean, after all, Father
Cartier is not a Jesuit but a parish priest in a large city
cathedral. Maybe you should ask him for help" Richard
was a trifle surprised by Father Breslin's suggestion. Father
Breslin sat back, relaxed and commented. "Well, that
sounds like a good idea. I'd go ahead". Richard nodded.

His plan was to return to Notre-Dame de Lourdes,
another Wednesday, which seemed to Richard to be the
schedule that Father Cartier kept to hear confessions.
Besides, Father Cartier had given him a week to respond
to his appeal for financial assistance. He was still not
certain that Father Cartier would be either willing or
able to provide Richard with any funds to help pay for

Mr. Tessier's services. After all, Father Cartier was the confessor who assigned to Richard the penance. He therefore would have an obvious motivation to assist his penitent in solving the puzzle of the dead man. Whether Father Cartier would act on that incentive was uncertain but Richard felt he had to make the attempt, particularly since his confessor had not only made the proposition himself and had assured Richard that he would consider helping him, promising giving him an answer in a week. That was six days ago.

As planned, he arrived a little after seven o'clock on Wednesday evening at the Notre- Dame de Lourdes for confession. Although there were less than several dozen congregants assembled, all three confessionals appeared to be ready to receive clients. Richard located Father Cartier in the same stall that he had been occupying during his previous visit. He was alone sitting in the confessional, stock still it appeared, holding something, a rosary perhaps or maybe a prayer book. Richard approached Father Cartier's confessional, opened the wooden door slowly, quietly climbed into the booth, and knelt down. The Father's lamp was extinguished and the partition slowly opened. Father Cartier turned toward Richard who opened with the predictable "Bless me, Father, for I have sinned. It has been...." He could see Father Cartier smiling. He then interrupted Richard. "No need, son, no need. I am guessing that you are here to follow up on last week's confession, I mean last week's discussion."

Richard replied to Father Cartier, "Yes, Father, I have been trying to pursue the question of the homeless man's death. I still need your answer, you know, about money to pay a private detective." Father Cartier shook his head, looking at Richard with a certain regrettable expression on his face, obvious through the screen of the divider between the two of them. Father Cartier had turned to face him and gave Richard the reply to his request for funding. "Unfortunately, I cannot possibly provide you with any money to help you engage a private detective. As I'm sure you know, or maybe should know, that I don't earn much money. Like most priests, I get a weekly stipend, like an honorarium from the church, for normal expenses. You'll realize I guess that it isn't much." Richard remarked, "Yes, I would imagine. Your normal expenses can't be very much, can they? Aside from rent maybe?" Father Cartier offered Richard a slight smile, almost a smirk and then disagreed with his observation. "Well, the church pays my rent, as low as it is, and my allowance is only for trivial expenses like cigarettes, coffees, items like that. So you appreciate that I am in no position to provide you with any funds." Father Cartier stopped for a moment and then continued with an explanation with respect to his opinion about whether he would help Richard if he could. "It would be akin to the confessor agreeing to reciting prayers that he has just provided a penitent as a penance." Richard nodded his head and realized that his quest was likely, if not futile. It was time for Richard to leave the confessional. He did not bother with an Act of Contrition.

Richard departed Notre-Dame de Lourdes somewhat dispirited. He was now without any way of resolving the mystery that with which he had allowed himself to be burdened. He had come to believe and still believed that, despite the occasional misgiving, a spiritual responsibility had been consecrated on him by the infinite conundrum of confession. He thought that he had little, if any alternative but to continue to pursue the riddle. What was he to do? As he had several previous times, he thought of abandoning the entire venture. That would mean, of course, that his entire preoccupation, his occupation, his pursuit with the sacrament of confession would have been a complete waste of time. After several days of deliberation, during which he realized that his continual musing about confession and penance would be pointless unless he somehow managed to continue his quest, he concluded that he would probably have to investigate the matter himself. He would have to proceed without Mr. Claude Tessier or any other private detective.

Final Proposal
On His Own

I t was several days later after he came to his most recent conclusion. Richard now seemed to be on his own, his responsibility solely without any possible support, included in particular that of a private detective or the police. He was therefore forced to conclude that he would have to investigate the nameless man's death by himself. He eventually decided that he would have to start by identifying the deceased. The only clue, albeit a significant one, available from the short article in the *Montreal Gazette,* was that the murdered man was encumbered with an artificial leg. Based on a film that he must have seen several times, he come to believe that he could explore the records of local hospitals that provided artificial limbs to the destitute. In that regard, Parc-Extension constable Bouchard, in their only telephone conversation, added another clue that Richard thought might be relevant to his search for the man's identity, i.e. the police had determined that the man's artificial leg appeared to be recently installed, a detail that would make his investigation of Montreal hospitals having installed artificial limbs less complicated than it would otherwise be. He would at least have a starting point.

As anxious as he was, he decided to begin his search with the Maisonneuve- Rosemont Hospital on L'Assumption Boulevard which was located in the same general area of Montreal that the deceased man he was attempting to identify was found dead. It was a large facility that served a good part of Montreal's population, or so said a sign that was erected in the front of the building. The sheer size of the place made Richard's task more daunting than he had expected. He stood in the lobby of the hospital, wondering how he could find the section of the hospital that provided treatment to patients who needed artificial limbs of one kind or another. He scanned the listing of the more than fifty various departments and sections in the hospital. By previously consulting the library, he was able to ascertain that the professionals who fashioned and fitted artificial limbs were called prosthetic, who he guessed must be indicated somewhere on the listing hanging on the wall of the lobby. He further determined, or at least imagined that such technicians worked for or reported to the orthopedic department although he could have been wrong. While the term "prosthetics" were not ascribed anywhere on the hospital listing on the lobby wall, there was an extensive listing under the orthopedic department, consisting of more than a dozen physician names and dozens of associated operations. He again was close to giving up.

Richard then decided that anything to do with social services was the most likely to have some relevant information about patients, less fortunate or not, who may have received a prosthetic of some sort. After all, he figured that anyone who may have lost a limb by accident rather than disease for example and, therefore, was in need of expeditious medical attention, would be handled by the part of the hospital which cared for people in circumstances which could have occurred to the dead homeless man. In that event, he would have to devise an appropriately convincing explanation for the relevant medical personnel so that they could tell Richard which patient, if any had recently lost a limb and then been outfitted with a prosthetic device, specifically an artificial leg. But where to look? Using those parameters, he managed to locate something entitled the Therapeutic Recreation Department, which had an office on the third floor of the main building. He was directed there by a volunteer who was sitting by the main entrance to the hospital. The volunteer was an older lady wearing a name tag identifying her as Margaret W. She was sitting behind a telephone, an index book, a small notebook, and a desk lamp. She had been reading a paperback novel when she wasn't dispensing information to people looking for direction.

While he was asking the volunteer for guidance, Margaret asked for the purpose of his inquiry, Richard stood silent for a moment, looking blankly at Margaret, and finally tried to offer an explanation. "Well, a friend of mine was recently hit by a car and unfortunately lost a leg. He and his family did not have the money to ensure that he would be outfitted with a decent artificial leg. But I heard that some hospitals, including this one I guess, have social programs that provide help to patients that may have the kind of problems that my friend may have." Richard moved a little closer to Margaret, casually gripping the edge of her table. "How do I take advantage of one of those programs? Does this hospital, the Maisonneuve-Rosemont for example, have such a program?" Margaret W nodded and smiled. "You'll have to talk to Doctor Boivon. He's the head of the prosthetic clinic. Here, Let me look." With that assurance, she picked up the index book and started to flip through its pages. The index finger on her right hand stopped half way down a certain page. "Here it is. He's in Room 612 on the sixth floor. Doctor Marcel Boivin, he runs the program."

Richard nodded, pulled a folded piece of paper out of his pocket and scribled Dr. Boivin's name on it. "What is the program by the way?" Margaret W slowly shook her head and answered as if she wasn't quite certain about her reply. "Well, I think he outfits the homeless, you know the destitute who have lost limbs with prosthetics, you know with artificial limbs, the cost of which is paid for by various charities. I know it sounds strange but Dr. Boivin started the program when he was a parishioner at Saint Anthony's church. Apparently, there were a lot of needy people in that parish and a lot of them had medical problems. Surprisingly, I heard that some of those people had lost limbs and had nowhere to go to receive help." Richard interrupted, "And Dr. Boivin offered to help, right?"

Within maybe ten minutes, Richard was knocking on the door to Dr. Boivon's office. His title, *Chief, Prosthetic Clinic,* was emblazoned underneath his name. His office was the only one which indicated a person rather than a function. The rest of the rooms included such activities as cosmetic consultation, implant repair, reconstruction, devices, fittings, design and manufacture, exercise, materials, and financing. There was little noise, scant commotion, the entire floor seemed more like a bureaucratic adjunct to physical work than physical work itself. Standing there, waiting for Dr. Boivin to answer the door, he came to realize that the sixth floor, or at least this section of the sixth floor, was the office for patients seeking artificial limbs or devices. The activities associated with designing, outfitting and financing selected patients for a prosthetic were conducted elsewhere while the arrangements to ensure that those activities were in fact conducted were made in one of the offices on this floor. Just as Richard was coming to that conclusion, the door to Dr. Boivin's office opened and a small, balding man stood in the doorway with a curious little smile on his face. He greeted Richard with the usual inquiry, "Can I help you?" Richard was prepared with an explanation for his visit. He had decided not to apply any creativity to it. In other words, he decided to tell Dr. Boivin the truth of the basis for his search, the identity of a vagrant found dead in the Little Burgundy area.

"Well, Dr. Boivin, I'm here to ask you about a patient who your clinic may have supplied with an artificial limb. He might have been somebody that I used to know. I had lost touch with him but was told that he was down on his luck. I was told that he took to begging for spare change in the street. He was then hit by a car and I understand he was outfitted with an artificial leg by your clinic. He eventually went back to asking for change and then was killed. I couldn't found out whether he was the man that I knew. You know, as far as the police are concerned, the man died nameless. I assume that was his status as he was buried. I just have to find out if I knew this man." Richard then looked at Dr. Boivin with a wishful look on his face. He was waiting for Dr. Boivin to respond.

Dr. Boivin stepped up and then gestured Richard toward the chair sitting before his desk. Richard slowly shuffled toward the chair and sat down. Dr. Boivin followed him and took his seat behind his desk. He still had that interesting smile on his face. "Well, we have had several itinerant as patients over the past six months or so. I think at least two of them may have received new prosthetics." Richard looked at Dr. Boivin as if he had just suggested that something profoundly unusual. "What do you mean, new prosthetics?" Dr. Boivin laughed a little. "I understand your skepticism. I should tell you that sometimes, particularly for people who may be derelict, we are forced to use artificial limbs that were previously worn by other patients who received newer equipment." Richard looked a little surprised and nodded his head. Dr. Boivin then continued to respond to Richard's question. "Anyway, I can let you take a look at a few files."

With that offer, Dr. Boivin turned in his chair, opened a file cabinet, removed some folders, turned back to face Richard and spread them out on the desk. Richard inspected the folders and noted that all three of them concerned individuals who were indigent. One of them, however, did not record any name. It documented that he has received an artificial leg after he lost a leg as a result of a collision with a taxicab. He was apparently bumming change from traffic on his usual locale on Saint Jacques Street. The folder also said that he was released, after appropriate rehabilitation in the Douglas Hospital in Verdun, to the Salvation Army shelter on Notre Dame Street. Dr. Boivin never discovered his name but people started calling him "Pegleg", which was ironically enough was what most of the street people who were also staying at the shelter."

With that admission, Dr. Boivin closed the file, looked at Richard with an apologetic look on his face, and summarized the information he had on the nameless man, aka "Pegleg". "I don't know what I can tell you, what advice I can give you. He was probably living in the shelter on Notre Dame. Either that or staying in a group home nearby. Furthermore, he was probably begging for money on Saint Jacques along with other street types. Maybe one of those people will remember his real name, if that is what you are looking for." Richard nodded and confirmed his intention. "Yes, Doctor I'm hoping that I can find out who that man is and maybe I can also find out who killed him and why he did it." Richard lingered for a moment, indecisive, wondering about whether he should expand on his explanation in any way. Dr. Boivin looked at him sympathetically, spread his hands out and stood up in apparent supplication. It looked like he was about to bid him farewell. Richard also stood up and offered Dr. Boivin his hand. Dr. Boivin shook it, smiled and wished him good luck.

Richard left the hospital with evident regret even though he at least had been provided with another hint of the departed's actual identity, a fact that so far had eluded him. It was his street moniker, "Pegleg" as well as a general idea of where he might have made his living, such as it was. Accordingly, he was to adjust his original plan, his exploration of "Pegleg" now less laborious than it was previously when Richard had no notion about the mystery man other than he had a prosthetic instead of a right leg. So he decided that he would start to interview, as distasteful as the prospect seemed, as many street beggars as could, hoping to find a former street associate of "Pegleg" who knew the deceased's real name. In addition, he could somehow canvas group homes or shelters on or near Notre Dame Street to determine whether "Pegleg" ever lived in any of them, although he was not sure how many possibilities there were in that area of the city.

After ruminating on this next project for several days, during which time he only once considered the implications of his pursuit of the mystery of the death of "Pegleg" on his studies. It was actually an accidental contemplation. He wondered whether an investigation of the library's provision of mystery novels could inspire his search for the identity of Pegleg. He consulted the library's card catalogue and other sources of research for titles of mystery novels that might provide him with a hint of another, more expeditious avenue of pursuit than simply approaching local street people who might have been associated with "Pegleg" for information. However, his exploration of the library's archives provided fruitless, the only result of his search the reminder that he had fallen seriously behind in his study of a survey of several American poets of the early twentieth century. In fact, he alone had come to the conclusion that he was now studying the death and possible life of a man nicknamed "Pegleg" rather than anything to do with the study of English literature. Admittedly, he would research the history of "Pegleg"' by soliciting the memories, in so far as they were retained, of those who shared his occupation of begging for change on Saint Jacques Street and its environs.

That evening, he invested his time contemplating the continuing collapse of his academic career as well as selection of an appropriate ensemble for seeking charity from strangers driving automobiles down city streets. He had realized that approaching dressed potential change donors dressed like a college man was not likely to be successful. As he had observed from his previous surveillance of local indigents imploring drivers to give them spare change on the corner of Atwater and Saint Jacques, Richard arrived there at eight o'clock two mornings later, after another partially sleepless night. There were a half dozen vagrants seeking charity, in varying modes of frightfully sloppy attire. All of them were wearing ill fitting, well stained and well worn dungarees of either black or coffee coloured, ripped sweaters and sweat shirts, barely serviceable footwear, and baseball type caps that looked like they had been worn in every type of unfortunate weather. Finally, all of them were missing more than several teeth and looked like they had not shaved or attended to their appearance in a number of years, if not decades. It was likely the standard panhandling image.

Of the six gentlemen asking for coins, four were standing on west side of Saint Jacques Street, which provided transportation to people headed downtown, while the other two were stationed on the east side, which had cars driving north toward the industrial district. Richard, who was suitably dressed for his new day job, chose to join the two soliciting for change on the east side of Saint Jacques Street, The two of them took little notice of his arrival, which Richard thought curious, since he was basically reducing the opportunities they had for charity, providing competition for handouts. One of the two, the older of the two, waved him to stand several feet away, ordering that he take up a position further away from the corner of the two streets, where the traffic lights stood. On the other hand, the other vagrant, who looked like a relatively new entrant to the corner, engaged Richard in conversation. It was a surprising action. He spoke directly to Richard.

"You're new here. We have never seen you here or on the other corner." It was evident that he was speaking for both him and his older colleague. Richard nodded, removed his own cap, and held it out to demonstrate his intention to seek change. He explained. "I am here because I do not have any money. Like you I guess. This is my first day. Some of the people who live in the group home up on Vinet Avenue, where I managed to secure a room, suggested that I might want to come up here to panhandle for spare change. So here I am." His new colleague smiled, only three or four front teeth showing, and turned to gesture for change as he held his cap out to and walked by the four or five cars who were stopped at the corner headed north. Only one of the cars rolled their windows down and dropped a coin or two in his cap. The other tramp looking for change just stood there looking disappointed. He looked across Saint Jacques Street where four beggars were trudging by the ten or twelve cars heading south were also waiting for the traffic lights to turn green. They seemed to be doing better, spare change wise.

That first morning went by without particular incident. Richard was able to collect several dollars, maybe five dollars by the time he was ready for lunch. Over the first few days, rather than join the other indigents in taking lunch at a nearby *Dilallo Burger* or *Mr Hot Dog*, where they usually received small discounts, Richard returned to either his group home on Vinet Avenue or the Salvation Army place on Notre Dame Street where he would have a free lunch and then invest a couple hours seeking change on Delisle Street where there were fewer competing vagrants than on Saint Jacques Street in the morning. The supervisor of his group home, a middle aged man with a beard named Steve, greeted him as he came through the door. Richard had been told by one of the officials at the Salvation Army office on Notre Dame Street that Steve was running a group home on Vinet Street and they could have a vacancy for a man down on his luck, the story that Richard had been peddling for the past weeks. Richard managed to secure a room for a day there after speaking to Steve. Aside from Steve the manager, the group home employed five staff members, four men and a woman named Maureen. Two days later, Richard arrived to secure a room with, carrying a small suitcase containing a few clothes, some bathroom items, and several books, including one, that Father Breslin mailed him after their last meeting. It was a short, self published book, more like a pamphlet really, he wrote entitled *Contrition*. In an accompanying note, Father Breslin had written that he had donated it as a retirement gift to the theology department.

Lunch was being served in the dining room of his new group home. Richard noticed that there were four out of the usual six inhabitants waiting for the soup and sandwich noon time repast, he and another resident, a guy named Lawrence being the only participants in street solicitation. One of residents enjoying luncheon, a barely five foot tall individual named Nelson who seldom spoke to anyone but fellow resident James, looked up with his usual demonic grin, and and whispered something to Nelson who was sitting beside him. Steve observed that it was likely that Nelson was wondering how the morning's panhandling on Saint Jacques Street went. In fact, Steve said that he and the other four residents enjoying lunch were curious about Richard's introductory efforts at seeking spare change. Interestingly enough, the four residents taking lunch did not participate.

Before sitting down to his soup and sandwich, Richard told the group that the morning went fairly well, collecting more than four dollars in coins. Nelson broke his usual reluctance to talk about anything to ask Richard to enumerate the number of distinct coins that he actually managed to receive. After he itemized the 27 coins, consisting of eleven quarters, nine dimes, and seven nickels. Nelson asked whether there were any pennies. Both Richard and Steve looked at each other with quizzical looks on their faces while the three residents looked interested in Nelson's question. On the other hand, Bruce put down his spoon and told Richard to make sure to hide the proceeds of the morning's begging from the residence's other panhandler Lawrence who sometimes was sad if his day's efforts amounted to less than two dollars, suggesting that he might want to add to his day's total by stealing change from his roommates. Richard responded to Bruce's advice with a blank look on his face while Steve shrugged and motioned to a seat besides Nelson. Richard sat down and Steve then served him soup, sandwich and a cup of coffee.

There was usual exchange of pointless conversations between the residents, usually concentrated on the movies and the television shows that always seemed to be playing in the living room. After lunch was almost finished, Richard asked Steve and his fellow diners whether any of them knew of anyone in the neighbourhood who was named "Pegleg". None of the five were able to identify anyone by that name although Steve remarked that he wouldn't be surprised since nicknames, of which he assumed "Pegleg" would qualify, were fairly common among so-called street people. Steve suggested to Richard that some of the panhandlers with whom Richard was becoming familiar might be acquainted with or know of anyone with such an epithet. He also said that there were more than one. Steve also suggested that Richard might consider approaching staff at some of the other local support homes if any of them had ever heard of someone nicknamed "Pegleg" or something similar. By the time lunch was finished, Richard had little to consider in so far as finding someone named "Pegleg" was concerned. There had to be an easier way to search for a man who was blessed with a nickname instead of a Christmas name.

By the time supper was served five hours later, the inhabitants were permitted their smoke breaks and sat down in the living room to catch a DVD, it was lights out in the residence. Richard was relatively pleased with his room, a single bed, a small desk, a narrow chair, and a little television set. The only inconvenience according to Richard was the fact that he had to share a washroom and shower/bath with the other residents, there being only one washroom and one bath on each of the two floors in the house. Although he intended to read Father Breslin's book, which would have taken Richard less than an hour, he never got the opportunity. The lights had gone out. Still, he had a fairly good night's sleep despite the mumbling of his next door neighbour Bruce who apparently had a tendency to talk in his sleep, a habit that according to Steve he had picked up in Shawbridge Youth Centre where his brief delinquency resulted in a stay for stealing a couple of cars. Richard woke up without incident, had breakfast and was the first out the door.

Over the next few days, he decided that he would maintain his post on the east side of Saint Jacques Street. His two associates on that corner would greet Richard with smirks and go back to pushing their caps toward the cars idling at the corner of Atwater and Saint Jacques. On the fourth day of his pursuit of spare change, after two hours or so of peddling his destitution, Richard looked at his cap with a certain gloomy expression, noting that his chapeau, which happened to be a worn cap that he wore when he was playing baseball for the Cedar Park pony league team more than ten years ago, contained 57 cents in change. It was a dreary day, cloudy and threatening rain. If it did rain, it would impede drivers from rolling down their windows. That would explain the change. His two deadbeat colleagues seemed to have similar looks on their faces. It had been an unfortunate day for all three of them. It was close to lunch time, and the three of them were discussing whether to take lunch at *Mr. Hot Dog*, despite the fact that they had had a bad day collecting change from strangers in cars. While they would enjoy a couple of hot dogs, whether they would pay for them or not, occasionally leaving the restaurant, which was formed in a horseshoe shape and attended by one waiter, a corpulent man named Denis, without paying for them. Sometimes, Denis would notice the thefts, sometimes he wouldn't. In event of the former, those who took advantage would avoid visiting *Mr. Hot Dog* for a week or so, hoping that Denis would not recognize any hot dog thief.

As Richard and his colleagues sat on the curb of Atwater and Saint Jacques Streets discussing lunch, he casually, or as casually as he could, asked them if either of them knew of a man that people called "Pegleg". One of them, the older one, seemed, at least for a moment, to recognize the epithet, a slight nod of the head the apparent indication. He never confirmed he knew the name. He did suggest, however, that he might consider asking one of the panhandlers on the other side of Saint Jacques Street if any of them knew the name. Richard thanked him and asked who of the four on the other side of the street had the most experience of asking for money on the street. He had told that his name was Benjamin and supposedly had been asking for spare change for years. Richard asked if he had a street name. It was Danger, origin unknown. Richard intended to approach him at some point.

Benjamin, aka Danger, having enjoyed his lunch at a local diner named Abby's rather than *Dilallo Burger* or *Mr Hot Dog,* returned to his usual roost, standing on the corner of Atwater and Saint Jacques Streets, lit up a cigarette and returned to begging motorists for change. Richard left his position on the other side of the street and took up a position adjacent to Benjamin. Fortunately for Richard, there was only one other derelict left to compete with Danger and now Richard for spare change from passing drivers. It was two o'clock in the afternoon and there were fewer cars than during rush hour to provide charity to men asking for money. Richard was therefore able to ask Benjamin/Danger whether he knew anyone named "Pegleg". He simply walked up to the man and asked if he had ever met "Pegleg".

He stated to explain as simply as he could. "I was told that a man, a supposedly a homeless man without a name, was killed some time ago. I have spent several months looking into his identity. I thought that I might have known him. I felt that I should investigate the matter.

Anyway, according to the press and police, the man was found killed, apparently murdered, in the Little Burgundy area one night. No one seemed to know his name and no one was able to discover his name but there was a clue, specifically that the man had an artificial leg, which he received after he had suffered a traffic accident. And then, like all unclaimed dead in Montreal, the man was later cremated and then interned in the Laval Cemetery. As you can understand, I am interested in anyone who might have known or knew of this man." Benjamin stood closer to Richard and stared in his eyes. He then spoke. "And you think that I may know something about this man?" he asked. Richard nodded and claimed that a man named "Pegleg" may have recently panhandled on the corner of Saint Jacques and maybe other corners as well. "Do you recall such a man?" asked Richard. Benjamin smiled and answered in the affirmative. "Yes, I remember him. A lot of people, both those asking for money and those giving it, probably remember "Pegleg". He was hard to forget."

Now that he had determined that someone actually was familiar with "Pegleg", Richard was uncertain as the next step in his quest. For some unanticipated reason, he had not been able to develop a plan should he actually find someone who knew "Pegleg". It should have been obvious what his next move should have been. In actuality, it was his source who supplied it. Benjamin, who had just ignited another cigarette butt, continued a slight smile and observed. "I assume you want to know the man's real name." Benjamin looked entertained, observing that it was obvious. "He was almost always anonymous but I think the guy's first name was Mark or Mike or Matthew or something like that. I also never knew his last name but I think he told me that at one time he lived at the Salvation Army shelter on Notre Dame Street." After that admission, Benjamin turned away from Richard, threw away his cigarette and stepped into the street with his cap extended as the traffic lights changed and several cars had to stop and wait. The other vagrant standing on the corner gave Benjamin some room, a signal of Benjamin's status as the elder of the street beggars. The driver of the second car, who had rolled down his window, gave some coins to Benjamin. The other three cars avoided his entreaties. Richard stood and watched. His next step was to visit the Salvation Army shelter on Notre Dame Street in Little Burgundy. Maybe the staff there knew "Pegleg"'s full name.

The Salvation Army shelter on Notre Dame Street in Little Burgundy was an older building that looked to have been constructed before the turn of the century. Still, it fit in well with the rest of the structures on the street. They all looked to have been erected at around the same period of time. In fact, there did not seem to be any buildings that were out of place. Richard arrived around lunch and there were a number of individuals, presumably staff members and various occupants of the shelter, milling about the counter beyond the main office. A man who introduced himself as Jack Farley greeted Richard as he walked up to the counter. Presumably because Richard was dressed a little better than most if not all of the bystanders waiting around the office, he was accorded a certain preferential attention from Mr. Farley who immediately asked Richard in a rather abrupt manner if he could be of service. In other words, however, he barked at him, asking him what he wanted. Mr. Farley was obviously a man who was accustomed to being bothered by irritating people. It was evident that whatever charitable elements in his psyche that may have inspired him to join the Salvation Army shelter in the first place had permanently faded, transforming him into the brusque individual who greeted anyone who asked him for anything with something approaching exasperation. Richard stepped back from the counter, likely with a disturbed look on his face. Farley looked at him for a moment and then looked away, another presumed inhabitant having attracted his attention.

It was predictable that Richard had not been prepared to deal with Farley, particularly since he intended to ask him for information, specifically if he knew or had known a resident with the nickname of "Pegleg". For a moment, he actually thought of offering Farley a couple of dollars, the idea of an inducement having occurred to him after a moment or so of consideration. That contemplation aside, Richard finally pushed his way to the edge of the counter, both hands gripping it and actually raising his voice to Mr. Farley. Amazingly enough, Farley acknowledged him and lifted his head. He was looking right at Richard. He then leaned forward and asked in a surprisingly calm voice, "Is there anything I can do for you?" It was an unexpected response from Mr. Farley, for which Richard was definitely not prepared. The latter was momentarily stunned into silence, standing there while the others waiting for Farley's attention stood by. They seemed perturbed but seemingly willing to stand by. Richard thought that the waiting residents probably were accustomed to Farley's general attitude toward pretty well everything.

In any event, he simply asked. "A man with whom I may have been acquainted may have been recently murdered by somebody in this general area. The man had a nickname, - "Pegleg", and I was told that he may have resided here in this shelter at one time. Do you remember a man with such a nickname?" Farley looked puzzled, which was hardly surprising. Richard just leaned in as if to press him for an answer. For his part, Farley continued to consider, seemingly pondering, as if he was not certain whether anyone named "Pegleg" ever existed at all, let alone ever lived in the shelter. And if he did, did Farley ever know his actual name? He wondered. And maybe so did Richard. After several minutes, during which the other presumed inhabitants waiting for Mr. Farley continued to grumble, Mr. Farley finally responded. Richard was pleased and surprised at the same time. "Did this guy have an artificial leg? I mean, with a nickname "Pegleg", it would fit, make sense, wouldn't it?" Richard was predictably overwhelmed, not certain how to respond to news that he had been pursuing for months. After stumbling for a few moments, he managed a question, the question. "First of all, do you remember his real name?" Farley looked at Richard with a thoughtful look on his face. "I think it was Ralph, Ralph something. I can't remember his last name." While disappointed, at least Richard felt he was closer to his objective although it seemed to be fading somewhat. But he had to continue. Predictable questions followed. "How long did he live here? I assume he wasn't living here when he died. So when did he leave and do you know where went when he left?"

Farley looked momentarily perplexed and then answered as best as he could. "Well, you have to realize that our residents can't stay here forever. Once a person is back on his feet so to speak, we usually find them some other place to live, you know, like a group home or one of the city's welfare shelters. Farley went silent for a moment and then asked Richard what prompted him to approach the Salvation Army office. "One of the panhandlers from the corner of Atwater and Saint Jacques told me that a guy named "Pegleg" might have stayed at your place here. So I came here to ask." Richard explained. Farley nodded and then responded as best he thought he could. Fortunately, a resident down on his luck with an artificial leg was not easily forgotten. He was asked to leave the shelter after a few months and found a group home somewhere in Little Burgundy. "I don't know where exactly, which street but I'd look for a place on either Blanchard or Quesnel. There may be four or five group homes in that general area. "Pegleg" may have ended up in one of them and if he did, they might have become aware that he wasn't there anymore when he was killed, or that maybe he just left the area. Anyway, it's probably worth a try."

Once again, Richard was looking for "Pegleg", this time in a series of group homes situated on one or two of the recommended streets in Little Burgundy. He started on Blanchard Street. Since such residences were not listed in the telephone book and he had not been astute enough to ask Mr. Farley for a list, that is of course if he kept one, he had to study each flat looking for a place in which indigents might have resided, the chief clue being a group of poorly dressed men who looked like they were not gainfully employed. They would laze on the stoop smoking cigarettes and perhaps exchanging stories about the day's events, hopefully panhandling. Having pursued street begging for several weeks, Richard had gained some appreciation of the art, thinking therefore that he could recognize purveyors of the profession. So he walked down the Blanchard Street, hoping to spot residences that provided lodging to men who were down on their luck, so to speak.

The first building he thought could have been likely had four men sitting on its steps passing what appeared to be pint of something between them. Three of them were smoking cigarettes while the fourth man was sucking on a half eaten cigar, something Richard thought looked like he might have picked up off the street. Richard stopped in front of the building, its address being 275 Blanchard. He didn't recognize any of the men sitting on the steps. He addressed the man who was sitting on the lowest step. "Hey, do any of your guys know a guy that people called "Pegleg."? Naturally, he's a guy who had an artificial leg. I was told that he used to ask for change on the corner of Atwater and Saint Jacques." The man sitting on the lowest step shrugged. Two of the other men sat blankly and stared while the remaining man, the one sitting on the top step ventured an answer, although he seemed unsure. "Maybe I saw a guy like that living at a place on Quesnel though I don't think he was living there long. I only saw him there one time. Maybe you should try talking to some of the residents in one of those homes." Richard thanked the man and moved on to a house that was four doors down. He was wearing a tattered hockey touque and a dirty woolen parka and apparently mumbling to himself. At first, Richard was reluctant to approach the man.

"Sir, can I speak to you for a moment?" Richard asked the man in the touque and dirty parka. The man, who suddenly stopped mumbling, looked up at Richard and smiled. He was missing two teeth on the bottom of his mouth and three on the top. He looked like he belonged in a horror movie. But surprisingly enough, he seemed cheerful and actually had a notion to reach out and shake his hand. But he stopped and then stepped down to the street. "About what?" He looked Richard straight in the face who then started his spiel. "I am looking for a guy whose nickname is "Pegleg" and who used to panhandle for spare change in this area. I have been told that he may live in a group home on one of the streets around here.

"Have you ever been familiar with a guy with that nickname?" The guy with the touque and the parka shook his head. Richard asked, "Are you sure?" The man nodded. Richard returned the nod and moved along to the rest of the street until he reached Quesnel Street where he continued his investigation.

Two buildings in from the corner with Quesnel, he came across a large building blessed with four stairs on which maybe eight vagrants were lounging at the end of a long industrious day of annoying motorists. Richard was more or less reluctant to approach the large building with the eight vagrant residents. So he simply announced his intention to seek "Pegleg" to the entire group, expecting maybe one or two or maybe more of the group to give him some information. "Yeah, I remember "Pegleg". He was a guy with a fake leg, right?" The man, who remembered "Pegleg" was dressed in a fake fur coat with bare patches, he then looked around to determine whether any of his colleagues recalled him as well. A guy who had been sitting on the top of the four stairs put up his hand and declared that he too had been acquainted with "Pegleg", claiming that he had called him "Moped" and then started cackling. Two or three other itinerants on the stoop repeated either "Pegleg" or "Moped" and laughed. Finally, Richard asked the throng if any of them knew "Pegleg"'s actual name. Apparently, none of them were aware of "Pegleg"'s real identity. Richard thought that curious.

Possible Absolution

He claimed that his one legged co-inhabitant's name was Robert Pope. His own name was Bob Smyth or he said, an alias that seemed fairly commonplace among the vagrant. For some unfathomable reason, Richard thought that he looked like he may have written poetry at one time or another but may have abandoned its pursuit in exchange for desolation and constant inebriation. Fact was that he looked exactly like what he appeared to be — a street bum. Eventually, almost before he knew it, he found himself living in supportive housing and group shelters with a collection of derelicts that also had a thousand possible excuses for their failures. Having testified to the knowledge of "Pegleg"'s actual name, the legitimacy of the admission had shocked his colleagues on the stairs. Richard responded to Smyth's revelation by offering to treat him to lunch at any local restaurant of his choice, hoping to somehow persuade him to provide Richard some background to knowing "Pegleg"s actual name. While some of his colleagues immediately agreed to the offer, even though they were not the intended recipients. Richard should not have been surprised but was nevertheless. "The invitation is only for Bob here." There was then a general groan coming from the stairs.

For his part, Smyth immediately jumped down from the second set of stairs only to land on a healthy expanse of dog excrement on the sidewalk of Quesnel Street. Predictably there were big laughs from the fellows, including nervous twitters from a couple of older ladies who had just happened to be walking past the building. Smyth didn't seem troubled by the laughter and then suggested that they consider dining at Ming's, a Chinese restaurant over on Vinet Street. It was commonly regarded, at least to the denizens of Quesnel Street, as an upscale eatery, at least compared to the usual fare available in the neighbourhood. He and Richard waved goodbye to his stair associates as they headed to Vinet Street and Ming's.

There were several dozen clientele already enjoying the fare at Ming's. A well stocked Chinese buffet was a well known specialty. A number of diners looked up from their meals and appeared to be momentarily annoyed, Richard speculating that the appearance of unknown customers the likely explanation. As soon as they walked in, standing in the lobby, while waiting to be greeted, both Richard and Smyth took to inspecting the place, noting that the walls, which were painted a faded, chipped maroon colour, were covered by dozens of illustrations depicting various scenes of what appeared to be for the most part China. Accordingly, most of the pictures showed Chinese peasants toiling the land and similar such occupations although none of them were shown to be panhandling for money, an art that was not prevalent Richard guessed in China. In fact, he thought that it might be illegal in China. Oddly enough, in that context, dominating the room at one end was a large picture of Chairman Mao Zedong. Richard thought it unlikely that any of the diners did not recognize the Chairman. But Bob Smyth did not recognize him.

They were shown to a table toward the rear of the room, handed two menus and sat down. Several of the diners who sitting next to the two of them looked up from their meals and stared at Smyth incredulously as if they had never seen such a character before, which may not have been surprising since Ming's was located in the Vinet Street locale commonly regarded as Chinatown. After all, denizens of Chinatown seldom came across street bums, particularly Occidental versions, and therefore were hardly ever asked for spare change, while either driving an automobile or simply walking down local streets. Although Bob Smyth noticed that he was being observed with unusual interest by other customers, he seemed nonplussed, as if he was often so regarded. In fact, Richard thought that Smyth may have winked at the curious individuals who were sitting at an adjacent table. The waiter, who did not appear to be particularly interested in Smyth came, both of them opting for the buffet, Smyth commenting that he was seldom able to take advantage of a buffet, wherever he dined, even at the group home or one of the restaurants that occasionally offered charity meals to the indigent. It was no surprise therefore when Smyth got in line for the buffet immediately after making his choice.

It was maybe fifteen minutes later, after Smyth had demolished a heap of food in record time and had already returned from the buffet with a second plate, Richard introduced the intended topic of his pursuit of Smyth. Interrupting him, whose consumption of his second plate from the buffet had slowed, Richard finally asked about Robert Pope. "Do you know anything about his background, what he did and where he was before you got to know him? Did he have any friends that you know of? And do you know what happened to him after he left?" Smyth smiled and answered the last question, even though he really didn't have to. He was hoping that maybe he was aware of details about which Richard did not know. He didn't. He simply commented. "Sure, I heard that he was killed. And that's all I know." They both allowed themselves to continue their meal for several moments, after which Richard returned to the pursuit of the story of Robert Pope, aka "Pegleg". He was most interested in anything that Smyth might know about his friends, that is of course if he had any. It was possible that Bob Smyth probably did not know much about Robert Pope's background but might be acquainted with any friend he may have. So he simply asked if he was aware of any that "Pegleg" may have had.

"Do you know if "Pegleg" was close to anyone in particular, when you know you were both living in the building on Quesnel Street?" Richard asked, leaning closer to Smyth, as if he was suggesting that he divulge confidential, if not secret information. Smyth was in the midst of shuffling another egg roll into his mouth. Smyth stopped, placed that half eaten egg roll on the plate, and then gave Richard another name, hopefully he thought a close friend of Robert Pope. This would be he thought another step closer to the explication of "Pegleg"'s death, his continuing obsession. Smyth went on to identify and explain. "The guy's name was Grayson. He lived in a room next to one that was occupied by "Pegleg" on the third floor of the place on Quesnel. For some reason, he left a couple of weeks before "Pegleg" died. Why he left I don't know but he seemed to be good friends with "Pegleg" while he was living there. "Pegleg" never said anything about it. And I don't know where Grayson went after he left the house. Maybe Mr. Provost, who runs the group home, can tell you. If anyone would know where Grayson went, he may."

So he had another person to pursue. After their lunch at Ming's, he accompanied Smyth back to the building on Quesnel Street. Perhaps Mr. Provost could fill him in on former resident Grayson. As he walked back to the building with Smyth, he realized that perhaps he should have contacted building manger Provost about "Pegleg" in the first place rather than interview Smyth. Not that it mattered much. By the time they arrived back at the building, the stairs were empty, the residents, having been served lunch, were presumably either back on the streets to bum spare change or investing whatever they were able to collect that morning in one of the many taverns spread around Little Burgundy like bus stops. Richard walked into the building, noting for the first time the actual address on Quesnel Street. Richard stood in the hallway of the first floor while Smyth said goodbye and started to climb the stair well to the second floor. A burly man with a beard suddenly appeared to greet Richard. He quietly inquired as to the purpose of Richard's visit. For a moment, Richard thought that maybe the burly man, who he assumed was in in charge of the home, considered him to be applying for any available room although he was too well attired to be so considered he thought.

"What can I do for you?" the burly man asked. Momentarily, Richard stood silent and then answered as firmly as he could. "My name is Richard O'Brien and I would like to ask you about one of your previous residents, a man named Grayson. Bob Smyth, who I just took to Ming's for lunch, told me that Grayson and Robert Pope, who you may know as "Pegleg", were fairly friendly with each other. Smyth told me, however, that no one, including himself, knew where he went. Do you have any idea?" The burly man, who had induced himself as Greg Desmond, delayed for a moment and then replied to Richard's question. "I think he may be living somewhere in Saint-Henri, near that bagel shop on the corner Saint-Antoine and Notre-Dame. Saint Vincent de Paul has a supportive home around there and I understand he may moved in there when he left here." Richard smiled and thanked Mr. Desmond.

It was the next Tuesday when he set out to look for Mr. Grayson in the Saint Vincent de Paul supportive house which he was certain was located somewhere near the corner of Saint-Antoine and Notre-Dame. It did not take long to find Saitn Vincent de Paul. It was housed in a squalling ramshackle building that looked like it was constructed sometime in the previous century. There was a large sign sitting over the entrance of the place, the address of which was 1295 Saint-Antoine, It was now located between a pharmacy and a newsstand that featured a one chair barbershop. Richard walked through the twin doors under the large sign announcing the Saint Vincent de Paul and the social assistance services it provided. There were a man standing in front of a group of mailbox slots. Richard assumed that they provided the sites for mail and messages for the building's residents. The man managing the mail turned toward Richard and stood with his hands on his hips, waiting for him to apprise him of the purpose of his visit. He had an irritated look on his face, as if whatever matter Richard planned to bring up with him, who aside from inspecting the mail, was plainly in charge of the building. He had a little plastic badge on his left breast pocket identifying him as Allan Turner, Manager.

"What I do somewhere for you?" the irritation on his face slowing fading, a grin started to materialized. "Yes you can." Richard replied, "My name is Richard and I am looking for a man named Grayson, who may have lived here at one time." It was obvious that Mr. Turner was expecting more of an explanation. "Grayson was a friend of a man who recently passed away and I'm looking for any friends who may want to be informed and may want to pay their respects to him on his death. I was told by one of the guys over at the one of the group homes on Quesnel Street that he may have been living here at Saint Vincent de Paul." Allan Turner started to stoke his chin and then replied to Richard. "Grayson has been living here off or on for maybe a year or so. Like most of the guys who live here, he supports himself with a government cheque, bumming spare change on the street, and occasionally bussing tables offer at the Elmdale." Richard was barely able to contain his enthusiasm with the news. He offered Allan Turner a broad smile and reached out to shake his hand. He then asked if Grayson was currently occupying a room in the building. "I'm not sure but if you come over at dinner time, you will be able to find out. If Grayson intends to stay over, he usually has dinner with us.", the implication being that if he doesn't appear for dinner, he would be staying somewhere else. Richard then asked if Allan Turner knew where Grayson stayed if he wasn't staying at Saint Vincent de Paul's. Allan Turner shook his head. "That's a mystery.", he said.

So Richard decided that he would turn up before dinner in Saint Vincent de Paul each evening until Mr. Grayson appeared to take dinner there. Initially he would have ensure that Mr. Turner would agree to allow Richard to consult with him on a daily basis to ascertain if George Grayson intended to attend Saint Vincent de Paul for dinner. He would simply repeat his initial explanation of his interest in Grayson, reminding him that the latter was a friend of an individual who recently passed away and that he may be interested. He did not tell him that he was primarily, if not entirely concerned with anything Grayson had to say about his friend Robert Pope, aka "Pegleg". He would start his regular consultations the next week. He would telephone Turner or his assistant, Fred Stevenson and ask if George Grayson was expected for dinner that night.

The first two times he called, he was told that Grayson had not shown up for dinner. The third time, Turner's assistant, a guy named Stevenson answered the telephone, compelling Richard to repeat his justification for seeking Grayson's presence in the first place. Stevenson was initially confused, asking more than once to explain his interest in Grayson's dinner plans. On the fourth day, he made a telephone call, Turner assured him that Grayson was slated to appear for dinner. Turner suggested that Richard wait until dinner was finished before approaching Grayson, a house directive based on the fact that liquor or beer was not permitted. With respect to house directive against drinks, Turner cautioned Richard against expecting that all residents would take it too seriously, mentioning that Grayson in particular often had difficulty following the directive, his propensity toward alcohol at times overwhelming. Mr. Turner added an obvious point. He advised Richard to try talking to Grayson right after dinner, thereby preventing him from sneaking a few drinks in his room right after dinner.

Richard arrived at Saint-Vincent de Paul about thirty minutes before seven o'clock. Dinner was over and most of the residents were leaving the dining room. Turner accompanied Grayson, a muscular looking six footer with a beard, into the building's reception area and introduced him to Richard. The two of them then retired to a small table and two chairs. It was obvious that Turner had briefed George Grayson on the purpose of Richard O'Brien's visit. Richard anticipated Grayson's opening observation. "So you want to know what I know about "Pegleg", right?". Richard nodded. So

Grayson continued. "Well, at first, I know that the man was killed. Everybody on the street, everybody in the neighbourhood, knows that." Richard interrupted to ask whether Grayson knew anything else about the death of "Pegleg". It was the main, if not the only point of his visit. "Well, nobody believes me, including the police but I think I know who killed "Pegleg" and why." Understandably, there was an eerie silence, the two of them looking at each other like neither of them knew what to say next.

Richard took to staring at the ceiling while Grayson just leaned back in his chair and waited for the presumably flabbergasted response. "I admit that it's difficult to believe. Are you telling me that you know who killed "Pegleg" and for what reason." Grayson smiled and nodded. "I can repeat it as many times as you like but I'm telling you it is true. I know that it seems difficult to believe but believe it." Again, there was a silence between the two of them until Richard asked another obvious question. "Why do you think that no one believes you?" Grayson shook his head again while a puzzled look came over his face. "Well, first of all, I haven't told that many people. Aside from the police, who didn't seem to have the time to pay attention to a story about the death of a nameless street bum with one leg, I only told a few people and I don't think any of them believed me." With that statement, Grayson waited for Richard to comment.

Richard then asked another obvious question, probably the most pertinent of the possible inquiries. "Well, why don't you tell me the story, the whole story. I mean, I am ready to believe you." Richard decided not to tell Grayson the basis for his pursuit of Grayson's story about the death of "Pegleg". It all led back to his preoccupation with confession. He wondered whether that preoccupation would survive.

FINALLY, A STORY

For whatever reason, curiosity being high on the list Richard thought, Allan Turner interrupted to ask the two of them were making any progress in whatever matter they were pursuing. It was not often that the house was host to any visitor that was not associated with either social services or at times, the police, the latter of course if one of the residents was in any trouble. Both Richard and George Grayson acknowledged by nodding and then exchanging puzzled expressions on their faces. Turner did not reply. He turned away and disappeared into the lobby of the building. The two of them went back to considering the story of the death of "Pegleg".

Grayson began his narrative with a certain sweep of expression. "Well, I had a buddy named Walter Michaels who was a fairly good friend of Robert Pope. At least according to Walt, who had known Pope for years, he had gradually become a street guy. He lost his leg, lost his job, his wife and kids left, he started to drink like he couldn't stop, and he ended up on the street, bumming spare change on the street with the rest of us. Guys on the street started calling him "Pegleg", a nickname that was predictable to say the least. He and Walter became good friends. One evening, Walter Michaels told me that "Pegleg" asked him for a very unusual favour. In fact, it was quite bizarre when you think about it, which I thought about a lot." Richard, who had been leaning over the table to listen carefully to what George was telling him, inclined closely and asked. "How bizarre?". Grayson put his head in his hands and answered as delicately as he could. "Well, he told Walter that he wanted to kill himself." Richard suddenly was spellbound and expressed something close to incredulity, if not shock. "Kill himself, you mean like suicide!" It was evident that Richard couldn't believe George who then made his story even more difficult to believe. "And he told me that he wanted someone to kill him rather than do it himself." Richard was no longer shocked, he was now irredeemably stunned. After lingering, Grayson continued with an unexpected development in the explanation, Richard waiting for a plot twist at the end of a horror movie. "Well, you may not believe it but "Pegleg" was a devout Catholic, or so I was told, and while he wanted to kill himself, which given his miserable existence I can fully appreciate, he believed that it was a mortal sin and therefore could not commit the act himself. He also said that he could not seek repentance, his death an obvious obstacle to confession and therefore contrition. So he decided that he would get someone else to kill him and therefore enter heaven without sin and therefore the need for forgiveness. It didn't make much sense to me but that's what he told me."

Richard could hardly believe it, that a Catholic would think that asking someone to kill him rather than doing it himself was not a sin. He wondered what Father Breslin would think. He would probably devout an entire class, if not more than one to discussing the matter. He recalled that Father Breslin, in elucidating about the commandments at one time, had observed that suicide was a grave matter, generally seeing the act as being contrary to the prohibition against murder as encapsulated in the sixth commandment. Father Breslin said, or should have said, that one's life was the property of God and to destroy it was a grave sin. Maybe it was some other member of the clergy who might have observed that suicide prevented believers from achieving eternal life, noting in particular that those who commit suicide are not subject to funeral services and cannot be buried in hallowed ground, that is in a Catholic cemetery.

Having quietly ruminated long enough in silence, he did continue the conversation with Grayson. "I assume that "Pegleg" found someone to kill him. I mean it was reported that the man was murdered, bludgeoned with a piece of lumber or steel rebar, and ended up buried in the Laval Cemetery. While you, some street guys and whoever did the deed knew his name, most people didn't, including newspaper men, and myself, not to mention the Parc-Extension cops, didn't know his name. Further, I assume that you know who killed "Pegleg". You may be the only person who does." With that suggestion, George was being requested by Richard to identify "Pegleg"'s killer. Richard was now prepared he concluded for the culmination of his search, whatever that was or had been.

George Grayson looked at Richard with a peculiar expression on his face. He should have expected the question but was still surprised. For maybe a couple of minutes or so, he sat there in speechless silence. Staring him straight in the face, George then identified the man that "Pegleg" had recruited to eliminate himself. "His name is Fred Ennis, some guy who he had known since they were both altar boys at Saint John Fisher out in Pointe Claire. They weren't in touch for years but somehow, I don't know how, they may have accidentally run into each other recently and then became friends. Perhaps, "Pegleg" was panhandling for spare change from passing traffic on the corner of Atwater and Saint Jacques Streets when Ennis drove up. "Pegleg" approached his car begging for change. They somehow recognized each other and then rekindled their relationship." Grayson's narrative lingered for a few moments while Richard gazed at nothing in particular, waiting for further explanation. "Apparently, they became surprisingly friendly after a relatively brief period of time and then I guess "Pegleg" felt congenial enough with Ennis to ask him for this — what can I call it — huge favour."

Richard felt that he had no choice to express extreme incredulity, as he had been hallucinating Grayson's story but wasn't. "And this guy Ennis, who "Pegleg" hadn't really seen for years, agreed to kill him. Now that's really strange, don't you think?" Richard still had this disbelieving look on his face. Grayson agreed. "Strange! It is even stranger when I tell you that he made a second appeal." Richard had calmed down long enough to ask another question. "Another request? I mean, did he want him to kill someone else?" Grayson looked at him, dropped his head like he was forlorn, and confessed to the second service. "This one is even more peculiar, if not outright more bizarre." Richard then predictably commented, "More peculiar? Jesus, what could be more peculiar than killing somebody as a request?" Smiling in an odd manner, Grayson then informed Richard of the second petition that "Pegleg" had made of Fred Ennis. "He asked him, if not demanded that if he killed him, that he confess the act to a priest and seek absolution for it. When I first heard about the request, I thought that "Pegleg" either did not make it or had invented it for some reason but maybe I was wrong. At least according to the man who, on a confidential basis of course, told him about the entire matter, said "Pegleg" knew that Ennis was a religious man who was more than willing to seek atonement for killing his old altar boy friend. Richard asked, "So do you think that Ennis actually sought redemption for his deed." Grayson nodded his head and replied with a certainty that convinced Richard that Ennis might have fulfilled the last request of Robert "Pegleg" Pope.

A CONCLUSION

As much as Richard was unwilling to actually believe Gregson's story about the conception, circumstances and consequences of the death of "Pegleg", he had no choice but to contemplate it. The idea that a devout Catholic, on the precipice of hopelessness, would convince someone to kill him rather than commit suicide and then have that someone seek contrition for the act through confession. After all his investigation of confession, during which he researched its subtleties, through the study of elementary and secondary school Catholic textbooks, a university course in theology, the analysis and examination of penance and the cleansing of the soul, and finally, a struggle with actual sin and the consequences of forgiveness, he was still pondering. So here he was, presented with an experience that would provide him with the wisdom about sin and forgiveness that he had been searching for since he first wondered about that older women waiting for pious declarations and serious repentances in the confessional. Sure, he had been educated in the practice of confession since he was six or seven years old, once he was celebrated with the ceremony of confirmation and therefore was prepared to accept absolution for one of many venal sins that any kid in grade one or two could commit.

He never quite understood his obsession, either then or now, but it was there nevertheless. Now, presented with an extraordinary precedent of the tale of the intentional demise of one man and the compelled confession of another, Richard was more bewildered than he was when wondering about counsel that selected members of the cloth had provided him on occasion about the doctrine of confession. He did not know whether to analyze his reaction and ruminations to the complexity of the story that Grayson had imparted to him about the theological tragedy of "Pegleg" or forget about the entire matter. He was still struggling with a university theology course, recalling Father Breslin waxing lyrically about the history of confession, theorizing about its meaning to the Catholic church or addressing the complexity of rectifying and forgiving any sin heard in confession.

He remembered his lunch with Father Breslin during which they discussed the responsibilities that both confessors and penitents had for any transgression against religious doctrine, including one as spiritually complex as the circumstances related to the death of "Pegleg". It did not matter that no matter what Father Breslin, any other confessor or even any theologian could suggest, he would not be in a position to elucidate about any serious sin, even a misdeed as unusual and perplexing as the death and subsequent drama associated with respect to Robert "Pegleg" Pope had been. He still remained in purgatory.

Printed in the United States
by Baker & Taylor Publisher Services